Dear Galaxy

Dear Galaxy

PAIGE LAVOIE

4 Horsemen
Publications, Inc.

4 Horsemen
Publications, Inc.

4 Horsemen Publications, Inc.
1497 Main St. Suite 169
Dunedin, FL 34698
4horsemenpublications.com
info@4horsemenpublications.com

Cover by Shea O' Connor
Typesetting by Niki Tantillo
Edited by SL Vargas

Library of Congress Control Number: 2023934999

Paperback ISBN-13: 978-1-64450-945-6
Hardcover ISBN-13: 978-1-64450-946-3
Audiobook ISBN-13: 978-1-64450-948-7
Ebook ISBN-13: 978-1-64450-947-0

Dedication

For Taylor Simonds, a friend
who always encourages me
to dream big and reach for
the stars!

Table of Contents

1.

There's nothing I love more than a secret, and when it comes to the halls of Galaxy High, I'm the holder of them all. I know about all the crushes, the wandering eyes, the heartaches and the budding romances; I address them all with the click-clack of my typewriter as the one and only advice columnist for the school paper.

The heavy Main Street lights reflect off the bubble dome that encases our small town on Ceres, the little planet I call home. It casts a glow across the crisp patches of astroturf that border the sidewalk. Shuffling past the flat angled roofs in cream, teal, and baby pink, I draw in a deep breath.

Just a few days 'til spring break means I need to get a handle on my article before we go to print. I pull out my heart-shaped compact before turning the corner to school. Hair? Perfect. The indigo curls frame my face and stay locked in place with the gallon of hairspray I used this morning. Face? A little shiny already. The star-shaped freckles dotted across my cheeks glow against the blue hue of my skin. My dad says my freckles tell a story; they're a piece of the universe inside me. It would all be very poetic if they weren't also a beacon for embarrassment. I quickly apply a bit of powder, knowing they'll illuminate like a million tiny light-bulbs if I'm not careful.

My new circle skirt flares out in front of me when I step onto the sidewalk. Even under the sunless sky of Ceres, I feel like I'm shining bright—*and not just my freckles.* I'm ready to meet whatever challenges the day brings. A challenge, an adventure, something I can finally sink my teeth into.

To most of my classmates, I'm just Susie. Friendly enough, decent in class (but not someone you'd copy home-work from), and absolutely not someone you'd spill your darkest secrets to. I'm entirely unremarkable. If I wanted, I could probably slip through the hallways unnoticed, without anyone saying so much as a word to me.

"Hey!" That is, anyone except for Oliva Oren. Her arm loops through mine before I even have a chance to respond to my best friend's greeting. When I look up, she scowls.

Perfect.

"Where the heck were you this morning?"

Besides the usual walk from school, uh...

"My house?"

"Well, not for long enough!" Olivia huffs. Flames flicker across her orange complexion while the end of her red pony-tail sparks with irritation. I'm glad that her flame-like folli-cles don't actually radiate heat. I can't imagine the number of times I would have gotten burned by now.

"I told you I'd be by at 7:30 to walk together," she insists, the fire in her eyes dancing with irritation.

"You said 7!"

"Did not!"

"You absolutely did!" I argue. It's always 7 a.m., and when it's not, I assume Olivia overslept and head out by myself.

We've been friends since, well, forever. There are three things I can always count on:

1. Olivia Oren is never on time,

2. She's hardly ever actually mad at me when she acts like this, and most importantly,

3. She'd never spill my secret identity to the rest of the school.

I don't think anyone at *The Gazette* would dare for fear of getting kicked off the paper. "Miss Galaxy" the school's long-running column, is the name I hide behind to bestow my timeless wisdom. It doesn't matter how lackluster my personal love life is. Miss Galaxy always has the answer—and I have a foolproof system to make sure I'm never wrong.

"Are you listening?" Olivia snaps my attention back to our 'argument.' "I just had to eat an entire stack of waffles—and your serving too—by myself!" she cries. A spot of syrup decorates on her collar, and a laugh escapes me. "Do you think I want to complain about my math homework to your parents?" Olivia continues, a hand on her hip.

"Yes?" I'm unsure why she'd even ask. Olivia is practically a part of the family. I think she's gotten my parents' help with homework just as much as I have.

"I mean, your dad did have some good advice on fractions ... but no!" Her scowl turns into a smile fast enough to give me whiplash. "They need to buy you a communicator, so you don't leave without me."

Or you could buy an alarm clock.

"They're so expensive." I shake my head as we walk toward the school entrance; it's hard not to notice almost every student with a shining wrist communicator. Of course, I'm not the only student without one, but sometimes it feels like it. I can just imagine the way a dainty silver band would look adorning my wrist. Olivia and I would be able to chat about anything, anytime, for better or worse.

A rush of wind nearly knocks me off balance. Olivia steadies me before I topple to the ground. *What was that?* Rouge sparks flicker like fireworks down the street. The source? Rocket boots attached to the feet of a middle-schooler. Now, that's a gadget I wouldn't mind disappearing off the face of the planet.

I shudder. Those pyrotechnics were way too close to my hairspray-drenched curls for comfort.

"Relax!" Olivia says, squeezing my now-tense shoulder. "They were yards away!"

"They could have set us on fire!"

"No one is getting set on fire."

"Because we ducked!" I point at the meticulous curl-set atop my head. "I am extremely flammable."

"In that case, you ended up paired with a dangerous best friend." Olivia smirks. I dodge before she has a chance to smack me with her sparking ponytail. My heels click across the glittering linoleum floors as we move through the curved pink doors of Galaxy High.

"Did you hear that Jason and Donna from Home Ec were spotted making out at Lester's?" she whispers. "Didn't you just answer a letter from Jason a few weeks ago?"

I smile. I guess my advice to "pour his feelings into a cake pan" and show her how he felt paid off.

"I can't believe he signed his name," she giggles softly. I know Olivia would never *willingly* spill my secret, but she could stand to whisper a little more quietly.

"It's more fun when I get to guess!" I whisper back. We continue to gossip dodging students dressed in swingline dresses in pastel hues with petticoats wide enough to block the hallway. Some of our classmates turn their heads and snicker at Olivia's exaggerated hand gestures. She doesn't seem to care or notice, but I shrink under all of the attention. Clouds of hairspray pollute the air as folks put the finishing touches on their looks. It's a good thing rocket boots aren't allowed inside; we'd all be doomed.

A wide smile plays across Olivia's face as she pulls us to a stop in front of her locker.

She's been like this since we were kids. I guess it means she isn't upset anymore, but I suspect she never really was.

By the time I pull the starburst shaped handle of my own locker to retrieve my books, I can't help but feel a little distracted by the spectacle going on across from me. PDA is nothing new in these hallways, but this couple is really going for it. My lips rise into a smirk. I can never be entirely sure, but this is yet another situation that has Miss Galaxy's name written all over it. A girl wrote in just last week asking if she should confess her feelings to the boy she'd been sharing a locker with.

I suspected it would be these two, by the way; I've caught the stolen, shy glances. Now, they look like they've been plucked straight out of the kind of campy romantic movies they play at the drive-in. The couple break away to stare into each other's eyes before their lips lock again. I'm sure a teacher or hall monitor will break it up soon.

I know I shouldn't stare. How could I possibly look away when pride radiates through me as bright as a shooting star? Two lonely students are now literally tangled together, and from where I stand, it looks like neither has a care in the world. It's funny—all my advice books say love is blinding, but I'm sure they don't mean it so literally. The thought of the whole world falling away, being the only two people in the universe, sounds way too unrealistic. No matter how much I've read, no matter how many crushes I've developed,

I've never liked someone as much as these two. They have to know everyone is gawking, right? Maybe they just don't care.

I square my shoulders, peeling my eyes away from the pair. As much as I had a hand in this affair, it's not mine; I'll have lots of romance to read about after spring break. Piles of heartache and first loves will be sitting on my desk. They always are, and this spring break won't be any different. So, why is my chest aching with each step to homeroom?

Mrs. Lux's hologram flickers in front of the class. It's not especially out of the ordinary. Our teachers are from all over the cosmos and often appear virtually—I suppose moving out to an ice planet in the middle of nowhere isn't appealing for most. The muffled laughter echoing throughout the classroom isn't because of the choppy signal that causes her voice to lag just a little behind the movements of her mouth. It's because she's forgotten to take off her fuzzy pink slippers and has a row of curlers forgotten on the back of her head.

"There is nothing funny about space travel!" our teacher suddenly snaps, and with that, the entire classroom roars.

In the chaos, students begin to pass a note to each other from the back row toward the front. The small piece of folded white paper travels from desk to desk, and for just a moment, I think it might make its way all the way back to me.

But it stops at the desk in front of mine and sits untouched in front of Skip Stone. My heart races just looking at the back of his head. I muffle a small sigh as I stare at the white and gold constellations that dot across his light grey skin. Sitting behind him in class, I think I may have each of them memorized. If he ever found out I thought about him like this, I wouldn't hesitate to throw myself directly into an ice volcano.

The thing about Skip is that he is so nice to everyone. He's always got a smile and a helping hand. Even with his busy schedule, the school's most popular boy tutored me last year when my grades started to slip in science. While Skip could have judged me for all of the silly questions I asked, he never did. He might be the most genuinely sweet boy in the school. The really terrible thing is that he's got this way of looking at me that makes it feel like he really sees me. I can't read into it—he's like that with everyone. He'll never see me as anything more than a classmate.

When Mrs. Lux has her head turned, he reaches down and picks up the note. Skip shifts in his seat just enough for me to see the edge of a smile flash across his perfect face. The note is neatly tucked in his pocket now, and I'm sure it's some kind of swooning confession. Half of the letters that land in Miss Galaxy's submission box are written by class-mates swooning over him, and Skip deserves every single gushing line.

I wonder what this one says.

"Susie? Will you pick up where I left off?" Ms. Lux suddenly asks. I should have been paying attention.

"Paragraph three," Skip's whisper comes quietly from his place in front of me. I stand up. I can feel everyone's eyes on me, Skip's included.

Cheeks burning, I turn my attention to the textbook.

"'After the establishment of starways across the galaxy, small planets were given the opportunity to interact with other planets, cities, and space stations, improving the way we travel, trade, and communicate across space.'"

Mrs. Lux's hologram nods in approval. "Wonderful Susie, and yes! Our planet, Ceres, is one of the many that benefited from this change. Before the starways, a small planet like ours would have been isolated. Although, that doesn't mean the system is finished. There are some rural stretches of starway in between planets that have become dumping grounds for waste, trash, and well... 'Cruising through the stars,' as you kids say, is not always a leisurely experience, and it can be dangerous—"

The bell rings, cutting off the rest of her sentence. Annoyed by the way everyone rushes off, I gather up my books, holding them tightly in front of my chest. But in the mad scramble of students, my shoulders slam into someone. I try to catch myself, but I topple over. My hips crash into a nearby desk, and before I know it, I'm staring up at Skip Stone's star-freckled face from the hard linoleum floor.

"Hi Skip," I gulp, completely frozen in place. It doesn't matter how many times we speak; he's much more intimidating up close. I can barely meet his golden eyes without feeling heat radiate from my face. His hand cups mine, pulling me off the ground. The fabric of his letterman jacket flexes, too tight for the muscles hiding underneath.

"Are you okay?" Skip asks, his lips quirking into a worried smile that knocks the wind right back out of my chest.

"Yeah, um, fine." My eyes fixate on his graceful movements as he pushes his one loose silver curl back into his perfectly coiffed hair.

"Thank you," I mumble, resisting the urge to bolt. How anyone can have a full conversation with him is beyond me. If I didn't have the textbook to focus on during our study sessions, I think I might have exploded. Skip sweeps my fallen books off of the floor and back into my arms while I gawk at him. Before I know it, the two of us are walking down the hallway together.

"Any plans for spring break?" he asks. "I already feel like I'm getting pulled in every direction." I can't help but notice how forced his laugh sounds. In some ways, it's got to be rough to be as popular as he is. I bet he has a party, date, or day trip scheduled for every day of vacation.

"I wish." My voice shakes. "Olivia and I will probably spend most of it in a booth at Lester's."

"What's spring break without an endless supply of fries and milkshakes?" Skip lets out a dreamy sigh. "Maybe we could meet up sometime. There's a science test after the break."

A science test.

Of course.

My heart spins out of orbit.

It doesn't matter how many daydreams I have about what it could be like between the two of us. Skip is only interested in one thing: my grades.

"Just the spring break adventure I need." I attempt to sound as though I'm teasing, but the words come out forced and awkward. Relief flows through me at the sound of the bell. I watch him confidently stroll down the hallway.

Yes, there's nothing I love more than secrets, but Skip Stone might be a close second.

2.

The submission box is light today. Most of the confessions are similar to stories we've recently featured; as much as I'd like to help, keeping Miss Galaxy's content fresh is essential. With spring break coming up, reading about all the dreamy places people are planning on exploring is almost too much. Olivia and I have been not-so-quietly lamenting our lack of travel plans. Seventeen years of my life and I've barely been off planet. I can't help it. I'm jealous.

"Dear Miss Galaxy, what should I pack for my family's celestial cruise?"

"Dear Miss Galaxy, how do I plan the perfect beach date?"

Letter to letter, everything in my slush pile is as stale as the cafeteria pizza. We print letters like this every season, and it's terrible, but I want something that feels new. I stretch my arms over my head and glance around the busy club room. Naturally, everyone clusters together with their classmates. The freshmen lump toward the front, sorting out photos and making collages. Once a week, they take turns to update our school's communicator system. It notifies students about tests, weather reports, and events, but it's a responsibility I'm glad I'm not tasked with. Blasting the entire school with a message? It's hard enough worrying about having a typo in the paper.

In our shoebox-sized office, everything from the desks to the atomic wallpaper is a shade of light blue. There's a mix of typewriters and outdated computers with large round screens at each workstation. The seniors are in the back, either goofing off or writing the "big articles"—local news, coverage of sporting events, or even short stories and poetry, depending on the week.

And then there's Olivia and I in the middle of the chaos. Though, we're not alone. I have one of the longest-running columns; it seems unfair that I'm the one sharing a desk. Luckily, my desk mate is usually late or in detention, so I spread out my books and notes accordingly.

I open the top drawer of my desk and pull out my secret weapon. The thing that helped me land the coveted title of "Miss Galaxy" as a freshman.

After all, how could someone like me be capable of advising the entire population of Galaxy High on the most intimate subjects?

Books. Obviously.

Books can teach you anything—even matters of the heart. Specifically, a second edition of *The Space Age Ladies' Guide to Romance and Social Affairs*, which sits tucked away in my desk drawer, ready to guide me to an answer when I need it. Admittedly, the title is a mouthful, but as the acronym TSALGTRSA isn't any easier to say, I just call it *The Guide*. That's what it is, after all. My guide to everything I could possibly need to know about the love I've never actually experienced myself.

The point is, it's never steered me wrong before.

BOOM.

I jerk up and see Wallace Webber, the unsung hero of all of us. His grammar skills have saved me more than once. Every good writer needs a proofreader, and Wallace, as Junior Editor, is that and more.

He's placed an awfully large houseplant on my desk—beads of sweat drip from his forehead. If I had to guess, he's carried it all the way across campus.

"Redecorating?" I ask, unable to keep the smirk off my face. I think I have an idea of where the houseplant came from.

Wallace shakes his head, still struggling to catch his breath, fiddling with the Wayfair glasses that take up half his face. His pink skin is flushed and dewy. I dash to the water cooler and grab a cup of water, placing it in his hands.

"Thanks," he gasps, chugging it down and slamming the cup onto the table. Wallace isn't exactly charming. Yet, there's something about him you can't help but be drawn to like the glimmer in his eyes behind his large horn-rimmed glasses or his broad smile. And it is disarmingly cute the way his pointed ears bobble up and down if you manage to make him laugh. Wallace has a bumbling sort of appeal. I'm not surprised he's found someone special.

"No—I mean, *yes*—the boyfriend gave it to me as a birthday present." His pink skin blushes a deeper shade. He looks like a valentine. Anytime he even thinks about Teddy, he swoons, and it's fun to watch someone who's always buttoned up loose his cool. I've only met Teddy a few times, but I suppose by the number of decorations amassing on Wallace's desk that they're pretty smitten with each other.

"Golly, I wish I'd known! I would have brought in a cake!" I exclaim. I'd baked one a few months back when Olivia turned seventeen, and I dare say it was a hit.

"Thanks, but I don't like to make a fuss." He shakes his head. "Besides, I don't think everyone would be keen on celebrating with me." His eyes dart toward Olivia, who lets out a huff from her desk.

"Your secretive nature has deprived us all of cake!" she snaps. I can't tell if she's actually angry or teasing. But seeing who she's talking to, it's probably the latter. Wallace didn't exactly love any of Olivia's first submissions for the newspaper; it took her three rejections to finally get accepted and claim her desk next to mine. Of course, she's more than proven herself since, but that doesn't matter. Wallace is always going to be the person who told her she wasn't good enough.

"You're just jealous no one is giving you plants and knick-knacks for your desk." He crosses his arms and smiles proudly at the neatly organized array of trinkets on his workspace. His eyes linger on her overflowing garbage can. "Not that you could find any place to put them."

"I have a system!"

Wallace stiffens his shoulders. "As Junior Editor of *The Galaxy Gazette*," he begins, "I think we should all strive for a clean and organized office, don't you?"

I personally can't argue. I like Wallace's logic. However, it's often delivered in a way that feels like the correct recipients won't receive the message.

By the way steam is beginning to pour out of Olivia's ears, I think we're about to have a situation on our hands. I have to do something.

"You know..." I pick up my pristine copy of *The Space Age Lady's Guide to Romance and Social Affairs* and quickly flip to the correct chapter. "As stated on page forty-two, 'Friends who often get into arguments should—'"

"For starters," Olivia interrupts, "we are not friends." With that, she sticks her tongue out and rolls her chair a few inches away. It's maybe the one thing she and Wallace can agree on.

A few of the upperclassmen glare in our direction. Their arguments typically last longer than this, so I'm personally relieved. But honestly, would trying a little harder to be friends hurt? Once Wallace retreats, I turn my sights back to my best friend.

"How's the movie review going?" I ask, glancing at Olivia's desk. I suddenly wish I had looked at her desk before asking.

I spy the crumpled pieces of paper torn out from her notebook, littered everywhere except the garbage can she was aiming for. We've been friends ever since she shared her new box of pencils with me in elementary school—long enough for me to be able to recognize writer's block when I see it.

"Mr. Junior Editor told me to tone it down after the hate mail I got from the last one!" she shouts, orange sparks spreading across her cheeks. "I said he should let me review the hate mail letters themselves. I mean, if they're going to write to tell me I'm terrible, they should have to be creative! Where are the standards?"

She's pretending to complain, but it's obvious she enjoys the way her reviews, whether they're on books, movies, or food, always seem to rub someone the wrong way. Just the idea of writing something that upsets one of my readers makes every muscle in my body tense up. Not that it's anything I'll ever have to worry about. Miss Galaxy's responses are constantly perfect, and I have *The Guide* to make sure of that. "I take it Wallace didn't go for the idea?"

"He just sighed a lot ... which wasn't exactly a no." Olivia brightens. I know that face. I hope she's not writing something she'll end up regretting.

"You just like making him angry," I tease, shaking my head.

"It's not my fault it's so easy!" She shrugs her shoulders, the devious smile never leaving her lips—until that is her eyes flick above my head.

Oh no.

A shadow creeps across the desk next to mine, silent scribbling peppered with sighs filling my ears. I can't believe he's actually here today. With Eugene Eris, it's a 50/50 chance. I slide my books back to my side of the desk and offer an apology that gets a shrug in response.

Boys like Eugene are all scowl, no substance. Others might call him the strong, silent type. Or, in a direct quote from the pile of letters on my desk, they might call him "cute bad boy," "the cool school loner," or "hottest guy in the cosmos."

No matter how attractive he is, that last one is going overboard. As far as I can tell, all he does is come to school to brood in corners, break hearts, and to my dismay, write a column for *The Galaxy Gazette*. And to add to my irritation, it's good—for being reviews of the school cafeteria's menu, that is.

Eugene transferred here last year, and his allure still hasn't worn off. Besides the pouty face, the leather jacket, and the fact that he writes most of his articles from a desk in detention, there's nothing that "bad" about him. He's just plain rude.

Last year, Wallace and I gave him a tour of the school on his first day, and he said a total of three words to us. At first, I chalked it up to a shy personality, but after an entire year, I'm done giving him the benefit of the doubt. I heard he transferred from a private school; part of me wonders if he thinks he's too good for us, but a simple "thank you" or "nice to meet you" goes a long way.

Wallace doesn't seem to hold it against him. Last semester, Eugene frequented the lunch table that Wallace and Teddy sit at. I think since Wallace is apparently okay with Eugene's creepy looming, he should be the one sharing a desk.

I scoot my chair away, determined not to let Mr. Cool Guy throw me off my correspondence A-game.

"That book takes me back," a proud voice says from behind me. I don't need to turn around to know that it's Ms. Loretta, our student advisor, and the former Miss Galaxy.

"Hi." My voice sounds so timid when I try to talk to her. Ms. Loretta's far-set eyes are worlds away despite her standing in front of me. The woman always looks like she's plotting something, and it's been my experience that that's because she is. Her shiny silver jumpsuit with a larger-than-life star-shaped belt buckle sparkles under the office light. It's so over the top that I have a hard time imagining her in the teachers' lounge, refilling her coffee mug. She looks more like she should be getting on a stage.

There's a rumor that she had a sort of superpower when she was Miss Galaxy. She could tell the contents of a letter before even opening it. Something about pinks and reds for love notes, blue for heartache; even the strokes of the pen could help her glean whether the writer was cautious or bold. I've thought about asking her to teach me, but I'm worried it would ruin the surprise. Each letter is like opening a tiny birthday present.

"Find a story in that pile of letters?" she asks, the same sparkle lingering in her eyes.

"Not yet." I look down at the slightly wrinkled pile and feel ashamed I haven't gotten more done today. "I was thinking of something with a little more wanderlust before break."

"That's the spirit!" She raises her coffee mug in a salute before making her way to her desk, a stack of papers from English class under her arm. "Now, unless any of you have an emergency..." She takes a seat.

"Back to it, people! We have a paper to make!" Wallace announces, clapping his hands together and pacing the length of the room.

"You are literally the only person who isn't working right now," Olivia hisses under her breath.

"Open communication and the willingness to listen to each other—" I begin, clutching my book to my chest.

"Not now!" the two shout in unison, glaring at each other as if the mere thought of thinking the same thing is repulsive.

I shrink back into my chair and close *The Guide* with a harsh thud, ignoring the feeling of Eugene's prying eyes. Wallace and Olivia never bother to take my advice. I can't hide behind Miss Galaxy with them. I let out a sigh, returning to letters about dates, crushes, and vacation plans. My shoulders slump forward in defeat. If the whole school knew who I really was, they probably wouldn't listen either.

"He's just so childish!" Olivia groans as she stomps through the neighborhood on the way back to my house. Her complaining is not untypical, especially when it comes to Wallace. I spend what should be a calm walk home enduring her rants about whatever "annoying" thing Wallace did that day. But I like walking with her just the same. We pass the pretty rows of pastel ranch-style houses with clean lines and geometric slanted roofs, complete with bright green astroturf lawns. The sidewalks are peppered with students all walking the same direction toward their homes.

We tumble in through the pastel pink door. The sound of Dad humming along to the radio instantly calms my nerves. I hang my jacket by the coat rack near the large front windows, while Olivia tosses her sweater overtop of an armchair and settles into the space. The large windows in the living room are floor to ceiling, giving a lovely view to the front lawn. It's a nice open concept, but sometimes it's like we're living in a fishbowl. Once I looked out the window and made eye contact with Skip while I was wearing my pajamas. I'm still mortified and think investing in curtains wouldn't be such a bad idea.

The kitchen is a disaster— with Dad, it always is. A pile of herbs cut from our live garden wall between the fridge and the pantry lay scattered across the shiny glitter-flecked countertop. This particular kitchen model is supposed to be sleek and clean, with hidden storage compartments and neat little places to cultivate an indoor garden, but with the way Dad cooks, chaotic is an understatement. He calls it his "happy place" while everyone else would probably use the word "messy." But that's a part of what makes this place feel like home.

I pop a blue tomato in my mouth, breezing past him while Olivia helps herself to a soda from the fridge.

"How do you like that?" he asks, holding his hand to his heart, as if wounded. His apron is covered in stains. "Not even a hug or a hello for your old man?"

I circle back, planting a kiss on his cheek. "Hi, Dad." I walk over to the pantry to get my apron while Oliva plops her homework on the table.

"Hi, Mr. Starshine!" Olivia raises her glass soda bottle in the air while Dad cheers back with the bottle of cooking oil in his hand. I count my lucky stars he doesn't take a sip. Hopping up on one of the barstools, he begins to ask us about our days.

His day at home, working the garden, was "fine."

My day at school was "fine."

The paper is "fine," as always.

I haven't told either of my parents that I'm the advice guru of Galaxy High. I'm not exactly lying; I'm just leaving out a few details. If either of them knew, they'd accidentally slip it to one of their friends or co-workers, who might tell their kids, and then boom, there goes my credibility at the paper. I can't be too careful, even if it's with my family.

Still, if anyone in the family is better at giving advice than I am, it's him. And it always helps, especially with something important, to have a second source. Olivia rants about Wallace, but it's nothing he hasn't heard before. Dad echoes the same advice I tried to give her earlier, and I can tell it's gone in one ear and out the other.

"Lots of people at school are talking about the right way to tell someone you have a crush on them ... it being spring break and all," I say, chopping up a few of the spare tomatoes to use as garnish.

"Oh?" Dad leans back, his brows knitted together. "I'd say as long as they're honest and being themselves... It is scary to put your heart on the line like that. It's not easy to recover from your first heartbreak."

I nod. That's precisely what *The Guide* would say too. I'm about to start setting the table when Dad raises his eyebrows.

"Is there someone at school who has caught your eye?" Dad asks. My mouth falls open. *Someone at school?* It's impossible to push the thought away before a pair of golden eyes flash to the forefront of my mind. I'm not going to waste Dad's time by talking about a pointless crush. Skip and I are study buddies at the very most, besides, knowing Dad, he'd make it a big thing.

"Hah! Just making conversation," I force out a laugh and look toward Olivia who is too busy stirring tomato sauce to save me from my fumbling. It's a wonder I haven't blown my secret all by myself at this point. We clear our things off the table, and Dad piles a serving dish of spaghetti drenched in blue tomato sauce in place of our backpacks.

"Would you mind setting the table?" Dad asks.

I click the shiny silver button on the side of the counter. Place settings rotate from the underside of the table, perfectly set with forks, spoons, plants, and glasses within seconds. I'm glad Dad got this fixed. Last time, it decided to unload all our plates simultaneously, which resulted in a lot of broken dishes. I'm pretty sure it got jammed up because I spilled a soda on the console, something I still feel a little guilty about.

Mom's fifteen minutes late, which isn't unusual. One of her many responsibilities at work is to monitor the ice volcanoes in sector five, and she spends her time sealing cracks in places where the ice has started to wear down the structure. They're not a threat to us—Mom is part of the reason for that. Not much of Ceres is livable, apart from our little town. Lots of scientists and researchers have relocated to here to study the unique biochemistry of the land. In fact, it's why the Oren family moved here when Olivia was still in preschool. Her dad works alongside my mom researching and reinforcing the dome, so that if something does erupt, even the smallest shard won't reach town. It's an important job, but that doesn't make it any less dangerous.

I can feel Dad's tension rising with the echoing tick from the starburst clock above the dining table. His face says the words neither of us want to utter out loud.

What if something happened?

"Mom's probably just caught up on an assignment—or the carpool is running late," I offer. That's true. It's about a half-hour commute, and she's hardly ever on time.

Dad lets out a heavy sigh, but the furrow in his brow doesn't go away. "You're probably starved. I'm sure your mom wouldn't mind if you got started."

I shake my head, determined not to have a single bite until every seat at the table is full. "If you're waiting, so am I," I say, ignoring the jab of Olivia elbowing me from under the table. I can't blame her. Steam billows off my full plate, and my mouth is already watering.

"If you couldn't tell, I snacked on my fair share while I was cooking." Dad leans back in his chair, gesturing for us to eat. It's evident from the blue stains around his mouth. Blue tomatoes are something only eaten in the comfort of your own home unless you mind stains on your teeth; they are definitely not a first date food.

My stomach betrays me with a loud gurgle. Olivia pushes food around her plate and gives me a small glare. Spaghetti night is her favorite, and clearly, she's tired of waiting. The sound of the front door unlocking causes us all to let out a deep breath collectively.

"Hey! Sorry, I'm late," Mom's voice rings through the house. Her light teal hair is down in messy curls, and the only makeup she's wearing is a swipe of red lipstick. Everyone always says I take after her, but I don't see it. She looks positively elegant, not at all like she's been reinforcing the bubble dome with power tools all day.

Everything about Mom is graceful, from her heart-shaped face to the gentle touch of stars across her cheeks. Only once in a while do I see a resemblance. My dad and I, however, are two peas in a spacepod. I have his dark indigo hair, the same bright splattering of freckles, and for better or worse, his people-pleasing personality.

The four of us don't waste any time digging into the heaps of noodles piled high on our plates. Mom chats about her busy day at work. Dad goes on and on about the garden. Olivia casually mentions her brother is "unexpectedly" back in town, which explains her appearance here for breakfast and dinner. I don't press her on the details, but it's probably not by choice if Rex is home from boarding school. "Tense" would be an understatement for the mood at the Oren household—especially since this is the second school in two years he's been sent home from.

The rest of the evening falls into the same comfortable routine. Before settling in front of the oblong TV set for a few hours, Olivia and I load up the dishwasher. Dad made a classic chocolate cake for dessert, and Olivia sips a cup of coffee while taking indulgent bites. Mom gives her the side-eye.

I'm still not allowed to drink coffee at home. Mom always makes it a big deal that it'll stunt my growth. I've been 5'2 since 6th grade, and I don't think I'm going to get any taller. I opt for a glass of milk and take my dessert into the living room. They're playing reruns of *Cara Cosmos*, a show based on one of our favorite book series when we were kids. The black and white picture goes in and out, but neither of us move to adjust the antenna. The lighthearted mysteries play in the background until we finish our homework, and Olivia heads out for the night.

"7 a.m. tomorrow, right?" I call out, watching her figure bounce from the doorway 'til it shrinks down the street.

"Save me a stack of pancakes," she shouts from behind her. I wave from the doorway, knowing full well I'll see her at 7:30 at best.

School, work at the paper, a week of slumber parties, and missed opportunities on the horizon. *The Guide* would tell me that if I wanted something bad enough, I should go out and make it happen. But I lie awake that night, the spaghetti dinner a lump in my stomach.

Miss Galaxy would know how to catch the eyes of their crush during a study date. Heck, if anyone could navigate the ups and downs of a spring fling, it would be her. So why can't I do it?

Is there anyone you have your eye on?

The question Dad asked before dinner knocks around in my head.

What I should have said is, "No one who's looking back."

3.

"Susie, can you go pick up the letterbox? Alice was supposed to get it, but she'll be writing her poetry column from detention." Wallace catches me in the doorway, before I have a chance to enter the room. There's a pencil tucked behind his pointed ear, and his pink antennae bobble with his frantic movements. The junior editor looks a little more stressed out than usual, which is saying a lot.

"No problem!" We normally switch off every day so that no one gets suspicious. I'm supposed to go tomorrow, but Alice will probably trade spaces with me if she doesn't have detention again. Why does the newspaper club attract so many delinquents anyway?

From the empty space at my desk, I assume Eugene is right there next to her. As I breeze back down the hallway toward the library, I catch a glimpse of his brooding frame. His navy eyes are distant and narrow as he approaches without as much as a nod. Ooof, he looks like he's in a worse mood than usual. His eyes flick over at me for long enough to make me pause. I shouldn't bother talking to him, but we *did* make eye contact. It would be rude not to say anything, right?

"Hey," I greet him, trying to be casual. "You're early today."

"Mmm." He nods.

One of the roaming trash cans knocks into my ankle before its little chrome frame wheels down the hall; someone drew a smiley face on it last week, and no one has been able to scrub it off. I think it gives it some personality.

"It's kind of cute, isn't it?" I ask, gesturing toward the trash can. "I think someone should give it a name or maybe a pair of googly eyes."

I have no idea why I'm torturing myself by being polite to him. He opens his mouth to say something before it falls into a straight expressionless line.

"No," he says curtly before breezing past me toward detention while shaking his head. My stars, who could hate a rolling trash can? Eugene's gloom knows no bounds.

The library is one of the few spaces at school that hasn't been updated to be shiny and new. The floors are a deep, yet vibrant, shade of green, and the desks are burnt orange. Full windows allow a glimpse outside where a group of students is permanently parked in front of the vending machines.

A few boxy computers sit in the corners on teal desks that clash with just about everything in the room. I make my way past the dark wood shelves 'til I reach the back of the library, where our humble submission box sits. A few years ago, the school tried to go digital with Dear Galaxy's submissions but found most students like the personalization of pen and paper. Seeing the different types of stationery and doodles always makes me smile, so I'm glad. Sometimes the easier thing isn't always better.

I catch a glimpse of silver hair, and my entire body freezes. I wasn't mentally prepared for a Skip encounter this afternoon, but there he is, studying quietly. The light from the windows glistens off his skin, making him shine brighter than usual. He's dressed in a pair of tan slacks and his letterman sweater; the sight is enough to make my knees weak. I tuck the box under my arm and make my way over to him.

"Hey!" He greets me with a goofy smile. It seems like I've caught him off guard somehow. "The freshman I'm tutoring is a no-show—can I interest you in some math flashcards?"

"That is a very tempting offer." I pause. Am I honestly considering doing math by choice just to be close to Skip?

"I have to get these back to the office. Miss Galaxy is waiting," I sing-song, turning to hide the way my face glows every time we're close.

He bites his bottom lip, averting his gaze for a moment. "Yeah, well, I hope there are some good ones in there for her." When his eyes lock on mine, it's like time has stopped. Does he actually read her—*my*—articles?

"Hah, I guess we'll see." I force a laugh, turning my back and giving him a half-hearted wave and an even worse goodbye before bolting as far from him as my legs will take me.

I'm always careful. There's no way I've dropped even the slightest hint. He thinks I help Wallace with editing. A sort of "junior editor-in-chief in training." It's my official title in the yearbook and an easy answer when talking about my role at the paper.

I return to the desk and dump the contents out. Beautiful colorful envelopes explode across the clean surface as well as a few crumpled notes I assume, from past experience, contain lewd pictures and profanities. I clear those away, close my eyes, and pick one at random.

Dear Miss Galaxy,

I have a crush on someone.

I've tried dozens of times to get closer to her, but I think she just sees me as a friend. What should I do?

xoxo,

Lovestruck Fool

The letter in my hands is crisp and red. The penmanship reads as nervous and messy. In a way, that has charm. It's earnest. Letters like this aren't trying to impress anyone—that's why they're usually my favorite. Today, however, it's expected. This question again. It pops up more often than anything else. But I suppose it will be a good refresher before spring break.

The corners are decorated with messy heart-shaped doodles. A little detail that leads me to believe the writer is probably younger than I am, with strong romantic feelings bubbling up inside them for the first time in their life. It's sweet but fills me with anxiety. The writer has it bad.

Messing up my response could be detrimental to the writer's high school future.

Luckily for this lovestruck fool, I *never* mess up. With determination, I pop a piece of paper in my typewriter. My fingers jump to the pink keys.

Dear Lovestruck—

I hesitate. I think addressing anyone as *a* "fool" feels too rude for Miss Galaxy's usual style. I'll leave it out.

If you don't let your crush know how you really feel, you'll be stuck on the sidelines forever. Don't be afraid to let your feelings be known. Be sincere and look for an opportunity to jump in and tell her how you feel! Worst case scenario, she wants to stay friends, right? Either way, you don't want to spend the rest of the school year wondering. Be bold!

Cheering you on,

Miss Galaxy

A great example of "Do as I say, not as I do." I roll my eyes, grabbing another letter from the stack. Something about this one is *odd*. Most of the people who write in choose bright envelopes and draw designs like hearts or planets, and scrawl "To Miss Galaxy" on the front. This envelope, however, grabs my attention for a different reason. It's plain white and sealed with a heart. If this is the amount of effort they put into the presentation, I can only imagine how boring this one is going to be.

Carefully, I begin to peel back the flap with my fingertips. Inside is a simple confession, typed out on what looks like a standard typewriter.

Dear Galaxy, I love you.

I read the words again and again. *It's a joke. It must be a joke.* I swallow hard, unable to let go of the thought. What if it isn't? My eyes return sharply to the paper.

Dear Galaxy, I love you.

I've read through all of your letters and still can't figure out how to tell you.

So, why don't I show you? Spots that shine bright in the darkness, paths to planets left unexplored. In the next 7 nights, I want to take you on an adventure. If you choose to accept, you'll be sent across planets. I've left a letter in each location that will lead you to the next. I don't know if this is too much or too little, but what do you say?

Would you like to explore the stars?
Anonymous

P.S. Your first clue is in The Park, just a few hours away from Ceres. You said in one of your articles that watching a meteor shower is one of the most romantic first dates. So, let's start with sparks in the sky that will hopefully end up in your heart. Look in the hollow tree on the hill.

My legs wobble, and I fall back against the desk. A pile of papers tumbles across the ground like the world's largest pieces of confetti.

An anonymous admirer. I... I can't think. I rush to *The Guide*, flipping through the pages. Wasn't there a paragraph about this somewhere? "Whoa! What's up?" Olivia asks, placing a hand on my shoulder. "Did someone write something gross or...?"

"I have to go!" I shout, unable to get a hold of my senses. She blinks slowly, nodding her head.

"Alright, I mean, we don't have to walk home together every day. It's—"

"Not home! *Here!*" I shake my head. My hair tangles around my fingers. Where *is* that paragraph?

"You're not making any sense!" She laughs, snatching the letter from my hands.

I'm dizzied by the words on the page. *Would you like to explore the stars?*

"I've never heard something so romantic in my whole life..." My body turns to gelatin; in one fluid motion, I sink down into my chair. I imagine myself hand in hand with a mysterious stranger. Our eyes locking, everything else melting away, our faces getting closer, and closer until—

"Susie, you're positively swooning." Olivia's cackle pulls me back to the present moment. She's looking at me with both amusement and maybe a little concern. I freeze, the blood draining out of my face. I'm acting like an utter fool. But at the same time—this is the most exciting thing that's ever happened to me.

"I am not! It's just a peculiar letter! That's all!" I throw my hands in the air, but even I can't keep the smile off my face. I snap up. She's right. I need to get a hold of myself. I close my eyes and take a deep breath. My hands jitter, making the letter slip from my fingers onto the table, where Olivia quickly snatches it up.

"Suppose I do it?" I muse out loud, my heart pounding with every thought. I know that everything I'm about to suggest is reckless. Maybe that's what makes it so exciting.

"Do what? What does 'it' mean?" Olivia squints at the words. "Actually go chase some stranger from planet to planet?"

"Right!" I agree with a firm nod. What about that is so hard to understand? I flip through *The Guide*, finally finding the passage I was looking for. "'When an admirer is too shy to approach their crush, they may opt to write a letter telling the recipient how they feel with a riddle, a clue, or just sweet words. This way, the admirer can gauge the way the recipient feels before acting.'"

"Uh... what?" Olivia is not following.

I fling my hands in the air. "Someone has a crush on m—!"

Someone has a crush on Miss Galaxy. Not Susie Starlight. Which means they could be expecting someone ... different. Like Olivia, or Wallace, or even Eugene or any of the other members of our club. After all, we do credit "Miss Galaxy" as an anonymous contributor in the yearbook each year.

"Someone has a crush on Miss Galaxy..." I repeat, softer this time. They don't have a crush on me. I need to remember that.

Olivia reads through the letter again. I watch her eyes dart back and forth, her brow furrowed like she's watching a game of tennis. "Any idea who it's from?"

"That's the thing!" I'm brimming with enthusiasm too strong to put a lid on. Every thought has me overflowing with questions. "I have no clue!"

She squeals as the pieces seem to have finally clicked together. "This is the coolest thing that's ever happened at school in the history of *ever*!"

It is.

Whoever wrote it was careful not to give anything away. I close my eyes, trying to picture the face of the author—stars, why can't I get Skip's smiling face out of my head?

It can't be that easy.

I lunge for my notebook and scribble down every point I can think of, trying to get my thoughts in order. I need to think, which isn't easy considering Olivia has materialized next to me, tapping her fingers against my desk.

"Wait, so what's happening?" Olivia asks impatiently, trying to peek over my shoulder. "Where are you going first?"

"I don't know!" I answer, snatching the pen from her hand and looking around for something to help—a current events calendar, maybe.

"What do you mean, you don't know? What are you going to do—just float around space until you figure it out?" Her voice gets higher with every unanswered question until she's practically shouting. "Do your parents even have transportation? Do you need my cruiser?"

I whirl around to see Olivia with the letter in her grasp. A sudden rush of jealousy takes hold as I suppress the urge to snatch it out of her hands. The letter is *mine*, and I don't want anyone taking it away.

My teeth dig into my bottom lip, sawing side to side while I try to think of a plan. "Okay, okay... so the meteor shower... and then... and then I'll go somewhere else? How is this going to work?" I'm stumped. "How am I going to get there?"

"Hello!" Olivia waves her arms around. "I *just* offered! I have Rex's old cruiser, remember?"

"It's awfully lively in here today." With all the excitement, I hadn't heard the clicking of Ms. Loretta's heels as she entered the room. "Does this have anything to do with your next submission?" The smirk on her face fills me with unease; if anyone has the power to drag my balloon string back into orbit, it's her.

She doesn't usually put her foot down. But Miss Galaxy chasing after her secret admirer? Something tells me we're going into uncharted territory. There's a chance even running the letter in *The Galaxy Gazette* is going to get vetoed.

But, Ms. Loretta always said that when the right story comes, you should take a leap. And she's never said no before. I have a better chance with her than I do with Wallace.

"Um, actually..." I try to grab at a single thought as they orbit around me. A road trip over spring break. A perfectly reasonable thing to plan with a friend. Except, how are we supposed to plan when we don't even know where we're going? And how am I supposed to convince my parents? Unless...

"Ms. Loretta! Can I follow up on this letter as a club trip?" I ask.

She's completely expressionless and unusually quiet. She studies the letter carefully, then smirks.

"Ms. Loretta?" I press in a smaller voice.

"I suppose... We don't have it in our budget this year to take a large-scale trip, so I had been debating on doing smaller outings for each grade. This could be yours if the four of you would like to go together. You're all responsible enough, so as long as your parents agree, I don't see why not. You don't need an advisor to go along with you ... and Mr. Wallace was just loudly lamenting about how dreadfully boring his spring break was going to be."

"Wait, *me*?" Wallace jumps up from his desk.

A sneaky smile crawls across Loretta's face. "Would it be an official club trip without the junior editor?"

"All of us ... together?" Olivia asks, side-eyeing Wallace.

"I guess that's what a club trip would mean, huh?" I nod. It's time to stop planning. I need to jump in headfirst and see what happens. Sure, Wallace and Olivia might try to destroy each other, but they could come out of this stronger, maybe even as friends. Though, that seems too much to hope for. I'm not sure I can survive even a day smashed between these two.

Ms. Loretta walks with a breezy sway before taking a seat at her desk. She hums thoughtfully before kicking up her feet. "It's the most logical solution, I assume. Besides, it'll give you each a chance to write about something outside of Ceres. The perfect cover for your little plan 'til you're home," she muses, then gives me a serious look "But are you sure you've thought this through?"

"Absolutely!" I jump on the answer eagerly, slipping my shaking hands into my pockets. In truth, this is the most reckless I've been in my entire life. It's exhilarating and terrifying and I feel like I'm going to throw up. But everything I've done before this point has been thought out and planned with list upon list.

I clench my hand into a fist. Maybe it's time to leave my guidebooks and lists behind and take a leap, trusting that wherever I land, I'll be happier.

"That is..." I turn to face Wallace and Olivia. The odds of them agreeing to travel together seems slim. A thought crosses my mind. If they agree, this could be the moment I need to get them to finally put aside their differences. Nothing bonds people like a road trip. "Will you come with me?" I ask.

"As the junior editor, I can't let you go unsupervised." Wallace straightens his collar. "Isn't that right, Ms. Loretta?"

To this, she says nothing, which makes Olivia laugh.

"You know he's only saying yes because his boyfriend will be out of town." Olivia shakes her head. "But I'm in! Besides, I'm the only one with wheels!"

I look down at the rest of the letters. Every kiss, every confession, every adventure...

Maybe it's time to write my own story. I pop a new piece of paper in my typewriter and let my hands fly to the keys before I have a chance to hesitate.

> Dear Anonymous,
>
> It's a date.
>
> Xoxo, Miss Galaxy

The door swings open, and I turn to look. A knowing smile spreads across Miss Loretta's face, and she spins around in her chair to greet Eugene.

Eugene.

Oh, no.

"Ah, Mr. Eris, it seems you're going on a trip."

My gut plummets. When I'd made my declaration, Ms. Loretta said this time would be for the *four* of us didn't she? Eugene is the only other member in our grade, it makes sense that he'd be included. I purse my lips to suppress a groan. I wanted to take a leap—an unplanned jump into the unknown. *This* is why I don't do that.

My head spins as Olivia throws her arms around me, pulling me into a hug.

"Road trip!" she exclaims in a piercing tone. Eugene's eyes bore into mine. I gulp.

Too bad *The Guide* doesn't have a chapter on travel.

4.

Seven days.

Six nights.

Traveling around space with Olivia, Wallace, and Eugene. What could possibly go wrong?

Except for, you know, everything.

Which is why I need to be as prepared as possible. Clothes are strewn around my bedroom, and no matter how many checklists I make, I can't seem to figure out how to cram everything I might possibly need into my suitcase. A minimal color palette would be smart, so that I can mix and match, but looking out at the expanse of pink and mint pastels doesn't really narrow it down. Any of these outfits could be the one I meet my secret admirer in. I need it to be perfect.

I wonder how Olivia is faring; her wardrobe is even more extensive than mine. While the main goal of our "club trip" is tracking down Anonymous, Olivia will be writing a travel guide we'll publish before summer break, Eugene will take his food reviews on the road, and I'll be using Olivia's communicator to post and respond to each new letter via the school's communication network. That way there's no way Anonymous will miss my replies, even if he's steps ahead of me. Lastly, for whatever reason, she's put Wallace in charge of photography. I've never so much as seen him with a camera in his hand, so that will be interesting.

Even if we end up with a million blurry snapshots, it won't matter to me. I topple backward onto the heap of clothes piled high on my bed. Tomorrow is my first trip off-planet, and I have no idea what to wear.

"Knock knock!" Mom sings from the doorway, "How's packing going for my space explorer?"

I groan, gesturing to the mess. I had thought it might be hard to convince her and Dad to let me go on a last minute trip, but they seemed excited to have the house to themselves for the next week and delighted that, for once, I'm actually doing something "fun" for spring break.

"Well, there is a little something else you might want to bring with you."

Her face lights up with a mischievous smile, standing with her hands behind her back.

"I'm not going to just let you gallivant out there without a way to check in," she says, and though her voice is firm, the warm smile that spreads across her face as she moves her hands forward makes my heart leap.

She can't mean... I hold my breath.

I'd been wanting to ask for a wrist communicator for every Christmas and birthday since they came out with the holographic series. But I knew it was a big ticket item, and as someone who barely uses the landline, it would be frivolous to say the least. Especially since the only people I'd be messaging were Olivia and my own parents.

"I was going to save this as a surprise for your birthday..." she begins. I spring up, unable to contain my excitement.

She hands me the box and I gasp as I open the lid. Sitting unceremoniously in the center is a shiny brass wrist cuff with a tiny screen in the center and four neon green glowing buttons on the top. My mouth falls open.

"Oh, honey, you're speechless!" Mom glows with pride, putting an arm around my shoulders. She's so pleased with herself. I don't want to do anything to make her lose that smile, but wow, it's *gigantic*—both her grin and the communicator.

She doesn't waste a second clipping it on my wrist. *Speechless.* That's the only polite option I have here.

The communicator takes up a fourth of my arm. It *would* have been considered cool ... when Mom was in high school. But nowadays, no one would be caught dead wearing something so outdated and unflattering. I open my mouth, trying to figure out how to respond. Mom proudly beams, but her eyes are on the communicator. My stomach twists into knots.

"I found some spare parts and managed to get my old model from when I was your age working. I've heard this style is really going to make a comeback."

Stars! She made it. That means I *really* can't tell her the truth. It's not that I don't appreciate it. It's just ... if I wear this to school, I'll be a laughingstock. I look up at her, and her eyes glimmer, waiting hopefully for a response.

"It's perfect." The words come out too sweet, the cherry on top of whatever lie my face is telling. I force a smile and try to act normal.

"It'll make me feel so much safer having a way for you to check in." She exhales. "A lot can happen on a road trip. Call if you need anything, okay? I don't care if you're planets away."

"Thanks, Mom." I sigh, letting her pull me into a hug that is way too tight. Maybe she's less cool with letting me go than I realized. Mom spends a few minutes helping me sort through the pile of clothing, and successfully convinces me I don't need to bring formal tea-length dresses with me—much less three. Still by the time she heads downstairs, I don't feel any closer to being finished.

A sharp chime startles me. When I look down, I see all the buttons on my communicator are blinking neon yellow. I tap one, but it doesn't work, then another, and another, until finally I touch the screen and my mom's small, pixelated face shows up.

"Hi, Mom." I don't know whether to laugh or scream. I'm amazed this thing even works, but her voice sounds like it's coming out of a blender.

"Your dad made pineapple upside-down cake when you're done packing!"

"Okay … thanks," I say, less enthused.

I hang up. At least, I think I hung up until I hear her laughing.

"You have to press the button on the left." Her voice echoes in stereo from down the stairs, delayed on my wrist.

Oh my stars!

I finally manage to end the call when it rings *again*. I press the button and see the return of her pixelated face alongside my dad.

"Remember: extra socks and a jacket."

"Okay, Mom."

I hang up, making sure I've done it properly this time. Echoes of laughter reach me at the top of the stairs. At least my parents are enjoying themselves.

My wrist chimes again.

"Yes?" I answer in a sharper tone than I ought to be speaking to either of them in. I'm relieved when I'm met with more laughter on the other end of the line.

"Love you!"

I sigh. "Love you too."

When it comes to putting together a wardrobe for the school year, *The Guide* says, "To be smart and well-dressed, you should pack items that can be re-worn and mixed and matched. I was on track with my color coordinated wardrobe—but stars! Nothing is going to match this beast of a communicator. With any luck, I can use my keen fashion sense to distract from it. I don't want my friends to see me like this.

I want Anonymous to see me like this even less.

I could just keep it in my purse. I was planning on using Olivia's communicator for the digital updates anyway. It'll be the first time we've done anything this big over the school's network. A mobile Miss Galaxy is a big change from weather reports and school events. The change will hopefully be an exciting change of pace for all of us, but it's nerve wracking to think that in a way I'll be taking the whole school with me on this adventure.

I decide on three skirts, three sweaters, an extra blouse, underthings, and a dress, just in case I end up somewhere fancy. And a swimsuit—everyone is bringing theirs "just in case." I certainly wouldn't mind if we ended up somewhere tropical. The swimming hole outside of town is freezing and better suited for ice skating all but a few months out of the year. I can't even imagine what a real beach might feel like.

My clothes lay next to my suitcase in a neatly folded pile of pastel blue and pink, along with a pink scarf and another in white. That should be more than enough. I hope so, at least.

It feels like I'm forgetting something, but I check, double check, and check again.

After clasping and unclasping my suitcase again and again, I decide there is absolutely nothing I forgot. Sure, my suitcase feels a little light, but that's probably normal for a one-week trip. And the guidebook would never steer me wrong.

It's just nerves, and I have earned a slice of pineapple upside-down cake.

5.

By the time I arrive at Olivia's place, the bags under my eyes are heavier than the suitcase I'm carrying. The sound of Olivia revving the engine fills my ears, and when I peer into the garage, I spot the giant smile playing across her face. She's been waiting for this moment ever since she and her older brother Rex fixed up the "hunk of junk" during a summer vacation, in the sweet spot right where she was learning to drive and he hadn't been forcibly transferred to a new high school yet. The "hunk of junk" was a Nebula Cruiser '55 with chipped mint paint, a sleek, curved body, and round lights.

I smirk. I didn't realize I'd be perfectly coordinated with our ride.

"I thought you had something sensible, like a flying saucer!" someone shouts from behind me. I stumble forward, whirling around to see Eugene and Wallace, their suitcases in tow. Wallace stares at the cruiser with wide eyes. I have to admit it's more suited for racing than it is for a road trip, but that's a part of its charm.

"Is it too late to leave without them?" Olivia crosses her arms. My shoulders tense. I didn't realize we'd get to the bickering quite so soon.

I wave hello to the boys, and Eugene sleepily waves back before rubbing his eyes.

It's disarmingly cute, and ugh, still Eugene—what am I thinking? Still, it's moments like this when I can see why people at school are still swooning over him. But that's not important right now. I turn my attention back to Wallace. Maybe this trip is what Olivia and Wallace need to finally get over whatever it is between them.

"Happy to see you too, Olivia!" Wallace says breezily, walking toward the passenger seat.

"Susie already called shotgun."

"I did?"

Flames flicker across Olivia's face as she glances back at me.

"Oh, I did!" I correct myself. "But if you'd rather..." I'm unsure of exactly how to navigate this. I want to help Olivia, but I don't want to offend Wallace. Not to mention that if he's in the front, I'll be stuck in the backseat with Eugene, who, if I'm not mistaken, I just heard laugh at me. I glare and feel disappointed when he doesn't notice my scorn, staring off in the distance with his dark, disinterested eyes.

"Nah, it's fine." Wallace shuffles to the backseat, and Eugene purses his lips at me—or was that supposed to be a smile? His face is so stiff, it's hard to tell. But knowing him, a smile is unlikely. I shake off the thought. It's too early to let him get under my skin.

Once we're all seated in the cruiser, there is an awkward silence that I didn't anticipate.

"Thanks for doing this," I say, but the tension doesn't melt away. Which is perfectly normal—besides Olivia, I only see them at school, and I only get along with one of them.

What did I expect? To climb into the cruiser and instantly become best friends, singing along to the radio? I knew it couldn't be that easy, but I could use a tad more enthusiasm.

"Beats spending the week at home with my folks!" Wallace offers from the backseat. Stretching his arms out, he yawns while Olivia thrusts the cruiser into gear, sending his body jolting forward.

The seats vibrate, and I resist the urge to scold my best friend. That was unexpected. Slightly muted laughter comes from the backseat, and I stiffen, shooting yet another glare toward Eugene. Then I realize *everyone* is laughing at Wallace's jumpiness except for me.

"Olivia, have you ever actually driven this thing before?" Wallace asks, his voice shooting up an octave.

"Well, sure! Tons of times on the driver's ed test track, and I go to Lester's Diner all the time." Her confidence is as wide as the smile on her face as the cruiser ascends into the air. Within seconds, home grows smaller and smaller—and stars this thing is fast. I gulp as darkness spreads around us. For a moment, the sky is a sheet of black velvet dotted with silver sequins.

"Lester's is barely two minutes away!" Wallace gasps, clutching his hand to his heart. With her enthusiasm, I hadn't given much thought to the possibility that maybe Olivia wasn't a competent driver. Wallace is right; Lester's tin-can diner hovers just outside the bubble-dome with its blinking neon sign and mouth-watering shakes. We've never really hovered more than a few miles off the planet.

The cruiser rocks from side to side, and I gulp, bracing myself on the armrests. We're far away from the main starways that surround and connect the big planets. Even still, I didn't expect it would be so ... dark. When Olivia and I cruise above town, there are always signs and streetlights.

Tension creeps up my spine until it grabs hold of my neck, and I push out a stiff breath. We're really leaving Ceres, the only place I've ever really known.

"It's fine! Susie trusts me. Don't you, Susie?"

Wallace and Eugene look at me with interest while Olivia's smile doesn't falter as she faces the vast emptiness ahead, a multitude of possibilities just a leap away. I trust Olivia implicitly as a friend—but driving on an open starway?

"Absolutely," I croak, knowing I want the statement to be the truth. Whether it is or not is yet to be determined.

"The Park" is a flat, grassy, bubble-domed field floating a few hours away from Ceres. They hold all sorts of concerts and events there. I've heard about it plenty of times but have never actually seen it with my own eyes. It's always been too far to justify doing a day trip, but too close to stay the night.

It was only supposed to be a three-hour drive, but after getting turned around a few times and having to wait in the massive line at the airlock, we arrive in four.

As described, it's a cute—yet overcrowded—patch of AstroTurf floating in the middle of space.

There are picnic blankets stretched out onto the grass, kids running around playing, and couples snuggled up as far as the eye can see. The meteor shower is happening so early, half of them are in their pajamas, and sipping coffee from small Melmac coffee mugs. With each small movement, their clothes appear to be suspended in time. The hem of my skirt floats with every step, as if it's dancing around my legs.

I'm surprised at just how crowded this place is. Familiar faces are mixed in with strangers. Letterman jackets in blue and purple, our school colors, are tossed over nightgowns and casual clothes. There's a game of low-gravity soccer going on in the distance.

Anonymous could be any of them.

I realize I'm searching for a tuft of silver hair in the crowd. But Skip is not why I'm here, I sternly remind myself, discreetly pulling the letter from my pocket to try to plan our next step. We're here—now what?

"Let's try to scope out a place to put our stuff down." I begin. We need some sort of home base, and I wouldn't mind looking around a little on my own to get my bearings. Still, we travel in a pack until we find an empty spot to lay down our picnic blankets. It's not hard to find the tree—if you can call it that.

At the center of the park, the shining metal structure is painted to look like bark with spindly branches that might have once held a swing set. Picnickers crowd all around it. I take a step forward and then falter, realizing I can't just walk up and start searching the tree for a letter. *Can I?* It doesn't look like any of the picnickers nearby go to our school...

"Is it rude to just go up there?" I whisper to Olivia, who rolls her eyes in response.

"We came all this way, and you're worried about stepping over a few picnic blankets?" She's right—of course she is. It just feels awkward.

"Come on." With a tug on my sleeve, she leads me toward the tree. "Wallace, camera!" Olivia holds out her hand expectantly. Wallace, however, doesn't budge; he clutches the clunky camera around his neck. His short pink hair hangs in the air for as he shakes his head.

"I'll handle the snapshots, thank you." Our junior editor bristles as the three of us leave Eugene to hold down the fort. We move past the crowd of people with Olivia explaining to anyone who stands as an obstacle in our way that we want to take pictures next to the tree.

Walter takes a photo of the metal structure by itself first, then gets close as I reach my hand into the hollow spot in the middle. Cool metal slides across my skin. I feel around past long abandoned pieces of gum and bits of chipped paint until I touch the smooth paper with my fingertips.

Wallace snaps a photo as I pull the letter out. I freeze in place, Miss Galaxy's identity is a closely guarded secret between all of us. Why would Wallace take a picture with me in it? He must see the hesitation on my face because I'm offered a reassuring smile.

"Don't worry. Your face is cropped out." His pointed ears flutter with what I guess is nerves. I wonder if he's ever done this sort of thing before.

The letter feels heavy in my hands. Now that I'm holding it, it's the only thing I can think about. Bickering between Wallace and Olivia crops up on our walk back, but the words might as well be static. I sit down with a thud on the edge of the picnic blanket.

My fingers tear into the envelope, as if opening even one second later will change the contents. But once it's in my hands, fear bubbles up. What if after all this effort, it really was just some prank? I take a deep breath. I'll never know until I open it.

I hesitate for just a moment longer until I can't take it anymore. I carefully lift the flap and slide the letter out, my heartbeat picking up with every passing second. My eyes jump to the carefully typed words.

"Dear Miss Galaxy," the letter reads, and it's as if the writer has taken a step back. They just called me "Galaxy" before, and somehow, that felt more personal. But maybe it had just been an error. It wouldn't be the first time. Still, the formal tone throws me off for a moment, but I keep reading.

> Dear Miss Galaxy,
>
> I've watched meteor showers like this one countless times—it's a strange feeling, isn't it? Watching something burn so bright right across the sky. The way the sparks flicker into fireworks always makes me wish I had someone to watch them with.
>
> For our next location, let's move on to what you called the most "ideal date spot for spring" in one of your articles. Go to the most popular beach where the orange sand sparkles brightly under the purple sky. Let's make this next one more challenging. The next clue will be behind where the marshmallows and popping rocks reside. That almost rhymed, didn't it? Maybe the next letter should be a poem...
>
> I hope you packed your sunglasses,
>
> Anonymous

I lie back on the blanket and let out a long sigh, pressing the letter to my chest. My face is flushed and glowing, my heart racing. Aliquam must be our next destination. It's the only beach I've ever recommended in my articles, and according to the travel guides, it matches the description perfectly. It's known for its bright sandy beaches and bubbly pink water. It's a popular vacation destination for most of the students of Galaxy High—at least according to the letters in Miss Galaxy's box.

"Just as goofy as the last one," Olivia says, lying next to me. "But I won't say no to a beach day." This time, I don't let her words get to me. I'd read about feeling lovesick countless times, but I never realized how much it would feel like an actual illness. I replay the letter over and over. Goofy? No, it's swoony perfection is made clear by the racing of my heart.

Now, I just need to figure out how to respond. I've been way too embarrassed to actually wear my communicator. It's stayed tucked safely in my purse, where I've discreetly sent Mom and Dad a few "I'm safe" updates.

Olivia passes me her communicator to work on my reply, though I think, in this case, I should wait until I've actually seen the meteor shower. It's the reason Anonymous chose this place after all. Wallace rummages through the picnic basket I brought along. My dad stuffed it full of bright pastel breakfast pastries that he must have stayed up half the night baking, along with some outdoorsy things we had lying around the garage. I can't fathom taking a single bite of anything, as appealing as the flakey crusts and pink and light green fillings look.

Wallace pulls out a ball and smiles. "Anyone up for a game of catch?"

I understand we're not all here to chase a secret admirer through the skies. But catch? Right now? After I've just consumed the most romantic love letter of my whole life?

"No... I just need to think." I don't remember when I stood up from the blanket; mid-step I realize I've been pacing. I stare down at Olivia's shiny new communicator.

Maybe I'll just brainstorm the start of my response...

I reach for my notebook.

The ball drifts through the air. Wallace has a better throwing arm than I would have thought, but then again, I think the low gravity might be making it look more impressive. The ball hangs in the air, floating above the AstroTurf.

I turn just in time to see Eugene's lanky frame spring off the ground in what looks like slow motion. He is all legs and arms, like noodles attached to his body. He catches the ball and throws it back to Wallace. They go back and forth, and for just a moment, Eugene's long limbs look almost graceful. Then he stumbles, and the ball lands right by the tree on the hill. The group picnicking there laugh. I think it fell in one of their drinks. It all seems so normal.

Is this what the two of them are like outside of school? There's an uncharacteristic smile on Eugene's face as they return to the blanket to dive into homemade pastries while I keep my attention fixed on my notebook.

Suddenly, it's dark.

All at once, the neon sign and overhead lighting switch off, and looking up in the blackness, all I can see is the flickering of stars—at first, that is. Then, the first comet zooms past, light streaking in its path, and tiny bits of debris crash on the glass of the dome. The sky turns shades of blue and purple.

We're a safe distance away. But having pieces of rock clanging away at the glass makes my heart race.

I never realized the sky could look so ... different. It's dangerous and beautiful—the light glowing brighter as the old rocks burn up in a cosmic light show. It's the end of their chapter, which means the start of a new one.

Shivers crawl along my skin. The ground shakes with the passing of every rock.

Falling back onto the ground, we watch them fly past in a silence only broken by the "oohs" and "ahhs" of the crowd.

Couples clutch each other. A smile pulls at my lips. *Maybe next time, Anonymous and I will be among them.*

A loud spark erupts outside of the dome, and the ground shakes. Startled, the four of us scramble from our places lying down to the center of the picnic blanket, colliding in a way that makes my shoulders brush into Eugene. His icy eyes meet mine in what I assume is disgust before he slinks away, sitting in an upright position.

A beep sounds from inside my bag. I realize I forgot to get in touch with Mom. Quietly, I reach into my bag. Thankfully, I've only missed one message from her.

[Mom: U OK?]

It reads in all caps. I wonder if she's messaging me from work.

It's still a little hard to get a hang of the controls. I make sure I type a quick, *I'm doing well, call you in the morning.*

[Mom: B SAFe]

[Me: I will]

By the time I snap my purse shut, I've earned Olivia's suspicion. Her orange eyes narrow for a moment, but she says nothing—so much for being discreet. I shake my head, mouthing, "I'll tell you later," and we go back to looking up at the stars. Our heads fall back on the picnic blanket. With a dreamy sigh, I switch to using Olivia's communicator to begin my response. I think that I finally know what I want to say.

Dear Anonymous,

There was both beauty and loneliness when I looked up at the sky. Living on Ceres for so long, it's embarrassing that I've never seen a meteor shower like that before. I'm not sure that I should even admit it on paper. (Readers, don't judge me!) I hope that, next time, when all this is done, we can watch one together.

I wouldn't mind a love poem or clearer instructions for that matter. Luckily, I know exactly where you're trying to send me next. Though, if I've read the guidebooks right, popping rocks and marshy waters aren't much of a clue.

I'll search all day if I have to. I can't wait to learn more about you.

Xo, Miss Galaxy

"Sus, I say this with love," Olivia sighs, peering over my shoulder, "but you write like an old lady."

"I do not!" I gasp. Miss Galaxy is supposed to sound worldly and mature! Ms. Loretta and I went over all the details in orientation. It's not dated; it's classic. Besides, Anonymous seems to be a fan. I hit the send button before I lose my nerve. Our communicators buzz in tandem, sending a ripple of light and chimes through the crowd. If Galaxy High is ever curious about what Miss Galaxy gets up to in her spare time, this week they're certainly finding out. Sending out the first letter and my response, I'm filled with both nerves and satisfaction. If Anonymous is paying attention at all, he has my response, and there's nothing "old lady" about it.

"When you meet, make sure you offer him a hard candy from your purse." Wallace snickers, reaching out to give Olivia a high-five that is immediately dismissed.

"They're cough drops! Who goes on a trip without cough drops?"

They roar with laughter while Eugene cracks a small smile. If this is what it takes for Olivia and Wallace to bond, I'll take it. Let's see who they turn to when someone's allergies act up because I'm not going to share!

6.

Being in the front seat of a '55 Nebula Cruiser is one thing when you're racing to the local diner or going for a cruise through town—but starways backed up with traffic is an eerie feeling. The cruiser is on a road in the middle of the sky with nothing but twinkling stars, the blackness of space, and hundreds of other cruisers and flying saucers chugging forward on the winding roads that connect each planet. The longer we're stuck, the more sick I feel.

"I've always wanted to visit the lemon drop beaches on vacation." Wallace sighs, shifting in his seat to look out the window.

"Lemon drop?" According to my research and the name on the navigation screen, the planet we're inching closer to is called Aliquam.

"Look to your left," he says, and I swivel to see beyond the cruisers stopped mid-air in traffic to the glowing yellow planet in front of us. It's oval shaped and pitched in at the ends with a large ring around the center, like a large lemon in the sky.

"Wow." I breathe, a smile lifting my lips before my stomach betrays me yet again. I've never been prone to motion sickness, but this drive is testing me.

I can't be sure if it's Olivia's driving or my nerves. Our first "mission," "date," whatever I'm supposed to call these excursions, went off without a hitch, but now hovering over our next stop? Golly, my insides are like a soda bottle that's been shaken. There's a chapter in *The Guide* about going on long drives. It says: "After just a little while, you should acclimate to space travel swimmingly, even if you're a novice space traveler."

I think I might be drowning.

As we crawl forward, I ground myself by staring at the strange-shaped planet as we're pulled into its orbit. After what feels like hours, we finally reach our destination— Aliquam. AKA Lemon Drop Beach.

The bright yellow planet is even smaller than Ceres. I know from my research that it is popular, but I had no idea just how busy it would be. After an hour queuing up for the parking garage, Olivia finally lowers us into a spot.

It's conveniently connected to the welcome center and locker rooms, making it easy for us to slip away to change into our swimwear.

I sit on a bench, nibbling at another sleeve of dry crackers. I didn't realize motion sickness pills should be a part of my travel bag.

I let my head hang to my knees for a minute, drawing in a few deep breaths. Somewhere out on this planet is another clue, leading me to another letter that'll make my heart ache. That's a thought that doesn't exactly inspire a feeling of calm.

Could Anonymous be somewhere nearby, watching? If it were me, I'd be waiting to see who was standing in the crowd, clutching a letter to their chest with hearts in their eyes.

I open my bag, unfolding the stretchy polka dot fabric of my swimsuit. I can't remember the last time I wore it and say a silent prayer that it still fits.

I wiggle into the high-waisted bikini bottoms and clasp the top behind my back. The idea of being out in public in the equivalent of my underwear makes me uneasy, but just as I've quoted many times from page 72 of *The Guide*, "Everyone at the beach is struggling with their own insecurities. They won't notice yours."

I give myself a little nod, mentally reciting the mantra before wrapping my curls up in a hot pink scarf.

When I step out of the changing room and find Olivia pinning her hair into a pile on top of her head, I can't believe my eyes. How I ended up with a best friend who looks like a movie star is beyond me.

"You look amazing!" I squeal, transfixed by her silver swimsuit with its matching high-collared cape that's certainly more for fashion than sun protection.

"Aww, so do you!" She pulls me over to pose in front of the mirror. "Like a proper beach bunny!"

She twirls around in the mirror and suddenly pauses, looking a little uncertain of herself. "Honestly, though, I've been waiting to wear this thing forever. You don't think I'm too much?"

"Never," I reassure her. "And if anyone says anything different, they'll have to answer to this beach bunny." I curl my hands into fists, trying to look as intimidating as possible. When I meet her gaze in the mirror, she throws her head back with laughter. Intimidation does not suit me.

But when it comes to actually stepping foot onto the beach, my nerves swell higher than a crashing waves.

As I exit the locker room, my sandals sink into powdery sand for the first time, the scents of salt water and sugary-sweet sugar cones from a nearby ice cream stall fill my nose, and is that citrus in the air? No wonder they call it Lemon Drop. With every step, the warm sun beats down on my exposed shoulders, and the idea of something cold sounds more and more refreshing.

Maybe after we find the next letter.

Wallace hops up from the distance, waving to get our attention. The two boys are waiting by the opposite locker room wall.

Wallace and Eugene are leaning on the locker room wall. Eugene looks...

Exactly how I'd expect, in the worst way possible.

His hair is coiffed into the perfect pompadour, and his square sunglasses are even darker than his demeanor. And he's still wearing a white t-shirt and his absurd leather jacket. Who wears a leather jacket to the beach?

Still, girls walk past and shamelessly glance up and down his slender body while he stands there, calm, cool, and completely uncaring. He doesn't bother to acknowledge a single passerby. I guess there weren't enough hearts to break at Galaxy High—he's expanding to the rest of the universe.

"You going to put that in the locker?" Olivia asks, obviously referring to the jacket. I try not to laugh.

"Nope," he answers briskly. *Stars*, what did I expect?

"Aren't you worried about the ... sand?" I ask. He says nothing. A chuckle escapes me. Despite how good it looks on him, it doesn't change the fact that he looks ridiculous.

The four of us head down through the powdery sand toward the ocean. With every step, I can't shake the feeling that Anonymous is out there somewhere looking for me. I straighten my posture, reminding myself to relax. Anonymous sent me out here to have fun. Besides, finding the letter should be at the top of my internal checklist. There are a few pastel and shiny chrome trailers parked on the outskirts of the beach. It must be incredible to wake up to a view like this. As we get closer, I'm able to really see the pink waves lapping against the creamsicle colored sand, while far in the distance, surfers ride the waves on the outer rings of the planet. Anonymous was right. This place really does sparkle.

We make our way toward the bubbling water. There are umbrellas plunged into the ground, the designs and colors bright, the tropical ones looking like they could have been sticking out of a drink in a fancy restaurant.

A group of kids run in between us, barreling toward the water. There are so many families camped out and splashing around, and everyone looks like they're straight out of a postcard—or at least like they're enjoying themselves. I am impressed to find that Olivia is walking calmly next to Wallace. Maybe it's just too beautiful here to fight with anyone, even your nemesis.

"Don't kick sand at me! What are you, five?" Wallace shouts. My posture deflates with a sigh. I guess I spoke too soon. However, I'm starting to see another problem.

For every star in the sky, there is a purple rock to match it. "The next clue will be behind where the marsh mallows and popping rocks reside," I mutter quietly to myself. Somewhere near the shore, but beyond that, it seems we're tasked with something impossible. Stars! The note could be anywhere...

There's a tap on my shoulder. Wallace stands in front of me, an encouraging smile decorating his pink face. "Guess we should start looking, huh?" he suggests before guiding the group forward. That's our junior-editor for you, always staying on task.

We drop our bags in a spot a little away from the rest of the crowd. Along the way, I turn over every single purple rock I stumble across. Most are about the size of my palm, smooth enough to skip over the water.

I find a crab, moss, and a few seashells ... but no letter.

We walk along the beach, dipping our toes in the bubbling pink water. It's a strange sensation, fizzing and popping with each step. The deeper we go, the more it feels like I'm submerged in a can of soda. This is incredible. I lean my head back and allow myself to relax in the glow of the sun. I wonder how the letter will be packaged this time. A message in a bottle? That would be fitting for the setting and so romantic.

A cold splash of water on my neck snaps me out of my daydream. "*Hey!*"

I whirl around, my blood boiling at the sight of Eugene just ... standing there. The school bad boy is not trying to look innocent; he wears no fun-loving smirk and isn't poised to splash again. He's just totally blank.

Does Eugene not understand how serious this is? Does he think my quest for true love is a joke?

"Fine!" Two can play at this game. If this is how it's going to be for the rest of the trip, I need to tell him once and for all that I'm not here for his shenanigans—with retaliation, of course, I stand back to launch my attack, getting ready to soak that ridiculous leather jacket. Giggling erupts from behind him, making me pause. Without warning, Olivia lurches forward from her hiding place, spraying me with water. "You are going down Olivia Oren!" I shout, chasing her out of the shallows.

Anonymous chose this place for a reason, right? Sure, it probably wasn't to annihilate my best friend in a splash war, but I'm not about to go down without a fight.

We continue down the beach while launching attacks, stopping to look under every rock in the shallows.

There's nothing here except for a beautiful beach and scenery. The splashing—whatever fun I'm having right now—is not bringing me any closer to Anonymous.

Stars. I'm wasting my time.

A cold splash of water soaks my face. It burns my eyes before trickling down my skin.

I sprint backward, almost stumbling over, and Olivia's laughter stops. She looks at me with the wide-eyed expression of someone who got caught passing notes in class.

"Maybe we should take a break," Olivia says softly.

"We just started looking!" I argue and realize my voice sounds harsher than I meant. A good traveling companion should be easy-going and carefree, and I had fully intended to be that way.

"It's been hours," she corrects.

Oh.

Well, that explains why my legs are starting to feel tired, but there's no way it's been *that* long. An hour, tops. She's overreacting. I'll relax plenty—after we find the letter. Besides, we've been having plenty of fun, haven't we?

"It's probably about time for lunch," Olivia suggests, and Eugene nods in agreement. "We got an early start, and we spent forever driving out here..."

How can they even think about food at a time like this? I shake my head. It's not important. I'll find the letter even if I have to do it alone.

"Maybe you should all take a rest. I'm going to wander around a bit."

"You really don't mind?" Olivia asks, not looking convinced. "Come on, Susie. Aren't you hungry?" She takes my arm, but I shake it away.

"I'm going to look by myself for a little while," I say with an unconvincing shrug of my shoulders. "Go ahead, really. I'm fine by myself."

I am not fine by myself. I am extremely irritated, but there's no reason they need to know that. If they want to have a normal spring break lounging on the beach, that's fine by me.

My legs carry me farther down the shore. There's still a lot of beach to comb through, and if I have to do it alone, so be it. I spy a cluster of rocks protruding from the deep water. It does draw my attention; there has to be a letter here some-where. I just need to walk farther in. It's shallow enough for me to walk to the cluster. Now that I'm alone, I finally take a deep breath and sink into the moment.

The milky pink water crashes against my legs. The bubbles rise and crack against my skin, and my feet sink down into the wet sand. The sound of a someone playing guitar melts into the cackling of rowdy teenagers. I close my eyes and try to drink in the moment, letting myself walk a little deeper.

Is this what you wanted me to feel, Anonymous? I wonder, savoring the cool citrus scented breeze as it messes my bangs away from my forehead.

A wave crashes against the back of my knees, and I stumble to keep my balance. My scarf flutters from around my neck. I try to catch it, but it floats right behind me. I dart after it, my curls whipping back.

"Got it!" a familiar voice shouts, and when I turn, I spot a figure standing at the edge of the water. He looks like he just came from muscle beach with a guitar slung over his back and the delicate fabric of my scarf dangling from his hand.

"Susie?"

I blink, and Skip's perfect face bathed in rosy light comes into focus.

"Skip?" I call out. What is he doing here?

"What are you doing here?" He echoes my question before I have a chance to ask it.

"I'm just—I, uh, I'm here with friends," I say, nervously pointing off into the distance. I've wandered too far off. I can't even see our spot anymore.

"Me too." He points to a group gathered around what looks like the makings of a bonfire that will surely be ablaze by the end of the night.

I hold out my hand, expecting him to return my scarf, but instead, his warm grasp envelops mine as we inch closer to the shore. With that small gesture, I'm steadied in the uneven sand. And the world feels like it's spinning.

Frustrated, I try to think of what to do or say. If he knows I wasn't reaching for his hand, he might feel embarrassed. And it's not exactly that I mind. No, I don't mind in the slightest.

"I was just about to grab an ice cream when I saw you." His bright gold eyes flicker down at me, and I wonder if my hair is doing something crazy.

"Oh, well... thanks again," I begin, but he's quick to cut me off.

"I'm asking if you want to come with me." He runs his hand absentmindedly through his messy silver hair that gleams in the sun as bright as any star. "My friends are all full from lunch, so I was planning on going by myself."

I look out toward the seemingly endless water, then back to Skip. I guess going with him might be a good excuse to see more of the beach and maybe find the spot I'm looking for. Plus, now that my stomach has settled from the drive, I *am* a little hungry, and ice cream sounds amazing.

I'm about to answer when my legs wobble under me. There are too many waves! Before I can react, Skip's arms wrap tightly around me. I'm pressed against his freckled chest, and it doesn't feel bad.

"Whoa! I got you!" he exclaims, holding me steady for a few moments. His heart is beating fast—or is that my heart? Our bodies are pressed so tightly together, I can't tell. I look up, and the bright light illuminates his eyes and hair. I shudder. He's too handsome for anyone's good. Carefully, he guides me out of the water, his hand never leaving the small of my back. I bask in it for just a moment, even though I know I shouldn't.

It's the second time I've had to remind myself that Skip is not the reason I'm out here. Right now, he's just a distraction.

A very cute distraction. But a distraction, nonetheless.

I look down at the pink scarf still swaying gently in his hand.

"Oh, um, my scarf..." I say, trying to manage my now hopelessly tangled curls with my fingers.

"This scarf?" A cheeky grin spreads across his face while he ties it around his neck and strikes a pose. "I believe the rules clearly state 'finders, keepers.'"

I expect him to untie it and hand it back to me, but instead, he strides forward. I don't have time for this! Still, I can't resist following behind him, knowing that it's not solely about getting my scarf back. The idea of walking along the beach with Skip is irresistible. Sure, I'm supposed to be looking for Anonymous, but could a little break really hurt? I'm not technically doing anything wrong... and it would be a shame to lose my favorite scarf.

"Hey!" I call, sand flying under the kick of my heels as I run after him.

"Ah, you change your mind about that ice cream?" he asks.

"The scarf around your neck," I manage, out of breath.

"Do you like it?" He poses again, his eyes twinkling down at me. "I just found it on the beach."

I can't help laughing. Only Skip Stone would be able to pull off a look like this: shirtless, shorts that don't quite cover his entire thighs, and my scarf. It's impossible to keep my eyes off him, but I have to.

"So, ice cream?" he asks with a childish laugh.

"Oh, um—" I am interrupted by a loud grumble from my stomach. Before I can explain it away, it grumbles again. I hide my face in my hands. I guess maybe I shouldn't have blown off taking a lunch break like Olivia suggested.

"I'll take that as a yes!" He's really ... enchanting. It's hard to believe that none of his friends made room for ice cream, even just as an excuse to be next to him.

"If the tide had sent us both tumbling, I'm afraid I would have ruined that guitar of yours," I say. The instrument is dry, save for a few pink droplets.

"I guess I rushed in without thinking." He smiles widely, running his fingers through his hair. Did he really risk damaging his guitar for me?

We chuckle. As we travel down the beach, I keep my eyes peeled, but none of the rocks look any different than what I've seen so far. We walk together, and despite my building nerves, I'm struck by how comfortable it feels to be this close. Before we know it, we've arrived at the overcrowded ice cream stand, making small talk as we wait in line together.

I bet to anyone watching, we look like a couple.

The daydream ends when we reach the front of the line, my fingers trace down my hips, searching for my wallet—which is in my purse.

Which I left back with everyone.

Perfect. Breathing out a sigh, I ignore the way my mouth waters at the scent of sugary baked waffle cones and step out of line, letting a group of the kids in front of me go. They excitedly bounce forward, clamoring over every free sample.

Skip whirls until he spots me on the sidelines. "What are you doing?"

"I don't have my purse," I explain, shrugging my shoulders.

"So?"

I stare at him blankly. Unless ice cream on this beach is free, I'm not sure what he's getting at.

The line is already moving. If I jump in now, it'll irritate everyone else waiting. Shaking my messy curls, I gesture for him to go on. He can just eat that very delicious looking ice cream in front of me, and I won't be jealous at all. I'm sure there are still some snacks back at the beach blanket.

In the meantime, I can keep looking for the letter. I hover over every little cluster of purple rocks. A hopeless feeling overtakes whatever hunger I had to begin with. But I press forward, wandering while trying to look as casual as possible.

"Whatcha looking at?" Skip asks.

"Collecting shells," I lie. I don't even have to look up to feel his gaze on my empty hands.

"You're not very good at it." When I look up, he's holding two black ice cream cones with swirls of blue and pink soft serve on top.

"I figured this matches your whole look?" he asks, his voice wavering with uncertainty.

That's—surprisingly thoughtful. "You didn't have to do that," I protest. "I'll pay you back as soon as—"

"I don't have to do anything." He winks and my entire face glows in response. Is Skip Stone flirting with me? No, no it's not possible. He's charming and friendly with everyone. I know that. Just because someone buys you ice cream, it doesn't mean they have a crush on you. But there's something about the spark in his eyes that makes me question everything.

What are the odds that both of us would be here on the same day?

"And don't worry about it. It was my treat." He places the ice cream cone in my hands, and I try to ignore the swoony feeling at the base of my forehead when our fingertips touch. "You know, I think this is the first time we've really hung out outside of school," Skip remarks with a hum.

"We studied together last year."

"Studying doesn't count." His lips twist up into a playful grin.

With every step, my sandals sink into the ground, caking sand over my wet toes. "How long have you been playing the guitar?"

"A few years," he says, his face falling a little. "My parents aren't exactly keen on it. They think I'm paying less attention to academics because of it. But it's just an outlet, you know?"

I nod. My parents have raised similar concerns about my spending too much time at the paper. It's the whole reason Skip started to tutor me in the first place. "Have you been falling behind?"

He shakes his head at first, but as soon as he meets my eyes, he nods. "Literature has been a nightmare."

"Well! In that case, maybe I can finally return the favor."

His arm has somehow linked its way in mine, and there's intrigue playing on his face. "Favor?"

I blush under his steady gaze. I look away, turning my attention to the sand. "You saved me in science last year."

"Oh." He throws his head back, laughing. "Is that all?"

"Is that all? I was about to fail!"

"You were barely averaging a B—"

"On a steady road to an F!"

He stops, spinning me around so that we're facing each other. "That's not how I remember it."

"Skip Stone! I'm trying to pay you a compliment."

He reaches out with his free hand to ruffle my bangs. "You sound like an old lady."

Not him too.

"Whatever the case, I'd be happy to help," I say, fearing that my grimace will be permanently stuck to my face if one more person calls me old.

"When are you free next?"

"Anytime for lunch, I suppose," I begin, then hesitate… by next week, I might have a regular standing date for lunch. A pain fills my stomach. I almost forgot to look for the letter. I've just been wandering aimlessly with Skip for the last half-hour.

"It's a date," he says happily.

"Oh! Um…"

"Relax! I meant as friends." Skip's laugh is startlingly louder than usual. Right, it was silly of me to think he meant anything else.

"Right. Of course."

He tilts his head curiously. "So, have you been following this Miss Galaxy stuff?" The question hits my chest like a rogue asteroid.

"What?" I choke. He did not just ask that question.

He gestures to his communicator. Oh, my stars. This is bad.

"We all got the blast this morning," he explains. "It's part of the reason the gang wanted to come out here."

"It is?" The ground might as well open up right now. I don't care how glittering and beautiful the sand is; I want to be swallowed up by it.

For all I know, the whole school could be out here looking for my—Miss Galaxy's—letters. What if someone intercepts it? What if I never get a chance to see the next clue?

"Yeah, I mean it's all kind of—"

Skip's voice is white noise. I look around, trying to count how many people I recognize from school, but they are all strangers, save for Wallace waving frantically in the distance.

My heart leaps into my chest. Did he find a clue?

"I should go," I say, gesturing toward Wallace who is already barreling toward us.

"Come sit by the fire pit later, and I'll dedicate a song to you and your friends!" It might be nice to sit by the fire on a beach with everyone, and they do seem to have snagged the best spot. And if one of them finds the letter before we do, it might be my only chance to hear about its contents.

"Hey, wait—my scarf!" I call back as the two of us part ways.

"I guess you'll just have to come to the bonfire!" he teases. I wish he wouldn't try to include me with his friends so much. It's not like I'm at the beach alone.

I run my fingers through my messy hair. At this point, I guess there's no saving it anyway. I race back toward Wallace.

"I've been looking all over for you! We all have!"

"Did you find something?" I ask eagerly.

He shakes his head. "No, but your bag started beeping like *crazy*. Olivia went into your purse and—"

Oh no.

"Well, she accidentally answered it, and your mom was … not happy that you weren't there! She was all, 'Bad things happen in good places!'"

Oh no!

"And then we couldn't find you! Olivia was worried, I was worried, and Eugene was worried."

"Eugene too?" I ask, highly doubting that.

"Susie, I mean this kindly," Wallace says slowly, his eyes widening as if he's worried whatever he says next will offend me, "but your mother's paranoia is very convincing."

"I'll take care of it," I say, but even I'm not convinced. If she called me that many times, I wouldn't be surprised if she's on her way here right this moment. I can't let that happen. Without a second thought, I race to our spot on the beach, only to find that it's deserted. Is everyone really out looking for me? I sink to the ground, pulling my communicator out of my purse.

Eighteen missed calls.

It's worse than I thought. I click on her name, and it barely rings before her pixelated face appears on the screen.

"Susie! I called you for *hours*. Why didn't you pick up?" Mom says all in one breath, the click of her heels echoes through the muffled speakers, and I imagine she's pacing the length of the living room.

"Oh, I guess I forgot," I mumble.

"The device is supposed to be on your wrist. How did you forget?"

"Oh, um... I took it off while I was washing my hands, and I guess I didn't put it back on," I lie, trying to figure out how to spare her feelings.

"Honey, it's waterproof! I understand wanting to protect it, and I know you're not used to having something like this or being away from home, but I need to be able to check on you."

"Sorry, Mom."

"You don't have to wear it twenty-four hours a day, but at least during daytime..."

"Were you worried?" I ask, my voice coming out smaller than expected.

"Are you really asking me that?" Her sharp tone is like a dagger to the chest. Ooof, I really messed this up. Both her and Dad hardly ever raise their voices. There's silence, then a loud sigh. "Anything could happen so far from home."

Which is exactly why I'm here. But I understand what she's getting at. I'm normally nothing to worry about—school, newspaper, home, every single day. But if something bad happens while I'm away, there's not much she can do. "I'll make sure I wear it all day tomorrow."

"Promise?"

Grimly, I nod.

"*Promise.*"

I look up and see Eugene looming a few feet away. He probably heard every single word. Great. Just what I needed—for him, of all people, to hear me get scolded like a child.

The call ends, and after a few moments, I give him a small wave, signaling that it's okay to come closer.

I remember, too late, that the communicator is still clipped to my wrist. I cringe, bracing myself for whatever snotty reaction he can muster. Eugene seems so trendy and judgmental. I hope he doesn't comment on the monstrosity on my wrist. It'd only make me feel even worse—especially since I should have been wearing it this whole time.

His eyes linger on it for a moment, but thankfully, he says nothing. We wait in silence until Olivia and Wallace return.

They've seen it now, anyway. The big brass bracelet is impossible to hide, like a ball and chain shackling me to home.

"Sorry, everyone," I say, staring down at the terrycloth towels. "It was a gift from my mom for the trip."

I should have just worn the silly thing. Now they've all had to deal with my mom and search high and low for me, all because I wanted to look cool.

Still, I'm relieved Skip didn't see me wearing it.

"None of us were *that* worried ... until your mom said she'd have you come straight home if we didn't find you," Olivia admits.

"*I* was that worried," Wallace corrects her, beads of sweat still decorating his forehead. His pointed ears lower; he must have gotten an earful from my mother.

The entire ordeal makes me feel so childish.

Suddenly, Wallace cracks a smile. "When Olivia pulled that thing from your purse, I thought it was a—well, I didn't know *what* it was."

I can't exactly blame him. It looks more like a small appliance than any of their fancy new communicators.

"It's so..." Wallace continues, his brows knitting together.

"Cool," Eugene interrupts. Wait, does he really mean that? Every worry I was holding onto melts away. I let out a small sigh. If too-cool-for-school Eugene approves, maybe it's not that bad, or he's teasing me. I choose to take the compliment. I have a feeling they're rare coming from him.

"Thanks, Eugene."

Olivia leans forward and thunks her communicator to mine, trying to link our numbers. In the newer models, all you have to do is tap the screens, and you're instantly added to each other's contact list.

"I guess yours doesn't do that, huh?"

"Guess not." I frown before we begin manually punching in each other's numbers.

"This will be perfect! Now I don't have to worry about you getting lost again," Olivia cheers, throwing her arm around me.

Guilt washes over me. The only thing I had lost was track of time ... with Skip.

"We can start a group chat!" Wallace exclaims tapping his device to Olivia's once we've finished.

"I'm not worried about losing *you* in a crowd." Olivia sits back.

"You know, tonight might be a good chance to—" I whisper, wondering if maybe the two of them could finally patch things up.

"If that sentence doesn't end with 'fill up on snacks,' I don't want to hear it. Any luck in love on the beach?" she asks.

"W-what?" I flush, thinking of Skip linking his arm in mine.

"Did you find another letter?" She raises an eyebrow, clearly gathering that I have more to tell.

"Oh... no, not yet, but I'm sure it's out there somewhere." I sink down. "Unless we got the location or the time wrong. Maybe Anonymous just decided it wasn't worth it, or it was carried away with the tide. Someone from school might have found it first."

"What?!" they shout at the same time. I fill them in on our new dilemma. Sending out the letters was one thing, but maybe next time, we should edit out the clue to the next location.

"Nice job, *Mr. Junior Editor.*" Olivia rolls her eyes at Wallace.

"Isn't stuff like this the reason you're here?"

"We'll just have to find it first!" Determined, Wallace hops off the picnic blanket with his fist in the air. But with the setting sun in the sky, I'm not so sure.

We might already be too late.

7.

As if it wasn't bad enough being scolded by my mother in front of Eugene, no matter how much we search, I can't find the next clue anywhere.

No one can. It's nightfall, and we are positively stumped. The bonfire is blazing down by the shoreline. A chill is in the air. Olivia, Wallace, and Eugene eye the warm, inviting flames. The day is almost over, and as we walk closer to Skip's group, it feels like accepting defeat.

I'm chilly without the warmth of the sun. I'm thinking of wrapping a towel around my shoulders when I suddenly hear Eugene's voice at my shoulder,

"Cold?"

I jump. "Just a little. I should have thought to bring a sweater to the beach, but I mean, it's the beach! So, I figured... well, I don't know. I didn't think we'd be here all day, and—"

The smooth leather of Eugene's jacket suddenly touches my skin. It's comfortable, just loose enough where it almost feels like there's a weighted blanket draped over my tired shoulders. My mouth falls slack. Did he just? He couldn't have just... I want to protest, but it's the most comfortable I've felt in hours.

"Thanks," I say. Maybe he's really not as bad as I thought.

He crosses his arms. Does he regret it? Was he just trying to be a gentleman? The notion of him doing something like that is surprising enough, and I'm not sure how to respond.

"If you were still cold, then you didn't have to...."

He shakes his head as if to stop me from saying anything else. It's the first time I've seen him without the heavy jacket, and I'm almost surprised by the lean body he's been hiding underneath. A long torso and lanky, willowy arms. He doesn't look as big and tough as I thought he would.

"Well, if you change your mind, just let me know. I don't want you being cold." I'm a lot warmer now, but I'll feel guilty if he's silently shivering beside me for the rest of the night.

We make our way to the bonfire. The flames flicker across our glowing faces. Skip waves us over happily—my scarf still tied around his neck. He makes a few clunky introductions, all while strumming the guitar in his lap. Most of us have met briefly or at least seen each other at school. I'm glad they don't seem to mind us joining their party. Skip did invite us, but *The Guide* states that this sort of joining of social groups can be awkward if not everyone is on board. No one mentions Miss Galaxy or finding a letter. I don't know whether I should be concerned or relieved.

"He's so cool," Wallace says under his breath. I nod, staring at Skip from across the fire pit. Between the way he's leaning back and the easygoing expression on his face, Skip is effortless. I can't take my eyes off him.

"Wait isn't that your scarf?" he whispers in a low voice.

"He caught it when we ran into each other earlier."

Wallace bites his lip, nodding.

"It looks better on Skip."

"I know."

"Oh stop," Olivia says, literally pushing our heads away from each other—considering we're whispering right between her, it's a fair response.

"Here," she says, shoving a bag of marshmallows at Wallace's chest. "Make yourself useful." And he does. The air is sugary sweet when he rips open a bag of marshmallows. Eugene reaches over me to grab a few, poking the tiny pillowy puffs onto a stick. Dad uses them all the time to top casseroles and cups of cocoa at home. But I've never had one toasted over an open flame before. I should be looking forward to this, but instead, it feels like a reward I haven't earned yet. Still, when Olivia slides an extra marshmallow on her stick for me, I don't object.

I look up and realize Skip has stopped playing music and is just staring across the flames at all of us.

"Oh! We have enough to share." It was honestly rude of us to not offer earlier. I hold up the bag of marshmallows. There's that same flirty glint at the edge of his smile. But the longer he looks, the longer I feel like there's more to this moment than just the flicker of the flames.

Golly, he must really like campfire snacks.

Skip hops up from his seat and beelines for the marshmallows. Before I have a moment to catch my breath, he's squeezing in between Eugene and me, and I can't say that I mind.

"What should I play next?" he asks. I turn to face him and realize how close our faces are.

"Didn't you want a marshmallow?" Olivia laughs, giving him a funny look that I can't quite pin down.

"Oh… right." He smiles, blushing gold and silver. I don't understand. What does he have to be embarrassed about? I wouldn't mind hearing another song, but the moment is gone.

Wallace passes out sticks to everyone interested in roasting marshmallows, and within a few minutes, we're huddled close by the fire watching the white pillowy treats puff up under the flames. Even with disappointment looming, even without the next love letter in my hands, nothing feels like it could ruin this moment. The sticky-sweet marshmallows melt in my mouth, coating my tongue in burnt sugar.

"Did you write the song you played earlier?" I ask, trying to diffuse the tension.

"I write a little. Don't think I'm a nerd or anything, but I'm a sucker for the poetic stuff." He's leaning in, talking just to me. His voice is tender, and I can't tell for sure, but I think he just winked. It must have been a trick of the light.

"Does he know he's talking to a bunch of writing nerds right now?" Olivia whispers under her breath.

Eugene lets out an unexpected laugh that he tries to disguise with a cough. It doesn't work. Now everyone is looking at us. Predictably, the stars across my cheeks glow with the sudden shift in attention. Soon, conversation picks up again.

Arleen laments about the new Dear Miss Galaxy column, and my face brightens with embarrassment. I cover my glowing freckles with my hands, hoping to feel the heat die down. "I still can't believe none of us found the letter." She groans.

The letter? They're all looking for the letter? Stars, this is bad. The glow from my face illuminates brighter with every sentence spoken.

"We combed this whole beach!" a boy with dark green hair who I don't recognize chimes in.

"I wonder if it was just a prank—Miss Galaxy is dabbling in fiction," Olivia says, trying to steer them all off-track. Bless her and her stone-cold game face.

"I don't know, gang; Miss Galaxy doesn't seem like the prank type." Skip shakes his head, looking off into the distance.

"You all work on the paper. Do you know who she is?" Peggy Sue, one of Skip's friends, asks from across the fire.

"No," Eugene answers, as indifferent as ever.

"No one does. She's an anonymous contributor." Olivia shrugs, matching his energy completely. She's way too good at keeping a straight face.

"HAH!" Wallace cackles, shaking his head. I swear I just saw his eyes twitch.

Oh boy. We're in trouble.

"Do WE know who Miss Galaxy is?" Wallace repeats. "HAH! Such a funny question. Olivia is right; it's the school's best kept secret. RIGHT, GANG?" His shoulders clench tight to his pointed ears, and he turns an even deeper shade of pink.

I need to get him out of here.

"Looks like our stock is running low," I observe, taking note of the fast-disappearing marshmallows in Olivia's lap. This is the perfect excuse to drag Wallace to safety.

"YES! We'll go grab some more snacks." Wallace pops up, his voice jittering with each word. If he keeps this up, everyone is going to think HE'S Miss Galaxy. We make a hasty getaway toward the vending machines. I'm sure Olivia will help smooth things over, and with any luck, will gather some much-needed intel. How is it possible that with all of us looking, none of us were able to find the letter?

"You don't keep secrets very often, do you?" Wallace asks when we are out of earshot.

"Me?"

"Your eyes got the size of flying saucers the minute someone said, 'Miss Galaxy!'" He laughs, shaking his head. "And your freckles are still shining like a lantern."

"Do you think they suspected anything?" I keep my palms clamped over my cheeks to dim the glow.

"No. Yes? No. No, we're fine." He seems to be doing a good job convincing himself. The shake is gone from his voice. "I think they're all too busy thinking about the school's latest piece of gossip to care about us. They're probably back to staring at Skip and wondering what kind of product he uses to make his hair do that swoopy thing."

"But what kind of product *does* make it do that swoopy thing?" I laugh, and the stars glow even brighter. I need to get a handle on this crush—but I can't say I haven't wondered about the secrets of Skip's haircare in class. My thoughts are always drifting to how it might feel to run my fingers through the perfect looking locks.

"Hey, what happens if we don't find the letter?" I ask. As Junior Editor, I'm sure he has a plan.

"Find a hotel and try tomorrow?" Wallace suggests. "Maybe comb a different beach?"

"And if it's not here at all?" I sigh. I was hoping for something a little more detailed from someone who delights in color-coding their planners as much as I do.

"Then I guess that's it for Miss Galaxy on the road."

My shoulders slump. That's it, huh? My first grand adventure washed away with the sparkling orange water. I wish there was something else we could do. But where else can we look? We've combed through the whole beach.

We make it to the row of glowing vending machines next to the restrooms. There's an assortment of goods in each—everything from extra swimsuits and sunscreen to snacks. This walk was just an excuse to get Wallace away from the awkward conversation, but we shouldn't come back empty handed. The selection is so different from what we have in the machines at school. Let's see... Marshmallows sit next to some kind of weird purple candy that looks like it's made out of sugar geodes.

There are chocolate bars at the bottom, and one packet of graham crackers left. We could do at least one round of s'mores with these.

I think of the way Skip's face lit up with his first bite of toasted marshmallows. This would probably make him even happier. I slip a few coins into the slot and wait for our snacks to tumble to the opening. It drops—well almost, getting stuck between a cosmic brownie and a mooncake.

Great. *Just great.*

I move to the side of the machine and try to shake it loose, but it doesn't budge.

"Maybe we can knock it loose when the chocolate bars fall?" Wallace suggests. It's a reasonable suggestion that for some reason makes me want to kick the front of the vending machine. Why can't this just go right?

I let out a frustrated growl, shaking the machine one more time. Weird. It seems like it's the only machine in the row that isn't pressed tightly against the wall. I wonder if unplugging it and plugging it in again would work. That seems to be my dad's fix for half our appliance problems, and it works at least 10% of the time.

I reach back for the plug and—what is that? Something crisp and white catches my attention. It can't be—it's got to be a warranty or warning label. I reach for it anyway. Within seconds, I'm holding a plain envelope sealed with a heart.

Anonymous's next clue. I can't decide if I want to laugh, scream, or cry. We spent all day searching, and it was behind a random vending machine! Why would they do that? I stare at the selection of snacks displayed. *"The next clue will be behind where the marsh mallows, and popping rocks reside."*

Marshmallows. Purple rock-shaped candies, that, now that I take a closer look, promise that they "pop and crack in your mouth." This writer is either trickier than I imagined, or I'm an idiot.

"Is that what I think it is?" Wallace, his arm halfway inside the vending machine, shimmies out and jumps to his feet. He peers over my shoulder as I trace the letters with shaky hands.

> Dear Miss Galaxy,
>
> I hope the day at the beach was as fun as the snacks this letter was hiding behind.
>
> The popping rocks have been one of my favorites since I was a kid and always hard to find back home on Ceres. In the same spirit, I dare you to drink a soda while eating them. It'll feel like your taste buds are about to blast off.
>
> The next location is also something I've always loved, and I suspect you'll love just as much: a place where you're surrounded by a million stories, but there are few people—each shelf a new adventure in the biggest collection of books this side of the galaxy. They say that while reading a book, you fall in Between Worlds. So, in the oldest copy of your most trusted tome is where you'll find your next clue.
>
> Sincerely,
>
> a boy at school who has a crush too big to know what to do with,
>
> Anonymous.

I hold the letter to my chest and let out a deep breath. It's finally in my hands and even better than I could have hoped for. We're heading to Between Worlds. The biggest library—ever? We'll have to stop at a hotel first, and then we can probably drive there first thing in the morning. It'll take a few hours I think, and considering our group, we're going to want all day to explore.

"Cute." Wallace shrugs. "A little childish with the snack recommendation, but all together something we can work with." I see the editor gears in his head already turning. A boy at school... it does narrow down the selection by a few, at least. I try not to let my thoughts turn to a certain silver-haired guitar-playing crush, that, try as I might, I can't stop thinking about. There are plenty of boys at school, and just because Skip is at the beach, it doesn't mean he wrote the letters. In fact, unlike his friends, he doesn't seem all that fazed by Miss Galaxy's adventures.

We manage to get the vending machine to give up the rest of our snacks, as well as the popping rocks and a cream soda in a glass bottle. Wallace artfully arranges them for a photo with the letter. We're the only ones out here, but he's taking so long to set up the shot, I can't help but feel nervous. Doesn't he care if we get caught?

He finally finishes, and I open a pack of the popping candy rocks. The chocolate-coated sugar crystals melt and spark against my tongue; the soda makes it worse—or better? I can't tell. It contrasts the chocolate in an almost sickeningly sweet syrup. I think I would have been obsessed with this as a kid; it's pure sugary sweet in a way that's nostalgic and a little sickening. While fun for a few bites, it's not going to make it onto my list of frequent snacks. I fish out my giant communicator and type on the tiny keys.

Dear Anonymous,

Marshmallows and Popping rocks are your favorite candies, huh? Well, after spending the entire day trying to find a "marsh" that looked "mellow" and beneath every single rock—I feel silly that we didn't raid the vending machines first thing. But you know the advice I give for all beach trips: always pack your own snacks ;) Still, you could have made the clue a little less obscure.

And a boy at school who likes soda and candy? You know, you could narrow it down just a little bit more next time.

Wallace leans over and looks at what I've written so far.

"Okay, I like the sass, but ask him more about himself! We need more to go off of if we're actually going to solve this."

"*This* is private." I shield my wrist so that he can't read the rest.

"It's official newspaper business, and as the junior editor—"

"I know, I know!" I groan "I just want to be genuine. I mean, as genuine as the all-knowing, all-seeing Miss Galaxy can be, right?"

Wallace gets it. He knows the branding. He knows exactly who I—I mean, Miss Galaxy—is supposed to be.

He shrugs, letting out an exasperated sigh.

"I think, considering the project, maybe you could give a little more of yourself." His tone is thoughtful as we walk back along the beach together. The letter is carefully concealed in my purse. "Plus, we're already editing out the clues this time, right? Let's give the readers something!"

I let out a huff, returning to my communicator for a small add on.

P.S. Tell me another fun fact about yourself, something silly or serious, I don't care—I just want to know who I'm writing to.

P.P.S. Dear readers, the clue has been edited out of this letter. As much as we at The Galaxy Gazette want you to follow along, we don't mean that literally.

I'll send it after we're safely off the planet and hopefully before Wallace has any more notes.

Anonymous' favorite candy. It's the only thing I really know about him. And I've never seen anyone at school eating these. If there's any place that will give us more information, it'll be our next stop. Where else do you look for answers if not a library?

We return to the firepit. Skip is back to leaning on one of the logs, gently strumming his guitar, picturesque and gleaming under the moon. His face lights up when he sees the pile of snacks we've returned with. "Find anything good?"

I can feel the weight of the letter in my purse, filled with promise.

"Yeah." I turn away from Skip and try to shake off my smile. *I hope so, at least.*

8.

etween Worlds is our next location. It's the largest and oldest library in all of existence. The mere thought of walking inside makes my chest ache.

I can hardly wait to get there, which means tossing and turning all night at the hotel. When we wake up in the morning, my clunky communicator is blinking on the nightstand.

[Mom: R u safe?]

[Me: Yes. Just waking up.]

[Mom: Check in again later.]

[Me: Okay.]

The weight of yesterday's embarrassment pulls me down the minute I clip the heavy communicator to my wrist. But at least I don't have to hide it anymore. I guess maybe it is kind of *cool* in a retro way. Even though it's uncomfortable, doesn't match my clothes, and the light blinking all night on the nightstand certainly didn't help me sleep.

Olivia, however, is enjoying having a way to text every backhanded comment she has toward Wallace when she can't just whisper in my ear—though it hadn't seemed like that had really been a barrier before.

The Guide dictates that forcing two people together is never a good idea, but then again, maybe they just need a little push. And who else is fit for the job but Miss Galaxy? I should at least try to fix this before we get any farther along in our trip.

I bounce to the cruiser with more of a spring in my step.

"Hey, Wallace, would you mind navigating for a little while? I'm getting tired," I ask. Hopefully, he'll take the bait. Proximity is a great way to get people closer.

"Sure! I'm pretty sure Eugene drooled on me when he was sleeping."

I raise my eyebrow. Eugene did ... *what?* Maybe this isn't such a good idea.

"What? Was I supposed to just push his head off my shoulder?" Wallace asks defensively, his shoulders lifting to the bottom of his ears. "I mean, I did after I saw the drool because I'm a good friend, but no one is *that* good of a friend, you know what I mean? He hardly even noticed. Who knew with his schedule that something like a beach day would knock him out?"

I've heard that Eugene goes right to work at Lester's after school. Between classes, detention, newspaper, and then a part-time job, I wouldn't be surprised if half his detentions are because he passed out in class. I don't know that I'd be able to handle a schedule like that.

Wallace is still talking, but the words are lost somewhere between my ears and my brain.

Eugene's face is glowing and tense, his shoulders straight and eyes wide. It's hard to imagine him relaxed enough to fall asleep on anyone.

"So, did you want to trade now?" Wallace waves his hand in front of my face. I nod silently, still feeling Eugene's eyes boring into me.

Wallace taking the front seat provides me with just the opportunity I've been waiting for. He and Olivia will be forced to work together, but that means that Eugene and I are going to be stuck together in the back seat.

He'd better not drool on me.

"Susie?"

I blink back to reality when he starts waving his hand in front of my face. *No! No!* I could *not* have been staring again. Except I was. My shoulders shrink. I hope Eugene didn't notice.

"Oh, of course!" I hand over the map, not expecting to have had an opportunity to work my magic so soon. "You are hereby promoted to navigation."

I force a nervous smile, turning my entire body away from Eugene. Right now, my focus should be on Wallace and Olivia's friendship.

Wallace raises his arm in a small salute with a goofy grin on his face. "I'll lead us well. You know, as the acting junior editor of *The Galaxy Gazette*, I've taken the necessary steps to make sure I've studied up on navigation. I can't have my club getting lost on an official outing." Behind the map, he looks confident, whereas I feel like I was floundering just trying to figure out north and south. This might work out better than expected, though I'm glad Olivia was out of earshot for his little speech.

She's still less than thrilled when she finds out.

"You're sure you're too tired? I mean, I can deal with him if you really need a break," she says, and I nod. Even though it's not entirely the truth.

It's not the start of a perfect team. But it's something. They can't go on fighting like this the entire trip—and now is as good a time as any for them to start getting along.

I take his spot in the backseat, accepting the ramifications of my decision. I try to make myself as small as possible, but Eugene doesn't seem to notice the space I'm creating to get as far from him as possible. His cool eyes stay fixed out the window. I try to do the same to distract myself from the knots forming in my stomach. Olivia and Wallace sit in absolute stubborn silence in the front; it's better than fighting but not the progress I'm hoping to see.

Baby steps, I remind myself.

I can't turn them into best friends in an hour. I close my eyes tight to block out the neon signs and stars we pass every few feet and try to picture Anonymous, but all I can think about is the way Skip looked smiling in the sunlight, my pink scarf tied around his neck. I wonder if he'll give it back to me once we're back from summer break. My lips rise in a small smirk. If I was his girlfriend, I bet he'd borrow my scarves all the time.

Once we've been on the road for a half hour, I allow myself to relax. Olivia and Wallace have claimed their seats as driver and navigator in calm indifference. They're not fighting yet. I count it as a win and shut my eyes, resting my head on the window. I doze, catching myself bobbing forward a few times. The muted sound of bickering becomes a familiar lullaby—they're not full-on yelling but I should intervene ... After I close my eyes for just one second.

I snap awake, feeling the impact of my head falling onto Eugene's shoulder. It's okay. This is fine. Maybe he didn't notice. He deliberately averts his gaze, his face glowing with embarrassment. Or is it anger? I wish I could tell. His mouth is pursed in a thin line, suggesting that he's disgusted by the mere thought of me being so close.

"Sorry!" I squeak and instantly hate myself for sounding so weak. I move as far to the opposite side as possible. I'm almost thankful Olivia and Wallace's bickering woke me up. That was too close for comfort. Sometimes he's annoying. Sometimes he's scary. Right now, he's both, but right now he's not the biggest problem.

The tension in the front seats is getting worse by the second. I couldn't have fallen asleep for that long, could I? Let's see, *The Guide* would say we need a bonding activity, some sort of mindless distraction. What do people do on road trips?

"Anyone want to play the license plate game?" I ask, fully aware of how goofy the idea is when spoken out loud.

"Well, we could, Susie! But we're in the *middle of nowhere!*" Wallace shouts from the front.

"We aren't. This is exactly what the map said," Olivia argues.

"We should have asked for directions as soon as the nav system cut out."

I straighten up, my head muddled with confusion. I really did clonk out, didn't I? All around us is pitch-black, and the magnetic pull of the starway is no longer keeping the cruiser on course. No billboards hover over the intersections, and the expansive sky around us is void of any light from passing ships or cruisers.

"We're fine, Wallace. Lay off." With each word, Olivia spews more venom in Wallace's direction.

"We're lost! Just admit it!"

"We. Are. Not," Olivia seethes through gritted teeth.

"We are so! When was the last time you even saw a fuel station?"

Olivia squints out into the blackness ahead. Looking out there's a dim sign that's impossible to read from my place in the backseat. Trash floats around us like tumbleweeds, and I get the sinking feeling we might be in one of the polluted areas Ms. Lux warned us about during that all-too-brief lesson on the starways. It should be fine. As long as Olivia drives carefully, we can stop at the next station and get back on track. "There! Fuel and lodging. Five miles ahead!" Olivia points, reading the tiny sign ahead of us.

"I meant *before* that! We're in the middle of nowhere!" Wallace lets out a heavy sigh, shaking his head. "Just admit we're lost!"

"Then blame Susie's admirer for sending us all the way out here!" she shouts back.

Oh.

I guess I did leap into this whole trip... My gut plummets, and my shoulders shrink instinctively. Guilt mixes with the nausea that's made itself at home in my stomach. Olivia doesn't really think this is my fault, does she?

"Hey! Now Susie's upset!" Wallace snaps. "Not cool, Olivia!"

"Sus—I didn't mean—"

"Let's just figure out where we are okay?" I sigh. I feel like a kid who's gotten dragged into a fight with their parents, shrinking second by second. The truth is we do seem lost. Why can't Olivia just admit that?

Another piece of garbage dings into my window, and I cringe. We're seriously in the middle of nowhere right now.

"And what is going on with that red light?" Wallace suddenly points at the dashboard. A red light sounds bad… really bad. I lean over to the middle seat and knock heads with Eugene, who apparently had the same idea. If he apologizes, I'm too distracted to hear him.

The light is right in the center of the console, big bold letters blinking "Warning." Stars, that's worse than I thought it would be.

"I told you, it's always like that!" Olivia argues.

It most certainly is not, but piping in now isn't going to help. Olivia's getting more and more defensive by the second.

"Well, it doesn't seem like it should be! I don't remember it being on when we started!" Wallace is practically screaming. Stars, this was a terrible idea.

"You were in the back goofing off with Eugene," Olivia hisses.

Wallace scoffs, holding a hand to his heart. "I do *not* goof off!"

"And are you aware that going this slow is a violation of the speed limit?" he nags, crossing his arms tight around his body. He shakes his head from side to side. "I thought that delinquent older brother of yours taught you to drive."

"Wallace…" I warn, but before I can say anything else, my back is forced up against the leather cushions as Olivia stomps her foot on the gas.

"Is this too slow for everyone?" Olivia's reflection in the rearview mirror twists with hot rage. "Do not—I repeat, do *not* talk about my brother." I've never seen her like this. The cruiser jolts into the darkness with a roar.

Eugene's arm juts out to hold me steady before my head makes contact with the back of Olivia's seat. Stunned, I meet his wide navy eyes, but he's focused on Olivia. His arm keeps me upright in my seat while he braces himself, his expression strained.

"H-*Hey*!" he shouts, and our panic matches. A dark blue lock of hair falls onto his forehead. His arm is still blocking me from any further impact, and when my body sways, it's right onto his chest.

Why is he trying to protect me?

I need to figure out how to fix this before it gets any worse. Except, my mind is blank. It's too loud. Eugene's arm remains outstretched, his eyes bulging. He's just as freaked out as I am. And there isn't so much as a paragraph in my guidebook on angry driving.

"PULL OVER!" I shout. I just want her to stop. "PULL OVER, PULL OVER!"

The cruiser jolts to the side.

I think we've hit something. A rock? Some more garbage? I can't tell, but it doesn't sound good.

I scream, but my voice is lost in the shouting match. "*Stop!*"

I force my head up and see Wallace scrambling for the manual button by the steering wheel. Olivia throttles us forward again, shoving him back into his seat.

"I thought you wanted me to go fast!" Olivia shouts. In all our years of friendship, I've never seen her this out of control.

Pressure builds in my ears, and sound becomes strange and muffled. Oh stars, I'm going to be sick! Is this one of those trash wastelands Ms. Lux talked about at the end of her lesson? If only the bell hadn't rang when she was in the middle of her speech, maybe just maybe she would have passed along some sort of advice.

The cruiser bumps and jolts with impact as if we're driving through an asteroid belt of space-waste. I close my eyes tight,

"Stop! Stop! Stop!" I shout. We jolt to the side, the impact of Eugene's body against mine is steady and warm. "OLIVIA!" I scream one final time, and finally, she listens.

We come to a sudden, quiet stop. The stillness is eerie.

When I open my eyes, Eugene is staring back at me. We're bathed in splotches of flashing red light.

Olivia is clicking every button within reach. "Come on, come on, come on!" she hisses, hitting the steering wheel.

My chest feels hollow and my stomach flips. She doesn't know what she's doing.

We weren't supposed to stop.

Eugene's arm is still protectively out in front of me, and suddenly I'm thankful that he's the one I'm sitting next to.

The cruiser tips forward, and without thinking, I clutch his chest, but the ship doesn't nosedive. It just floats weightless and hopeless in the stars. The large pieces of debris slowly drift toward us. They close in, ready to smash through our windows and suck the four of us out into the dark expanse of space.

I think of the communicator on my wrist, how it's too late to say goodbye. If I called my mom now, all she'd hear is a crash.

This was a bad idea.

A really, *really* bad idea.

The sound of my scream harmonizes with the others, bouncing around the glass dome. A million thoughts hit me all at the same time.

Are we going to fall?

No... no, we'll just float.

Float or crash into something.

Oh, we're *definitely* going to crash into something.

We're going to crash and die.

Or run out of air.

Or freeze to death.

I'll never see my parents again.

I'm going to die never having kissed anyone.

I'm going to die never having gone to a school dance.

I won't know who Anonymous is.

Olivia and I won't go to college together.

Because we'll be dead.

Floating in space forever, and no one will ever find us.

Eugene's arms tighten around me, and I brace myself against him for impact.

And the moment we crash, I wonder what he's worried he'll miss.

9.

When I open my eyes, I'm crushed between the back of the front seat and Eugene's body.

I gasp and gasp again, but my breath is gone; no matter what I do, I can't catch it.

This is why Mom didn't want me to leave Ceres. This is why she said it was dangerous. We were about to crash into a pile of space junk, and no one would have even known!

But we didn't. We're okay. I'm okay.

Eugene brushes a hair away from my face, and his eyes say it all. He's just as scared as I am. But he seems okay too. I'm glad—so do both Olivia and Wallace, thank the stars.

Eugene... I can't believe he tried to protect me.

We seem to be calmly floating downward in a soft glow of green light. How? A tractor beam? Are we caught in an actual tractor beam right now? I've never read about this situation in *The Guide*. I don't know what to do.

Eugene and I scramble apart and toward the windows. I squint and see a rusted service plaza below, and an old man in coveralls holding a remote. He waves at us.

The closer we get, the more the grin on his face unsettles me. He looks a little too pleased with our situation.

The four of us topple out of the cruiser.

"Thanks," I mumble at Eugene. His wide eyes scan over me before he turns away with the same tight-lined expression as before Olivia tried to kill us all.

"Are you okay?" I ask, looking him over. He seems like he's back to his usual self, but still, he seemed pretty shaken back there.

"Mhmm."

It takes only a glance to see that we're in the middle of nowhere. Instead of the mint tones and shiny chrome I'm used to, everything looks like it's covered in rusty shades of brown and gold. We are surrounded by discarded pieces of cruisers that I'm assuming met worse fates than ours.

Olivia crosses her arms. She's not making eye contact with any of us, and I get why. Even if she blames Wallace on the surface, deep down, she's got to know that driving recklessly is what got us here. I would be inconsolable if I were her. I push down my own anger; we're safe, and she's hurting. I can at least offer some comfort.

I put my hand on her shoulder and feel her tense under my touch. She doesn't say anything, just lets out a loud sigh and eyes her cruiser as it gets pulled into the garage. It's bathed in green light, floating farther and farther away from us. Her fists clenched, she rushes toward it.

"Hey, wait!" I'm on her heels the minute she charges forward. With every hurried step, anxiety balls in my chest. What's going to happen if we can't get her cruiser fixed? Anonymous has no idea where we are! What if the letter isn't waiting for us when we finally arrive at the library? The letter said it would be hiding in a book! And we're supposed to be there *today!* This throws the entire timeline off.

Someone—anyone—could check it out, and there goes my next clue. And then what? We catch a bus home? Pretend none of this ever happened? Will I just go back to answering normal letters again?

I kick the gravel under my shoe and take in the miles of glittering stars. Despite everything, we can't go home without the rest of the letters. I can't let that happen.

The old man standing behind the console stands to greet us. He must be the one who pulled us into this strange way-station. His toothy smile is wide and reassuring. His wiry hair sticks out straight from beneath a baseball cab.

"Looks like I caught you kids just in time." He shakes his head. "First time off the main starway? Folks around here call me Bub."

"Okay... Bub. I don't know what happened. I just took her into the shop a few months ago. She should be working fine." Olivia's voice sounds harsh, but I can hear it crack. If she speaks any softer, she's going to cry.

Still, I can't have us coming off as rude. "Mr. Bub, I'm really sorry, but we happen to be on a tight timeline and unfortunately, budget. Um, we're really, *really* grateful you pulled us in, so first of all thank you, but—"

"We can fix anything!" he says with gusto. "Your friend's cruiser will be a piece of cake. And speaking of cake, you kids should all go grab a bite. We'll give you ten percent off the box lunch special while we see to the repairs. I already told her it shouldn't be but a jiffy."

He gestures to the rusted tin building.

"Oh, is there a restaurant behind that old building?" I ask, already feeling my stomach rumble despite our uneasy landing. We didn't stop for lunch, and I barely ate break-fast. Olivia laughs, then covers her mouth with a shake of her head.

I know that look. What did I say?

"Nope," Mr. Bub replies matter-of-factly, the smile on his face starting to fade.

We turn away and start to walk back toward Wallace and Eugene.

"Darn city kids..." I hear Mr. Bub grumble. Back home on Ceres, being called a "city kid" would be a compliment. It would mean you're hip and fashionable. Like Skip. He's a prime example of someone like that. But from the old man's tone, I don't think he means it in a nice way.

I squint and see the blinking "open" sign hanging on the rusted door.

The old building *is* the restaurant.

Oh, my stars.

Nothing edible looks like it would come out of that building, but we're kind of stuck. Despite appearances, my stomach lets out another loud rumble.

"Can you believe him?" Olivia growls in my ear.

"I mean, we shouldn't judge a book by its cover," I say. "But I don't think he likes 'city kids.'"

"Not the repair man! Wallace! This wouldn't have happened if he—"

"What?" I gasp. Pushing the blame on Wallace is unacceptable. I mean, by that logic, it's my fault for asking him to be the navigator—and this is certainly not my fault!

"Well, what was I supposed to do? Let him tell me how to drive?" She crosses her arms.

"Yes. He was being the navigator," I say through gritted teeth. Wallace wasn't the one speeding. Wallace wasn't the one who was cruising through space junk as though they were mere bumps in a road.

Wallace didn't put us in danger.

"Olivia, this was your fault." The words lack the softness she's used to from me, and from the way her body snaps to its full height, my edge seems to cut deeper than intended.

"So, you're taking his side in this? He called my brother—"

"*This* isn't about Rex!" I shout, stomping my saddle shoes upon the rough pavement. "I was really scared!" I continue, my heart still pounding out of my chest. "Like, I understand he gets under your skin, but you can't just..." Tears pull at the corners of my eyes. If I keep forcing words out, I'm going to break down. I'm cracking with each passing second.

"Hey, we're okay," she sounds too snippy to be reassuring, "and 'Bub' over there said it shouldn't take more than a jiffy."

"And then I'm supposed to trust you behind the wheel again?" I cross my arms, refusing to make eye contact until she apologizes. I'm one step away from demanding she sets the cruiser to autopilot for the rest of our trip—I vaguely remember Olivia's brother mentioning doing a few upgrades, and I think that was one of them.

"Fine! You're right. I overreacted, okay?"

My arms stay firmly crossed.

"It was—I just—I uh," she grumbles, kicking gravel from beneath the toe of her shoe. "I'm sorry I scared you."

"And?" I ask, loosening my crossed arms ever so slightly.

"For letting my anger get the best of me." She rolls her eyes, which I choose to ignore. "I'm sorry, okay?"

Considering how heated she is, I'll take it. I wrap my arms around her in a hug and feel her melt into it.

"I forgive you." I sigh, letting go of my pride, and gesture across the lot to Wallace and Eugene. "But those two might not."

She lets out the loudest groan I've ever heard, accepting defeat. We rejoin the boys who are idling a few feet from the rusted diner.

I perk up as she wrings her hands anxiously in front of her chest. She's actually going to apologize to Wallace.

"Hey... I, um... already said this to Susie, but that was..." Olivia begins, and oh my stars, it's finally happening.

All we needed to do was crash on another planet for the two of them to finally get over whatever it is. But as soon as her eyes meet Wallace's, her expression changes. "Eugene, I'm sorry. Wallace, maybe don't tell me how to drive, okay? And don't you ever call my brother a delinquent again, got it?"

Stars. Here we go again.

Wallace stumbles backward, his mouth agape.

"What?" he snaps. "You are not—"

"*Got it?*" she repeats, her ponytail flaring with sparks that shoot into the air like we've stepped into a welding shop.

"Yeah, fine. Sorry! Geez!" Wallace huffs, taking a step back from the rest of the group.

I guess that was almost an effort—except it wasn't, not by a long shot. Biting down on my bottom lip, the grim realization that my meddling might have made things a million times worse sets in. I mean, what kind of an apology was that? For them, I suppose it might count as progress, but not enough.

She strides toward the diner. I don't go after her.

At least she apologized to Eugene. He didn't do anything wrong. But then again, neither did Wallace. Sure, he shouldn't have egged her on. But that's not an excuse for putting us all in danger.

Wallace looks at me with his jaw slack, then shrugs his shoulders. I wonder if he is pretending to be unfazed. "She'd better not blow our budget out here on that hunk of junk is all I'll say," he grumbles. I don't think our club's emergency funds are supposed to be used for auto repairs. He heads toward the diner, Eugene in tow.

I let myself fall behind. When it comes to setbacks, *The Guide* instructs that optimism should be kept close, and I really do want to look on the bright side, but the brightest thing on this asteroid is the rusted streetlamp above my head—and I'm worried it'll crush me with the next strong gust of wind.

"It's fine. We're fine. We're fine," I whisper to myself before following.

They say that shared experiences, good or bad, bring people together. And for better or worse, the boxed lunch special seems to be our best bet. Still, it would have to be something *really special* to make this stop. And I doubt anything special could come from a place that looks like a rusted tin can on a planet filled with dust and old cruiser parts.

Let's just hope that the shared experience doesn't happen to be a stomach bug.

Four trays slam down onto the rust-toned table, threatening to break it in half. "Enjoy," grunts our waiter before slouch away. I try to resist wrinkling my nose. I can't imagine people come here for either the service or the food—the "box lunch special" the man outside mentioned turned out to be the only thing on the menu—but the grimy restaurant is positively hopping.

The "special" is a divided lunch tray of clear, bouncy cubes. I've never seen anything like it. It smells of comfort food—flaky biscuits and casseroles. But appearance-wise, it looks no more appealing than an ice cube. It jiggles on its own accord, almost like it has a life of its own. Tentatively,

I poke my fork inside. It isn't alive, is it? There are no veins or organs. From what I can tell, it's plant-based.

"Are these tiny gelatin molds?" Olivia asks.

Oh! That's a little less scary.

Her fork hovers around her mouth like she's trying to make up her mind.

Every gelatin mold my dad has made has fruit or sometimes even noodles floating inside to give you an idea of the flavor. These are a blank canvas.

Plain gelatin, though not exactly appetizing, is something I can handle.

Carefully, I dig my fork in, cutting the smallest slice off the top. *Group experience*, I remind myself, looking around the table. Eugene has already started. I raise my forkful in the air.

"Cheers," I offer. It's less enthusiastic than I mean it to be, but Wallace and Olivia follow my lead. Even Eugene joins us in raising our forks in the air until the strange, clear globs meet.

"Cheers," they grumble, no more excited than I am. Still, the small interaction almost makes it feel like we're getting along.

Almost.

We each take a bite. Then, silence.

Savory flavors coat my tongue. I can't recognize them. I go in for another bite and try to figure out if I've had anything similar before. The texture is smooth, but somehow satisfying. It should be a tasteless, gelatinous mush. But instead, every bite is bursting with a different complex flavor.

I go in for another bite and realize I've already finished my first cube.

"What are we eating?" Olivia has almost cleared her plate.

"I have no idea!" But it's the best thing I've ever tasted. I'm starting to understand the crowd.

Eugene pulls out his notebook and starts jotting something down.

"Oh! Are you writing your article on this place?" I ask.

"Mhmm," he replies with his mouth half-full.

I should have known that's as far as the conversation would go. The mood stays tense until we're finished up.

Mr. Bub is outside. He has a creased expression he didn't have before, and I worry something has changed.

"Bad news, kids. Cruiser's not a big fix, but it's going to take 'til tomorrow," he says, sticking his hands in his pockets.

I couldn't have heard him right. A *jiffy* means no time at all. A *jiffy* means we should be getting back on the road!

"Til ... tomorrow?" I echo, my heart sinking right along with every hope I had of getting to Between Worlds before the end of the day. I feel betrayed. But it's late, and we're off-course. If anything else goes wrong, nothing is going to stop me from bursting into tears. There's already pricking at the corner of my eyes. "Do you have any rooms available?"

He starts to laugh. "Well, we've got one, but—"

"We'll take it." Olivia puts her arm around me. I slink away. Clearly, she's trying to make up with me, but despite her apology, I'm still cooling down from earlier.

"Hey!" Wallace says waving his arms in the air. "What about us?"

"Sleep in the hallway!" Olivia shrugs, crossing her arms. Considering she's the reason we're here, I'd appreciate it if she toned down her feud for at least the next 24 hours.

Bub sucks in a quick breath through his teeth. "Wouldn't do that."

"Why not?" Olivia shoots back.

"We turn off the gravity stabilizers at night. Saves money, keeps costs down. They're on the fritz," he explains.

"...okay."

"Don't want you boys floating away."

"I wouldn't mind," Olivia grumbles so that only I can hear.

"Olivia!" I hiss before turning my attention back to Mr. Bub. "And there's only one room?" I clarify.

He puts his hands in the pockets of his coveralls. "Last bus just left, so that's all we can offer. Unless you want me to call you a cab."

A cab ... this far away from home? That would just about tank whatever funds we have left. This is our only option. And staying in one hotel room isn't the worst thing. It's not like we're going to be piled on top of each other! Four people, one hotel room. It'll be awkward to put my hair in rollers and slather cold cream on my face in front of the boys, but...

"We'll take it," I say with hearty determination.

He lets out a laugh and shakes his head. "Good luck."

10.

I stare at the small cubicle before us. *The Guide* certainly didn't say anything about *this* predicament. This has got to be a mistake, right? Mr. Bub couldn't have possibly thought we could—

"How are we doing this—horizontally, vertically?" Wallace muses, tilting his head.

"There's got to be a mistake," Olivia says, shaking her head. "Where's the bed?"

"This *is* the bed."

"Shut up, Wallace." Olivia once again huffs, the negativity wearing on my last nerve.

"What? It is! I can't be the only one who's stayed in a space pod before," he says, continuing to study the impossibly small space.

He is. And his certainty that this is the only option is not calming any of us down. The pod is no larger than a closet, with white padding on each side. There's hardly enough space for one person, let alone four.

"Maybe we can get another room?" There's got to be a sensible and logical solution here.

"This is literally the only room they have; Bub said so!" Olivia shoots back.

"I don't care what Bub said—it's a closet!" I snap, then sigh. "Sorry, I'm just really tired."

"Whoa, Susie, you must be really mad. You didn't even call him 'Mister,'" Olivia teases. Eugene unexpectedly snickers.

Rude.

Thankfully, Wallace ignores our commentary, squinting under his horn-rimmed glasses at the small, padded space. He might be the only one trying to make this work.

"Horizontally definitely won't work. Eugene's legs will hang out, which is no good."

Olivia throws her arms up in the air. "We can't all fit in that room!"

"Yes. No. Yes. Huh." Wallace paces the small doorway of the cube, his antennae springing and falling with every word.

"Haven't you ever played the telephone booth game? It'll be fine." Wallace brushes her off with an anxious smile. The guidebook says that when road trip mishaps happen, to go with the flow and maintain a relaxed and easygoing attitude, but this situation is pushing past my limit.

All of us? Together? In here? All night? Being in the cruiser together is tense enough.

Eugene's eyes are boring into my soul. Despite myself, my cheeks start to glow. Why is he looking at me like that? I know I nearly fell asleep on his shoulder in the cruiser, but I'm not about to make the same mistake again!

Without another word, he walks into the small cubicle and, in typical Eugene fashion, immediately sulks to the corner. He turns away and presses his face against the padded wall. He seems to be totally passed out within seconds. I'm impressed and incredibly jealous.

All I want in this moment is to be able to fall asleep like that.

"I'm not sleeping next to Wallace," Olivia grumbles under her breath.

"Well, I don't want to sleep next to you either!" he argues back.

"In case you didn't realize, we are all sleeping next to each other," I huff. I want to remind them that the reason we got into this mess in the first place was because of their arguing, but I'm too exhausted. There's no privacy; we're going to be shoulder to shoulder.

The lights blink. My heart seizes in my chest. They're not turning the gravity stabilizers off now, are they? I imagine floating aimlessly like balloons without string and rush into the pod, pulling Olivia and Wallace with me. The door shuts with a thud, locking into place. I feel my feet lifting off the ground. There are straps on the walls, though none of us can figure out how, and if, we're supposed to use them.

"Wallace, get your elbow out of my face!"

"Only if you get your knee out of my stomach!"

"It's *not!*" Olivia's hair brushes up against my cheek as she turns to look down. "Oh no, you're right... sorry."

"So, you'll apologize for that..." he grumbles.

"Look, I'm *sorry,* okay? I accept my punishment of having to sleep in close proximity to you. I am justly suffering, okay?"

I try to act as a buffer between them, but my body keeps drifting between the padded walls.

"Sorry!"

"That was my foot!"

"Hey!"

"Watch your elbow!"

It goes on like this for what feels like hours. No matter how hard we try, our bodies float into each other effortlessly.

Someone's elbow is on my shoulder, and there's a foot on my hip. *The Guide* had insisted that situations like this should not only be avoided but are ... well, *suggestive* in nature. I mean, four entangled bodies is a recipe for romantic complications. If I saw a letter on my desk describing this situation, I can only imagine the way my freckles would glow at the mental image.

I shrink closer into the corner, trying to keep my arms and legs in a straight line. The only complication here is how any of us are going to manage to get to sleep. There is nothing—absolutely *nothing*—romantic about this, especially given the present company. It's just impossible.

And speaking of impossible, Eugene has remained still, his back turned to all of us, breathing steadily. It seems like he isn't having any trouble staying asleep. I'm envious and angry, smashed between Olivia and Wallace.

"Alright, this isn't working for me!" Olivia whispers, letting her body drift up to the ceiling. There, she curls into a tight ball. I'm jealous I didn't think of it first. Her hair floats around her head like a halo of fire, a nightlight in our dim cube.

Wallace squints his sleepy eyes and shakes his head. He grabs a corner of the padded floor and manages to strap himself in.

Now there's me up against the left wall, Olivia on the ceiling, Wallace hovering in the corner, and Eugene stretched out on the other side.

"Night, everyone," I say quietly. It feels weird just going to sleep without saying anything.

"Night, Susie," Wallace replies, stifling a yawn.

"Night, Susie," Olivia mumbles from the ceiling.

CHAPTER 10

"Night," Eugene whispers. Huh. I guess he wasn't asleep after all. I shift uncomfortably. It's hard enough trying to sleep vertically.

I try to shift closer to the wall, threading my arm through one of the loops of fabric in the corner.

After all this, the next letter had better be incredible.

11.

We're plummeting.

Pins and needles dance across my skin while stars streak outside the window. I try to look forward, but the images are cloudy. I can't see Olivia or Wallace in front of me. Squeezing my eyes closed, I wait for it to stop.

Arms wrap around me, pulling me close. I should feel safe.

But we're falling faster and faster, and my stomach balls into a pit.

I'm going to die.

I don't want to die.

The arms hold me tighter.

When we crash, they'll soften the blow. I crack my eyes open and look into Eugene's face. He looks just as scared as I am, shaking in my grasp, but his embrace is also warm. So warm. Light sparks all around us, and I brace myself for an impact that never comes.

I jerk awake. A dream, just a terrible dream. No—not all of it at least.

Eugene's face is millimeters away from mine, but he's asleep. His long eyelashes flutter ever so slightly but don't open. I gulp, trying to shift my weight. There's nowhere to go. Wallace has drifted up to my left side, and Olivia is over my head. I'm boxed in.

Closing my eyes tight, I hope that the two of us will just naturally drift apart. Maybe I don't need to do anything.

When I open my eyes, he'll be pushed into the corner again. *One, two, three.*

We're closer now, close enough to kiss. Wait—no— why would I even think that? I don't like Eugene. He did one nice thing for me! One! Nothing that warrants a dream or a kiss. Maybe *The Guide* was right about situations like this. Still, I can't help but think about the way he tried to protect me. His deep navy eyes had been wide and serious; he thought we were going to crash too.

A lump in my throat forms. His face is restful until the soft expression suddenly tenses. A twitch begins with his lip and drifts down his jaw.

Is he having a nightmare too? His eyes close tightly. Slowly, I reach out, unsure of what to do, and place my hand on his shoulder. The fabric of his jacket is cold; there's warmth from his skin radiating underneath, a contradiction that seems to fit him perfectly.

The shuddering comes to a slow stop, and I'm pulled into his arms like an oversized teddy bear. Oh stars, wait a minute, maybe the arms in my dream weren't just a memory of us almost crashing. Maybe he'd been holding me in my sleep all night. I gulp. The worst thing is it kind of feels nice.

Nope!

Nope! Never ever again will I question *The Guide.*

We should not be this close, not now, *not ever.*

"Eugene..." I whisper, tapping his shoulder. He groans in response, spinning both of our bodies away from Wallace. My head falls onto his chest, which is rising and falling with a gentle rhythm. "Eugene." I tap him once more, heat rising to my face.

He's dead asleep. I let myself relax. At least with his arms around me, I'm not drifting around the pod anymore. His soft cotton shirt presses against my skin, and it honestly might be the most comfortable I've been all night. Just like in the dream. Only there's no threat of crashing.

We're here. We're safe. My eyes grow heavy, tempting me to fall asleep right here in his arms. I mean, would that really be so terrible? Guilt pours through me. Oh jeez. Eugene has no idea that he's holding me, and that's wrong.

Besides, what would Anonymous think, knowing that while trying to discover their identity, I was in the arms of another? However accidental it might be.

I let out a determined huff.

"Eugene," I say, just a little louder this time. The front two pin curls of my hair come undone, and a few blue strands dance in front of his face.

He stirs, just barely opening his eyes. When he sees me, his expression hardens.

His muscles tense around me. Suddenly his eyes widen, and his arms pinwheel, hitting Wallace in the chest. The two of us float up toward the ceiling, Wallace's sleeping body seconds from crashing into Olivia. I try to maneuver in between them, but I'm too late. He barrels right into her.

"Susie—*what*?" She clearly hasn't opened her eyes yet.

"Wha—?" Wallace's sleepy voice comes next. His legs swing, nearly kicking Eugene in the head. In an instant, the three of us are mashed to the ceiling. Eugene stares at me in horror. He opens his mouth as if to speak, but then my ears pop and the lights flicker. My stomach rolls, and within a second, we slam onto the ground.

We're a sea of limbs and groans. When the door slides open, Eugene is the first to sprint out.

It's morning.

And I've never felt more tired in my life.

"Morning, kids," Mr. Bub greets us at the front desk. "Cruiser's as good as new."

"What exactly was wrong with it?" Olivia asks, doing nothing to hide her impatience.

Everything he says in response might as well be in a different language, but with every word, Olivia shrinks into herself, nodding along—glad someone understands this diagnosis because I am positively lost.

"So, if I had been going slower..." she begins, her face shining bright red.

"You needed a tune-up regardless! But it certainly didn't help. You see..."

There he goes again, rattling off an explanation that makes absolutely no sense to me, but I nod politely.

I'm eager to get back on the road. As soon as the keys are back in Olivia's hands, I take the front seat to be as far away from Eugene as possible. Olivia looks relieved. Eugene looks mortified. And Wallace—poor Wallace needs a cup of coffee.

But it's Eugene I'm fixated on as his shocked expression cuts through me again. He woke up holding me. I wonder if he was dreaming about someone else. Was he disappointed? No, I can't let myself think about that. It's just awkward. We're not friends. And now he won't even look at me. Which is fine because I don't want to look at him either, not if he's going to be like this. It wasn't like I squeezed into his arms by choice! He was the one holding me like a teddy bear.

We're farther off course than I could have imagined, but I hope we'll arrive before dinner at least.

After everything that's happened, I could use another love letter, sure, but what I really need is a good night's sleep.

12.

y neck hurts.
  My shoulders hurt.
  Stars, everything hurts.

I'd heard that microgravity is supposed to be good for your back. Some folks even have sleeping pods installed in their houses. The advertisements always say you'll wake up refreshed...

Guess that doesn't work if you have four people crammed inside.

We stand in the doorway of the largest library in the cosmos, a place I have dreamed of going ever since I found out it existed. I should be excited. But all I want in this moment is... well, let's just say that if the next letter leads us to a mysterious comfy mattress planet, I would not be upset.

As long as I don't have to share.

Unlike our school's library, this place is all sleek and white. The bookshelves are streamlined and well organized with only front facing titles. There seems to be a system of transparent tubes on the roofline zipping titles across the large building. At the entrance, a large computer stands from floor to ceiling with an oval screen and shiny buttons. I stare at the spectacle in front of me, the white on white color palette is broken up by the color of books, and brightly dressed readers who mill about the space. It's a lot to take in, and I'm unsure where to start.

The more I stare at the fully stocked shelves, the more each book starts to look like a pillow. I shake my head, trying to focus. Maybe if I open my eyes really wide, that'll keep me awake.

But it doesn't. In fact, the wider I open my eyes, the more I want to close them. With every step toward the shelf, I'm dizzy with the limitless options. I've never seen so many books in one place—one for each of the stars in the sky and just as dazzling. Normally, I would want to dive into as many as possible.

But now, I'm wondering if there's a comfy couch in a corner so that I can take a nap.

"Sleeping in the doorway?" Olivia asks. Before I can straighten up my slumped shoulders, she reaches out for my hand and guides me forward. This is the longest I've ever been mad at her. I mean, yes, she could have doomed us to a miserable death in the void of space. But she is my best friend, and she did kind of—*mostly*—apologize to me. As she pulls me into the large shimmering alcove of books, my irritation washes away like I've been hit with a wave from Lemon Drop beach.

Wallace and Eugene have already started to wander, pulled into the maze of bookshelves. I'm overwhelmed, lucky to have Olivia guiding me over to the massive computer database.

A keyboard sticks out of the wall. The oval screen swivels down when we approach, and we're greeted with a pixelated smiley face who blinks, awaiting instructions.

"Welcome to Between Worlds," The computer greets, the white pixels forming into a half-circle grin. "How may I direct you?"

"Do you think it knows how to make coffee?" Olivia asks with a nod.

"You will find out café on the second level with an array of teas and drinks from around the galaxy," the melodic voice answers. "With over one hundred options, there is sure to be something to satisfy your needs. Would you like me to read the menu?"

"Sur—"

"No thank you!" I say, jumping in front of Olivia. Stars, is she trying to get on my last nerve? Still, I can't help but smirk up at the computer. We definitely don't have anything this advanced at school.

"How may I direct you?" the computer prompts again, patiently waiting for our directions.

I mull over the clue before answering. The oldest copy of my most trusted tome, huh? There's only one book the next clue could possibly be in. Anyone familiar with the book would recognize the way I tend to quote it in my articles. But still, if this is right, it means Anonymous has been paying more attention than I thought.

"Please direct us to *The Space Age Guide to Romance and Social Affairs,*" I say with confidence that if we find that book, we find our next letter from Anonymous.

"A first edition of *The Space Age Guide to Romance and Social Affairs* can be found in teen nonfiction 4312," the computer replies. "Would you like it to be deposited in the bin below?"

Looking up at the complicated system of tubes, with books whooshing across the library, I freeze—at that speed, a letter would topple right out of the pages.

"No!" I shout. "Uh—no thank you!"

Now I'm the one pulling Olivia along as I race to the elevator.

"Running in a library! Susie, you're wild!" she teases me. But her voice is too loud, and we're instantly hushed by Wallace and a shiny metal robotic librarian perched at a corner desk. Unlike the pixilated face of the supercomputer, this robot is not smiling. By the time we get to the elevator and the doors shut, we're doubled over with laughter; the promise of the next clue has chased my bad mood away.

"I can be rebellious!" I say, sticking my tongue out. "Besides, it says the book is here, but that doesn't mean someone won't check it out first! Or worse, maybe it got filed in the wrong area or stolen or—"

Olivia places her hand on my shoulder. "Relax. I don't think it's in high demand." What does she mean by that? *The Guide* is the most respected and reputable source of information for any problem you could encounter in your high school career. Who wouldn't want to hold a copy of the first edition? I bristle, shooting a small glare in her direction.

We charge forward, though I have to remind myself not to run. *4312… 4312…*

There!

I could recognize the pale pink spine anywhere. It stands out against the earth tones, right in the center of the shelf.

I rush forward, then pause.

This is a first edition. Should I be wearing gloves? Carefully, I start to remove the book from the shelf. Just as soon as I cradle it in my hands, Olivia shifts awkwardly from side to side, catching my attention.

"Hey, are you still mad?" she asks.

Really? She's going to ask me this now. I'm literally holding the book containing the next clue, and she picks now for a heart-to-heart? Because of her, our budget is all messed up, and we're going to be bunking together for the rest of the trip.

The four of us in one room. And that's a detail that still hasn't fully sunk in. Nothing can be as bad as last night, but I'd like a little more privacy. If Eugene gives me one more dirty look, I might explode.

But am I mad? I don't know. Disappointed? Yes. In desperate need of a nap and coffee? Absolutely. I'm as worn as the pages of this old book.

"I'm just so tired," I admit. "I'm sorry. I know I should be having the time of my life, but if I slept thirty minutes last night..."

I flip through the book while trying—and failing—to suppress a yawn. Despite how awful and achy I think, this is exactly where I need to be.

There's a small paragraph regarding anonymous admirers, and just as I thought, that's exactly the spot where Anonymous tucked the letter.

"Admirers are often closer than you'd imagine..." it reads. Cracking open the envelope, I envision the way Skip's eyes sparkled at the ocean. The way he looked at me, it almost seemed like—

No! My fingers dig into the crease of the envelope. Frantically, I pull out the letter, unsure of who my heart is pounding for.

> Dear Miss Galaxy,
>
> As your favorite book has taught me, "A poem is a sweet, simple way to express affection," so here goes:
>
> Milkshakes, malts, and jukebox waltz.
> Chrome and neon brighter than the shiniest star.
> This blue and cream destination will really raise the bar.

"Out of this world" is what they say.
The same and different. We're so far away.
I wish I could tell you, but no... not today.
'Til I see you again tomorrow, and I can't wait 'til I do.
Now I think this poem is through.

I don't know if poetry is where my talents lie, but at the very least, maybe it'll make you laugh.

XO,

Anonymous

P.S. A fun fact about myself, huh? When I was young, I loved the Cara Cosmo book series.

My face is radiating.

This letter is so ... *cute*. I still don't know who this person is, but Skip or no Skip, I think I could like the writer. Really, *really* like him.

"Can we get a better hint?" Olivia laughs. "Everyone loved Cara Cosmos."

I shake my head. She's right. I remember running around the playground pretending to be the characters with our whole class.

"Well, we're not supposed to be there until tomorrow," Oliva says. "What do you say we hit up the cafe on the third floor and look at some books?"

I nod. In this moment, the rush of adrenaline feels like it's piloting my body just as well as a full night of sleep would. The third floor is an endless row of cookbooks with a rotating cafe in the center. People sit at silver flecked tables, sipping frothy pastel drinks in clear mugs while they read their books.

We get in line, and I read through the letter again while we wait. After the embarrassment, I'm not sure I can stomach anything. Olivia orders some sort of hot drink coated in light pink foam. I order something called a "Star Gazer," the prettiest-looking one on the menu, though I don't know what flavor it'll be—only that it's light purple with specks of white, with a chrome star and a delicate flying saucer beveled on the top.

I don't like it. But I'm not sure if that's because it's just too bitter for the mood I'm in. I want something sweet and dreamy.

I want Anonymous.

Olivia takes out her notebook, but I don't want to write. Not right now, at least. A million thoughts are swirling around in my head.

I need to walk around a little.

I go back to where I found the letter. There are all sorts of advice books. Some old and outdated, some shiny and new—just like the copy I have at home, only in nicer shape.

I accidentally wander right into the *Cara Cosmos* section. I'm sure the plucky, outspoken, brilliant detective would know exactly how to catch a secret admirer.

It's more crowded down here. The aisle of popular titles most be closer to the center.

I scan the shelves; in the dozens of books, I try to remember if there was ever a similar plot. I don't remember the series ever being particularly romantic. The closest thing she ever got to an anonymous love letter was probably a ransom note.

I reach up, expecting to pull at the spine of an old book, but instead I brush hands with someone else.

I jump back, and the book falls between us. Eugene reaches down to pick it up.

Of course he's here brooding while I'm trying to find peace of mind.

He leans down, extending the book to me, and I refuse, leading to an awkward push, and before the book clatters to the floor, he takes a quick step back. My eyes fall on the old book, scanning it for damage. The crack in the spine wasn't there before, was it? A few loose pages have slipped out of place.

I scramble to pick the book up but freeze. I'm suddenly very aware of the space he's created between us. Eugene opens his mouth to speak, and then promptly closes it, sinking down to grab the book off the floor.

"Do you want to uh ... talk?" I ask, shifting my weight onto the balls of my feet. "Olivia and I just went up to the cafe, and honestly I wouldn't mind trying something different before we leave."

He doesn't say anything.

Huh.

Maybe he's mulling it over.

"The Star Gazer is pretty, but it tastes like chalk," I continue, trying to fill the silence.

"Okay." But it doesn't sound like he's agreeing to go with me. No, it feels like the sort of "okay" you give someone who is telling a rambling story or that you manage to spit out during an argument.

"Okay..." I trail off, waiting to see if he moves toward the elevators. Oh stars, we're going to have to address the issue, aren't we?

"I get that you're probably just as embarrassed as I am about last night," I say in a hushed tone. I understand that I'm the last person he'd want to wake up next to, but he doesn't have to keep looking at me with ... whatever that expression is. I'm not the one who was trying to cuddle in a spacepod!

This whole trip, Eugene has barely said two words to any of us. I'm sick of it. I'm sick of *him*. The sideways looks. The brooding. All of it, especially when it started to feel like maybe I was seeing a different side of him.

Clearly that was just the adrenaline of almost dying.

"Do you not want to be here or something?" I add more quietly, turning my head away. "If that's the case, you should have just said something."

"I-I..." he begins, his face falling into a grimace, offering yet another stretch of silence between us. Why won't he just say what he's thinking?

He opens his mouth and closes it again.

Stars! I can't deal with him anymore.

"Y-you what?" I snap, and am immediately met with a loud shush from the library-bot.

His face flushes, his eyes growing wider and wider.

"Just say whatever you're thinking." I cross my arms, averting my eyes to the book with the cracked spine. "It shouldn't be that hard."

I earn another shush before I look up. He's gone. My chest tightens with a feeling of regret and guilt. I didn't mean to snap.

Now that's he's gone, I'm suddenly very aware of all the eyes on me.

Eugene and I don't speak for the rest of the day.

13.

We eat a silent dinner of sad pizza in the hotel room. Olivia tries to fill the void with forced chatter. Wallace helps too. But nothing they say can cut through the thick tension between us. Eugene gets up to leave after dinner, and then he's just gone. Hours tick by, and I realize my window to apologize might have disappeared with the pink sun of the small planet we found lodging on. What if he doesn't come back?

"Do you think he's okay?" I ask Wallace. I told myself I wouldn't feel guilty. But I do. And with every minute that passes, the lump in my chest gets worse. We're planets away from home, and Eugene is just gone.

Did he hitch a ride back home?

Did he get his own hotel room?

What if he gets into some sort of trouble wandering around out there?

"He said he just wanted some space. I told him, 'It's all around you! Don't go far!' but he didn't really respond to the joke. Which was fine." Wallace shrugs his shoulders. "But he did seem pretty upset."

"Because it's a terrible joke," Olivia says with a yawn. "Mr. Cool Guy can take care of himself. He's got to sleep sometime, so I'm sure he'll be back soon." She seems so confident that he'll return, but I'm not so sure.

I don't think he wanted to be here in the first place.

Wallace snores. Olivia snores. And even in their sleep, they're competing on who can be louder.

Hours pass, and with every creak, I glance toward the door.

Eugene still hasn't shown back up.

I wonder if he's gone for good. He seems like the type who would hop on a bus home without saying goodbye. I don't get it. It's not like I said something terrible to him. Sure, I shouldn't have been so rude. But isn't him storming off like this just as much of an overreaction? Besides, he's rude to me all the time! I can't be rude once?

I hope that if he tried to get back to Ceres, he made it there safe. But it's hard to think about anything with the sound of snoring.

Overtired and unwilling to have two sleepless nights, I grab the keys from Olivia's purse. I just can't handle it anymore.

At least in her cruiser, it'll be quiet. Stars, after a night crammed in that space pod, it might feel like a luxury hotel. Plus, if I put down the seats in the back, there'll be way more space to stretch out.

I grab my blanket and make my way through the mostly empty hotel. There's one robotic valet still powered on in the front, but even its sleek silver humanoid shape doesn't acknowledge me any more than a microwave oven would.

I make my way to the cruiser and hit the unlock button on Olivia's keys, only to see a shadowy figure sit up. There's someone inside! Did she forget to lock it? The figure groans as it smacks its head on the roof. In quick, jittery movements, the door flings open and a very sleepy-looking Eugene stares back at me with half-lidded eyes.

"W-w-what—" he stammers, his mouth hanging open.

"I'm sorry! I, uh—I couldn't sleep in there, so uh… I, well, I figured I could come to the cruiser, but I didn't know you'd be here." I fumble, then finally admit, "I was worried when you didn't come back."

He blinks. I just stand there, clutching my pillow over my chest. I'm intruding. I start to turn around, and a thought occurs to me. "You've been out here the whole time?" I ask.

"Yup." His voice is firm. Eugene's lanky body is shuffled over to the other side of the cruiser. Is he … making room for me? The backseat is spacious enough for two people. The seats are down. This would be a good opportunity to clear the air between us, and I'm not exactly sure what to say to him. Olivia and Wallace have always been the buffer between us, and after the way I blew up at him at the library, I'm surprised he wants to be next to me at all.

"Thanks, uh, Olivia and Wallace are snoring. A lot." I take the space next to him and set my pillow next to the window. It's quiet and comfortable, and completely undeserved, considering he's undoubtedly still mad at me.

He leans over the front seat to the center console. "Music?" he asks with a tone gravelly from sleep.

"Yes!" I squeak before turning my attention back toward the parking lot. How can he be so casual?

"Sorry if I was kind of harsh earlier," I start, unsure of where I want to go with the rest of my sentence. Honesty is supposed to be the way to get past misunderstandings, but sharing a desk with Eugene has resulted in a year of fake smiles and conversation. I've never actually told him how frustrating it is to coexist.

"The truth is, you're pretty hard to read." I finally turn toward him. "And now, this is awkward, isn't it? We've never really been alone together." The words sound more intimate than I mean them to. "Uh, I mean, I..."

Nope. There's no saving myself from how that sounded. I don't even try.

Together, under the stars like this! For two people who have no interest in each other, it's an awfully romantic scene. The stars on his cheeks shine in the darkness, illuminating the rest of his face. I watch his Adam's apple bob up and down with a hard swallow.

Embarrassment washes over his face until finally he turns away from me, rolling over so that he faces the trunk of the cruiser. I just need to come out and say it.

"I'm sorry..." I shift toward my own window. "I shouldn't have yelled at you like that. It just feels like maybe you don't... I don't know. Do you think I'm annoying or something?"

He sits straighter, assessing me from eyes to torso, and despite myself, the freckles on my cheek glow, illuminating the space between us. We're a foot away from each other, but it feels too close.

"No," he whispers. There's tension strung high in his shoulders. Then, Eugene suddenly melts with the speed of an ice cream cone, shifting away with slumped shoulders.

"Okay..." I trail off, I assumed we both adamantly disliked each other, but if that's not the case... "Then why?"

Silence again. I shouldn't expect anything more.

"If you're not a chatty person, that's fine." Maybe I've been taking all his one-word replies too personally. "I just—I don't know, a nod or something would be helpful once in a while."

"That's not..." His voice is so low it's hard to make out above the hum of the music. It's the closest thing to a full sentence I've ever heard out of his mouth.

"I-I stutter..." The words come out under his breath.

"You ... what?" I heard him, but I don't understand. Is that the reason he's barely said three words since we met?

"Is that why you're so quiet?" I ask. My throat feels dry. I hope he won't think I'm prying too much.

"Mhmm," he mumbles, and I relax back in my seat. Eugene still hasn't turned back. Nervously, I reach out, gently touching his shoulder. He timidly looks back at me.

"I always just thought you hated me!" I blurt before I can stop myself. "I—oh, I shouldn't have said that. It's just—I don't get it. Why keep it a secret? I think half the school is terrified of you." Before I can say anything else, I'm distracted by the messy tuft of his hair swaying back and forth.

My eyes trail to his lips, watching them quiver.

"No." He shakes his head. Leaning forward, he switches the music off. "Rather they're scared than laughing."

"Is that why you transferred to Galaxy High?" I ask and watch as the color drains from his skin. It's hard to imagine anyone being brave enough to make fun of Eugene—to his face, at least. I've always had the decency of doing it behind his back, but right now, even that is starting to make me feel guilty. He averts his dark eyes before finally nodding.

"What happened?" I ask before I realize I'm entirely overstepping. "I'm sorry. You don't have to talk about it if you don't want to."

He bites his bottom lip before letting out a gut-wrenching sigh, his head tipping toward the ceiling.

"It w-w-asn't," he pauses, clamping his mouth shut. "It's not something I like to think about."

His voice is so low, I wonder if it's easier for him when he's talking quietly. Whatever happened at his old school, he seems traumatized by it. I imagine his lanky body being pretzeled into a locker, or his classmates mocking the way his voice catches on the first sound of certain words.

"So that's why you have this whole bad boy persona?" I ask, trying to wrap my head around the way he presents himself at school. "Why not just try to be yourself?"

"A name like Eugene *and* a stutter? No." He shrugs his shoulders, forcing a laugh.

"I've never thought about your name."

"Right," he replies, clearly proud that the walls he put up have worked so far. He lets out a sigh and shakes his head. "It-w-wa- It got bad. Called names, shoved, you know those mmm-moving trash cans?"

I cringe, unsure of where this might be going. We have them roaming around the hallways at school between classes. It's been a great way to make sure the hallways stay clean.

"Imagine being sh-sh- pushed face down in one." His dark eyes swell like pools of liquid before he bitterly turns away. I imagine his long legs helplessly kicking as the trash can wheeled him down a crowded hallway for everyone to see.

"Didn't anyone help you?" I gasp. I can't imagine how mortifying that must have been. He shrugs, shaking his head as if the answer is simple, as if I should have known better than to ask at all. How could his old classmates be so cruel?

"No one should have ever teased you about something you can't control!" I huff. It's terrible that the bullies from his old school made him feel like he needed to create this untouchable image.

He arches an eyebrow. Even in the dim light, I can see the hurt on his face. Why is he looking at me like that? I never... Oh stars! My thoughts plummet back to the library. What was it I had said? Echoing his stutter...

Telling him to just *say it.*

I'm no better than the kids who drove him out of his old school.

"I..." My mind races to find something that'll excuse the behavior. He's right. It was terrible, awful, inexcusable. "I'm so sorry." Our eyes meet, and he smiles tenderly. But it's not enough.

"I was awful."

"You w-were mad."

"That doesn't matter." I shake my head from side to side, unable to get rid of the pit growing in my stomach.

He reaches out to touch my shoulder. It's wrong. He shouldn't be comforting me. I thought nothing could be as bad as Eugene's cold, stoic expression, but this... I never want to see him make this face again.

"Everyone does it."

My heart sinks.

No one deserves to be bullied—especially in a place everyone should feel safe.

"I'm really sorry that happened to you, Eugene." The words feel a little too stiff, but I'm not sure what else to say. "I'll never tease you again, I promise. I won't be like them."

"Thanks." And for the first time, he smiles, a bashful grin that spreads across his lips and all the way up to his sparkling eyes. His voice is gentle when he lets himself speak but filled with emotion. The stutter jars the sentences unevenly, but the tone itself is softer than the one-word replies I'm used to. It's like he's a different person. "You're forgiven."

"Why?" The blunt word creeps from my lips, and for whatever reason, he laughs.

"You mean it." His freckles shine across the cruiser.

Now I see what all the girls at school whisper about. He *is* cute, but not in the way they describe. He feels *different*—softer.

Tonight, we're meeting for the very first time. We sit in silence for a while, with only the sound of the nearly silent radio between us.

"So, w-why are you doing this?" Eugene asks, breaking the stretch of silence.

"I told you. Olivia and Wallace snore."

He laughs again, this time throwing his head back, messing up his already tousled hair.

"No, *this*." He vaguely gestures, and it takes me a moment to understand. Why am I out here, chasing down my first romance?

"I just..." I begin, trying to figure out the best way to explain. I hug my knees to my chest and let my head fall back to look up at the sky.

"It's goofy." I shake my head, wanting to get out of answering the question.

Eugene props himself up on his elbows, looking even more intrigued than before. He did just tell me a secret he's been hiding since he transferred to Galaxy High. I can at least tell him why I'm leading us to what feels like the edge of the universe.

"Okay, so I get dozens of these letters a week, right? They flood my desk, and they vary in tone, experience, and seriousness, but when it comes to love—real love—they all have something in common. That Feeling—you know the one. It's supposed to be dizzy, bubbling, nervous; it makes you feel excited, happy, and sick all at the same time?"

It's too embarrassing to look at him. I don't want to know if he's going to laugh in my face, or nodding along, so I keep my eyes fixed on the cruiser's worn seat.

"*The Guide*—it talks about the Feeling too. The thing is, that book is the only proof that it's real. These letters are the closest thing I've ever felt to it. They make me feel ... like something might really be out there for me."

The stars on my cheeks illuminate the entire backseat, and the heat on my skin is too much to bear. When I finally look back at Eugene, he just nods. I haven't talked to anyone about this, not even Olivia.

"I sort of expected you to laugh or something." I clamp my hands to my cheeks to dampen some of the glow. "Stars, it's embarrassing. I can't believe I just blurted all of that out."

We stare at each other in the dark. Somehow his silence doesn't feel as intimidating as it did before. "You're actually pretty easy to talk to." I look back up at the glittering stars overhead.

Eugene seems surprised. "No one has ever said that to me b-before."

"Well! I'm saying it right now." I roll over to face him and gulp. I ended up closer than I thought I would. "You're not how I thought you'd be, with your black coffee and your leather jacket."

"Can I-I-uh tell you a secret?"

I nod, my heart racing as he leans forward ever so slightly. I didn't realize we could get closer in this tight space. "I-I don't even like coffee that much. I just know I can say it without stuttering."

"Wait, so you've just been suffering through cups of coffee you never wanted in the first place?"

"Sometimes," he says in voice so low it's almost a whisper. "Sometimes I want the coffee."

"Now I'm sorry."

"No."

"But it's—"

"My choice."

"Right." I let out a sigh. "I guess I just… I don't know. It'd be nice if you had a good time. I mean, I dragged you all out here, and well, I'm just worried about every little thing, I guess."

I slump into the cushions of the seat. He's chewing on his bottom lip. The skin is cracked and rough when he finally releases his teeth.

It looks like there was something he wanted to say, but he's holding back. I can't blame him. He's already opened up in ways I never would have expected. I don't want to push him, but I want to know what he's thinking. Now that I know he doesn't hate me, that's one thing I can cross off my worry list.

Silence falls between us, and we shift back to looking at the stars beyond the domed roof of Olivia's cruiser. "Do you have a favorite?" I ask.

"Star?"

"Drink." I laugh. "But let's do your question. It's better."

He shakes his head. I can't believe this is the same brooding boy from school. He thoughtfully looks up at the sky and then at me. I suddenly feel out of breath, wondering if he's studying the pattern of glowing freckles on my face.

Do you have a favorite star?

"All of them," he replies. I want to tell him that's cheating, but looking out at the endless galaxy, glittering with possibility, I don't think I can pick a favorite either.

"Hey…" I whisper after a long stretch of silence, unsure if he's asleep or not. I don't really want to wake him.

"Mhmm," he mumbles, with a yawn. His eyes are beginning to close, and I smirk, realizing he's falling asleep.

"You know I'll keep your secret safe, right?" I'm glad the wall between us is finally broken, but I want him to know he can trust me. "I promise to never make fun of you."

"Yes."
I smile ear to ear.
That's a one-word answer that I'm finally happy with.

14.

"A stutter! Why didn't you say so?" Wallace exclaims, wrapping an arm around Eugene. *Why didn't you say so?* Oh, Wallace.

"I mean, I get why you didn't say so. I just mean ... well ... being, uh—" The more he talks, the more his rosy face tints a deeper shade of pink. "You know what I mean!" He pulls Eugene into a full-on hug. I wonder if I should try to help him escape. Eugene doesn't seem like the touchy type, but just when I take a step forward, Eugene's stiffness melts into Wallace's shoulders. Wallace is the closest thing he has to a friend at school; it must feel good to finally get this secret off his chest.

It's nice to see this side of Eugene. For two nights now, I've woken up entangled with Eugene Eris. Today, he greeted me with a "good morning." We stayed up late just talking— about school, what it's like working at his parents' diner, the paper, our favorite books and movies. The reason he's so quiet was surprising, but even more than that, I can't believe how much we have in common. Eugene's not half bad.

I just wish Olivia would stop giving me that funny look. She's had it on her face ever since she found the two of us in the back of her cruiser this morning. Her eyes narrowed and lips quirked up in a sly smile. Even after the four of us loaded into the cruiser and head toward our next destination, she kept glancing over at me. I wish she would just focus on driving instead of whatever she's trying to imply.

"Do we even know where the next location is?" Wallace jumps in, and I rummage through my purse until my fingertips land on the most recent letter. I'd been so distracted at the library, I'd kind of forgotten about the whole "submitting live updates" thing. I hope Anonymous doesn't think I've forgotten about it.

"Susie figured it out at the library." Olivia makes a face. "Jukebox Diner. Their slogan is 'Milkshakes out of this world.'"

"They're famous for one with marshmallow stars and a color-changing formula!" At least that's what I could find out when I looked it up at the library. It's an hour drive taking the main starway, so we grab a quick breakfast of brightly colored pastries and coffee fizz from the hotel vending machine to tide us over. Eating snacks in the backseat with the radio blasting—it's starting to feel like the road trip I dreamed of. If I tune out the sound of Wallace and Olivia bickering at least. With the two of them, it's never ending.

Olivia sings along with the radio.

"Less singing and more driving, please?" Wallace groans from the backseat.

Eugene pops a hard candy in his mouth. It's the kind Dad always gave me when I had a sore throat. Dad still keeps a handful of them in his bag at all times. I can't help but wonder if he's uncomfortable. His throat probably isn't used to so much talking.

Is there anything I can do to help? He could just have a sweet tooth. No, Eugene doesn't seem like the type, but nothing about Eugene should surprise me at this point.

I don't say anything. My eyes stay fixed on the scenery, watching the colorful billboards go by.

"So, Eugene, did you write for the paper at your other school? I'd been wanting to ask, but..." Wallace trails off. "Anyway, your articles are always organized and on time, and I always kind of wondered if you'd been doing this for a while."

Eugene shrugs. "I-I um... mostly for fun."

"Did you belong to any other clubs?" Olivia asks.

"No." His reply is sharper than I expect it to be.

"Does the stutter happen all the time, or just when you're nervous?" Wallace asks, and my jaw drops. That doesn't seem like something you're *supposed* to ask.

"Um, w-well..."

"Are you nervous right now? Because you don't have to be! We're all friends here—except for me and Olivia."

"Obviously," she replies coolly with a small nod. Something they finally agree on.

He laughs. I can't tell if it's uncomfortable laughter or if it's genuine. But now that they've found out why he doesn't talk, it seems like talking is all they want him to do. Maybe this is one of the reasons he didn't want anyone to find out.

Silence falls across the cruiser again. Olivia goes back to singing along with the radio, louder after the comment Wallace made. Her voice is nice, and I'd much rather have the singing than speeding. A familiar melody picks up, and my heart flutters. This is one of our favorites, frequently sung in Olivia's bedroom using hairbrushes as microphones and not caring how silly we look.

Without me even having to ask, she cranks the volume up, and we sing along with the nonsensical lyrics about dating a robot.

She takes her hands off the wheel to dance more than I would like, offering me an apologetic smile and clicking autopilot. I bobble my head while keeping an eye on the emergency controls. Just in case.

At least, that's the plan, but the song is so catchy that, by the second verse, I'm full-on shimmying in my seat.

We keep the cruiser karaoke going, and I keep having to remind myself that we're not the only two people in the cruiser.

A deep voice from the backseat makes my hair stand on end.

Eugene is singing.

Eugene—the school "bad boy"—is singing right now.

Eugene and Olivia's voices mingle together well for the next song. I join in on the chorus, but mostly I can't do anything but just listen. Even Wallace starts to sway his shoulders along after the next song. It's short-lived, however. The blinking neon sign of The Jukebox Diner draws us into the small parking lot. It looks like a tin can floating in the middle of darkness, on its own little patch of AstroTurf, with the same artificial glow that reminds me of home. We get through the airlock and find a parking spot. The closer we get, the more I can see the paint flaking off the sides, but it looks impressive, nonetheless.

"Race you inside!" Olivia shouts with a sudden burst of energy I'm not prepared for. We rush forward until we're standing in front of the large, shining doors.

The blue and cream color scheme is consistent throughout the restaurant right down to the checkerboard floor. Anonymous was right. The booths are packed with groups of girls with high ponytails and poodle skirts and boys in leather jackets, slicked-back hair, and tight pants.

There's an empty table way in the back, and a seat or two at the bar. Stealing a glance around the bar, I spy one of the famed giant milkshakes in almost every booth.

They're twice the size of anything you'd get back home, with blue and black ice cream swirls and tiny gleaming stars that twist and pop; small candy planets orbit the glass. My mouth is watering by the time we reach the booth.

Our waitress dances over to a song that blares from the jukebox. Her hair is styled in a bright pink beehive and looks like it could have a gravitational pull of its own. "Hey, kids, what can I get you?" she greets us with barely a glance.

"Oh! Um... did anyone leave a note for a customer? Someone named Miss Galaxy, by chance?"

"Do I look like the postman?" Her hand rests lazily on her hip, and she gazes at me with annoyance and amusement. She smirks.

This wasn't part of an Anonymous poem.

My shoulders tense up to my ears, and I shake my head.

"What'll you have to eat?" she corrects herself, glancing around at the table before locking eyes with Eugene.

Eugene starts to open his mouth and then shuts it, and I notice the creasing on his brow.

"Coffee," he says finally.

"And I was thinking maybe the four of us could share the signature milkshake," I say, not thinking before I jump in. "It's pretty big, isn't it?"

"Out of this world," the waitress says dryly. It's a line that clearly loses its punch the more you say it.

"And fries!" Olivia adds.

"Large fries!" Wallace pointedly corrects her. "You ate all of them last time."

"I did not," she huffs, crossing her arms dramatically. "Did too."

The waitress's eyes widen, and her head snaps back to me. "Anything else?"

"I think that's all. Thank you." I practically have to shout over their bickering.

She folds up her pen and paper and leaves. There's a soft nudge on my shoulder from Eugene.

"Do you want a coffee?" His voice catches me off guard. He's leaning in close, dark hair falling into his face. I could use all the caffeine and sugar I can get right now. Leaning back against the worn vinyl of the booth, I let myself relax. I try to, at least. After spending so much time together, being this close to Eugene shouldn't affect me at all, but I can still feel every inch of the space between us. I slide farther into the booth, even though something tells me I secretly wish I were moving in the opposite direction.

"This place is a scream!" Olivia exclaims. "Not to mention the atmosphere."

"The blue and cream are very complimentary," I agree looking around. Everything is shiny and matching.

Wallace and Olivia let out a cackle.

"She wasn't talking about the color scheme." He waggles his eyebrows up and down, and I glance around the room. A few people with perfect curls and outfits hang out around the jukebox. They bobble to the music, their freckles gleaming under the fluorescent light. With looks like this, they'd give even Skip a run for his money. Stars, who am I kidding? They look like they stepped out of a magazine! But the most remarkable thing about the group is that they're eyeing our table like a plate of cheese fries and a malt.

Ah, *that* kind of atmosphere. An uncomfortable laugh escapes me.

We're far from Ceres, and I doubt any of them have a connection with Anonymous, but I can't help but wonder if they might know something. My face burns at the idea of approaching a group that good looking.

Wallace crosses his arms. "Not that I would be paying attention to that sort of thing." He fiddles with the locket around his neck. "But really, Teddy would love this place." He frowns. After going steady for a whole year, it would make sense that he's missing his boyfriend during their week apart. But this is the first time he's let it show.

"You could get him a souvenir mug!" I suggest, pointing at the logo-printed mugs near the counter.

"Yeah, I think I might on the way out," he murmurs dreamily.

I prop my head up on my elbows. "How did you two meet, anyway?" For all the bragging Wallace does, he's never actually talked to us about how they got together.

"I had a crush on Teddy since elementary school," he says, a cute, bashful expression on his face. "But we only started really talking when we got paired up in science class. I offered to carry his books home from school one day." He's blushing. It's so unlike him, but then again, everyone has those things that make their faces glow. For Wallace, that soft spot is Teddy.

"Then what?" I ask.

He covers his face with his hands. "He kissed me on the porch." He shakes his head. "He liked me too; he just wasn't sure if I felt the same. He didn't want to get rejected, and neither did I. But then one day, it just happened."

"That's a really cute story, Wallace." It's simple, but lovely. I can't help but wonder if Teddy had been pining for Wallace just as long as he had. A kiss after a walk home is just so classic.

A thud interrupts our swooning. Our waitress dropped our order in the center of the table. I know the sign said "out of this world" but...

"Am I crazy, or is this bigger than the ones at the other tables?" Olivia looks absolutely shocked as she stares at the massive milkshake.

The planet-shaped candies bobble ever so slightly as they circle around and around. The stars bursting up against the glass look even prettier up close.

"Well, she wasn't kidding. It's plenty to share." I'm mesmerized by the planets orbiting the glass.

"All together?" Wallace asks. He's the first to lean forward with his straw, stabbing it into the whipped cream on top.

We all lean forward and do the same, and I tense at the feeling of my shoulders brushing up against Eugene's.

"Three..." Wallace counts down, "two ... one!"

Clunk!

The tops of our heads knock together. I laugh.

"Let's try that one more time." We lean forward, more cautious this time.

Our faces are close. Like really, really close. I can feel the heat of Eugene's face next to mine, I glance over and can't help but notice the almost delicate slope of his button nose, his lips curved into a slight smile. I turn my attention back to the milkshake, taking a slow sip with the others.

A burst of raspberry and chocolate coats my tongue, followed by a fizzy sensation that I guess are the stars. A soft marshmallow blends with the other flavors.

It's delicious. I smile, watching the colors in the glass turn from blue to purple right in front of my eyes.

"Oh, that is way too sweet!" Wallace's face twists into a grimace, and he reaches for his water.

"For once, you and I agree about something." Olivia nods aggressively and pushes the milkshake across the table toward Eugene and me.

"You two are missing out!" I exclaim. "This is delicious!"

Eugene nods, and I'm glad someone else at this table has some sense.

"Thank goodness he agrees! Because if you tried to finish that entire thing yourself, you would explode," Wallace says through his laughter.

"Susie, that sounds like a challenge!" Olivia pressures, wiggling her eyebrows. "I dare you!"

"I kindly decline." I pick one of the rotating planets and pop it in my mouth. A fizzy candy rock pops and melts on my tongue. I wonder if that's why Anonymous chose this place. The orbiting confections are similar to the purple rock candies I tried on Lemon Drop Beach.

"Brain freeze?" Olivia asks, dipping a french fry into the whipped cream, then tossing it in her mouth.

I've seen her do this dozens of times, but the boys just stare.

"Oh, come on, Eugene! You work in your parents' diner. You seriously have never tried this?" I personally prefer it with chocolate and vanilla, but it still works with fruity flavors. The sweet and salty combination is surprisingly nice.

Wallace tentatively grabs a fry but fumbles. It tumbles out of his hands, but lands in the milkshake's orbit, shaking more and more with every turn. My eyes track the french fry around and around. We watch closely, waiting for it to plummet onto the table, but it doesn't. It orbits around the glass again and again as giggles build in my chest.

This long awkward french fry barrels around the glass alongside the candy planets, clunking into the rim at every chance. My lips crack into a smile, wider and wider until I can't contain it anymore, I throw my head back and laugh until tears pool in the corners of my eyes.

The rest of the table joins in, but I can't tell if they're laughing at me or the fry at this point. I feel like a sleep-deprived middle schooler hopped up on sugar at a slumber party. Even when Wallace plucks the fry out of orbit, I can't stop.

"It's not that funny," Wallace whispers, his face suddenly a rosier shade of pink. I look up and realize that a few nearby tables are glaring in our direction.

I try to rein it in, hoping the last of my giggles fall out with the shake of my head. Then suddenly there's a roar of laughter beside me. It sounds strange and forced. I think Eugene might be making fun of me at first. Then I realize that the attention isn't just on me anymore. He's not going to let me make a fool out of myself alone—or he's finally just realized that the orbiting french fry is the funniest thing we've seen this entire trip. A cutting glare toward the rest of the patrons suggest it was the first thing though.

I calm down and take another sip of the shake. This time, my straw bumps into something hard at the bottom.

I poke around. There's something in there. Candy? No, it feels too large for that. I try to scoop it up with the spoon, and it slips, but not before I catch a glimpse of plastic.

No way.

I pull the milkshake closer, enthusiastically diving in with the spoon. Chocolate sloshes down the side of the glass, creating a small puddle on the laminate table.

Just as I thought, it's a plastic capsule, and just as I hoped, there's a paper inside. I don't bother to wipe it clean before I pop the capsule open. My ice cream-covered hands create fingerprints across the small note. Wallace is quick to snap a photo before I'm handed a napkin.

Dear Miss Galaxy,

This frozen treat was awfully sweet, but not as cold as
the place you and the next clue will finally meet. A place
where folks go to ski and play is the next place that I'll
have a chance to say I'm smitten with you. Really, truly.
I hope when you find out who I am, you'll feel the same
way. But until then…

XO,

Anonymous

P.S. I tried the rhyming thing again. I really wish you
could tell me if it's working or not because it feels a little
funny, like I'm writing a kid's book. I hope you like it
anyway. This one is tricky, so I've given you an extra clue.

Just as cute as last time. It really seems like Anonymous
is loosening up. For the first time, there are coordinates
at the bottom. I stop to think. Cold planet—it's got to be
Glacies, which, from what I remember in class, is huge. I'm
glad we at least have a place to start.

I look around frantically, trying to find a familiar face
from school, but instead I lock eyes with our waitress.
"Excuse me!" I shout, motioning her over. She looks at me.
"Did anyone come into your kitchen today?"

She puts a hand on her hip. Oh, no, I was too vague. She's
wrinkling her nose, her pen tapping on her notepad.

"Lots." Then her eyes wander down to the milkshake. She
knows! The sides of her mouth lift into a smirk.

"Ah, that." She shakes her head, letting out an unim-
pressed laugh. "Teenagers! When I was your age, it was
enough to just ask someone out for a malt, but now everything's gotta be a big production!" She huffs, turning away
from our table. "Better get a move on, Miss Galaxy."

Oh stars, does that mean she read it? I can't believe she would do that. But then again, if I were in her position, I don't know if I'd be strong enough to resist the temptation. I mean, I already spend my time reading other people's love letters. But at least I have permission!

Olivia is quiet.

"What's wrong?" I ask.

"We're going to Glacies." She pouts.

"And?"

"It's a planet literally made of ice."

"And?" I don't know where she's going with this.

"Susie! I am made of fire!"

"You can still go to cold places," I argue back. Ceres has Ice Volcanos for Stars' sake! "There'll be a suit rental for all of us."

"But I don't like them!" she whines, more comically this time.

"Yeah! And she's already around enough stuff she doesn't like," Wallace jabs.

"Exactly!"

I cock my head at Wallace.

Is his tactic to get her to agree with him to just be self-deprecating? I can't say I agree with the method, but it's interesting, to say the least.

I reach across the table and squeeze her hand. "I will buy you all of the hot chocolate you want."

"I mean, I'll go, but I'm not happy about it." She crosses her arms. "It's going to be so cold."

15.

Anonymous,

Do you have a teleportation machine? I don't understand how you managed to get the last clue inside of the milkshake I was drinking. You're always one step ahead, but I guess that's the whole point of a scavenger hunt, isn't it? Everywhere you've led me to so far has been a surprise. I'm still thinking about the wall-to-wall books at the library, and that milkshake was a thing of dreams.

And by the way, so are each of your letters. You may be sending me somewhere cold next, but I'm warmed up by each of your words.

'Til next time,

Xoxo,

Miss Galaxy

-send-

The motel room is silent and awkward, and for once, it's not because anyone is fighting. This is the most tired I've ever felt in my life. Judging by the heavy bags under everyone's eyes and our matching sets of slumped shoulders, I don't think I'm alone in that feeling. On the way to the motel, I slept in the cruiser for an hour or so; Eugene took up the mantle of co-navigator. I think we're all too scared to have Wallace sit in the front with Olivia again.

When Mom messages me asking if I'm safe, I want to tell her every little detail about the trip, but instead I just tell her I'm fine. It's the understatement of the century, but still the truth. I'm finer than I've ever been, and soon, I'll find out who's writing these letters.

Wallace gingerly sits on the edge of the bed he and Eugene will be sharing, polishing the lens of his camera. I haven't had a chance to ask exactly how he ended up getting that camera in his hands.

"I was a little surprised when Ms. Loretta suggested you as the photographer," I admit with a small yawn. He raises his eyebrows, looking slightly offended. "Don't get me wrong! You've been doing amazing so far. It seems like you've taken some really interesting shots. I just didn't realize it was a hobby of yours."

"I guess I've been dabbling for a while." He shifts his gaze away. "We all have our hobbies outside of the newspaper, right?"

"No," Eugene and I answer in unison. I catch his smirk from across the room. I shake my head; we have more in common than I realized.

"I'm the only one without a regular column, so I'm sure that's all there is to it." Wallace shrugs. "I don't know that I'm any good." I've never seen him so unsure of himself. His shoulders have fallen forward in a dramatic shrug.

"Well, whatever you decide, we'll be here to cheer you on." I smile. Stars know we could use another good photographer at the paper.

"Are you kidding me?" Olivia snaps from beside me. Her voice is so loud I jump Oh, when I said "we," I was really just talking about Eugene and me. Though, I still don't know why a comment like that would get her this heated. I was just trying to encourage him.

A silence fills the room until she speaks again.

"Pedestrian," she says pointedly. "Does that sound like cheering someone on?"

Wallace's face is blank, giving me zero clue to what in the stars Olivia's talking about.

"You don't even remember, do you?" She shrugs. "Figures."

Suddenly, his eyebrows knit together, and a loud sigh mixes with the tension building in room. "That's what this is about?" His voice is soft, barely an echo, and then his eyes widen. "That was for your first submission!"

"So, I'm supposed to just get over it?"

"That's not what I'm saying."

I look between the two of them. I thought once they started talking things out, everything would be clear. But now, I could really use a context clue.

"You can't pretend to be this goody-goody 'yay, you can do it' person and then call my piece 'pedestrian,' okay?!" she snaps. "And don't pretend you were any better for my submissions after that." I've heard this story, not necessarily the details, only that Wallace rejected her time and time again.

I thought maybe we were just overstaffed, or the pieces didn't fit with the paper at the time. But calling her writing pedestrian? Even for Wallace, that's harsh.

"Look!" Wallace begins. "I was in a different headspace back then. If I had known—"

"Well, you should have known!" Olivia cuts him off before he has a chance to say anything else. I never realized that his rejections had cut her so deep. I'm her best friend. I should have been able to see this earlier.

But wait—

I gasp.

Their dispute is out in the open! This is my chance to help them resolve the situation! I practically lunge for *The Guide* before Olivia shakes her head.

"Nothing in your book is going to fix this, Susie." Her hand rests firmly on my shoulder, and the look in her eyes is deathly serious. "Just because you're friends with Mr. Perfect Editor and Chief doesn't mean I have to be or even want to be, okay?!"

Both Olivia and Wallace's arms are crossed, and they refuse to look at each other. *The Guide* has a whole chapter on getting friends to make up, tactics to use to reignite that spark of your platonic love, to remember why you became friends in the first place. But Wallace and Olivia don't even have a broken foundation to stand on. The relationships I've built with them are completely separate.

"Okay," I say, putting *The Guide* back in my bag. I draw in a deep breath. A real-life Dear Miss Galaxy letter is standing in front of me, the first one I'll ever answer without my trusted book for reference.

"Maybe just go back and forth and try to clear the air, even if it's just, like, one sentence at a time. Try to get each other's perspective. I don't expect you to be friends after this, or even like each other, but Olivia, you have some understandable hurt—"

"I'm not hurt! I'm mad," she huffs.

"Okay, and now Wallace, you say something in response," I coach, my heart beating faster and faster by the second.

I'm not sure if this is going to work. I'm just making stuff up as I go along. If they weren't so focused on each other, I'd worry they could see my hands starting to shake. Conflict on paper is so much easier. I want the comfort of my book, but I don't want Olivia to get upset again if I reach for it. I'll have to act as moderator without it.

"You've been insufferable to work with the entire time you've been at *The Gazette*." Wallace paces the room, his chin tipped up to the ceiling. "Isn't that enough payback?"

"You just don't get it!"

Alright, this isn't great, but no one has stormed off yet, and they're not full-on yelling at each other. They continue to go back and forth with variations of the same statements while I look for my next opening to steer the conversation.

"Maybe you two could try putting your feelings in letters," I suggest, unsure if either of them has heard me. "It always helps to just start writi—"

Before I can finish the thought, there's a tap on my shoulder and Eugene is at my side, an ice bucket tucked under his arm.

"Ice," he says in a low whisper.

Doesn't he see we're kind of in the middle of something here?

"And that's a two-person job?"

"Yeah."

I ignore him, turning my attention back to Wallace and Olivia, who have worked themselves into a full-on shouting match at this point. I need to get in there.

"So, what you two should—" I begin, but my voice is completely lost. Eugene's hands pull me gently toward the doorway, and before I can protest, the door closes. We're on the wrong side of it.

"Eugene Eris! How am I supposed to fix this if I'm not in the room?" I whirl around, pointing at the teal-colored door.

"Not your job." He shrugs and motions for me to take the ice bucket. And just like that, he's the too-cool, aloof guy from school again.

"Funny, because that sounds a lot like my job! Fixing problems is what I do, in case you've forgotten!" I say pointedly, pulling at the door handle.

Neither of us have the key. And they're screaming too loudly to hear me knocking.

I glare back at Eugene, crossing my arms.

"We don't even need ice, do we?" I grumble, taking the bucket out of his hands and setting it down. Anger rumbles in my chest. How am I supposed to help if I'm literally locked out of the situation?

"W-want to go for a walk?" he asks.

"No," I answer flatly, keeping my arms firmly crossed over my chest. I'm not even going to try to pretend I'm not mad at him.

Of course I don't want to go for a walk. I want to get back into the room and help Wallace and Olivia. I wait by the doorway until their shouting picks up again. Defeated, I slide down the door, sitting on the hotel's doormat. They're never going to be able to handle this without someone to steer the rest of the conversation.

After a few moments, Eugene offers me his hand. Glaring up, I decide the aforementioned walk is probably better than listening to my friends yell at each other from the other side of the door.

There isn't all that much to look here in the parking lot—just a bunch of cruisers and airships docked next to each other, all in different shapes and sizes. One looks like a massive hot air balloon with souvenirs pinned all around the interior like a scrapbook. The rest are shining steel and chrome that reflect our pajama-clad bodies as we walk past them.

On the other side of the motel, there's a pool. With no other destination in mind, we wander over to it, taking seats in the lawn chairs.

How am I supposed to just sit here? "What if they're fighting?"

Eugene shoots me a look.

"Well, what if they're fighting *more*?" I snap, then realize I'm yelling at him—again. "Sorry. I can't relax."

Popping up from my chair, I walk out toward the pool. I need a plan. I need my book! Everything I need is in that room right now. I pace back and forth while I try to figure out a plan. What if Wallace and Olivia need me right now?

"I mean, this whole time I've been trying to get them to talk! I know some people just don't get along, and that's alright, but to go on *hating* each other? Well, I guess Wallace never hated Olivia, but—"

"Susie!"

I pivot on my heel, but it's too late. Everything happens in slow motion. Eugene's outstretched hand is getting farther and farther from my own. I reach, but there's nothing to hold onto. Time catches up before I can get my footing. The water slaps the back of my head. It drags me under until suddenly, I'm weightless.

The sky reflects in the water. When I open my eyes, my blurry vision makes it seem like I'm floating in the stars. A shocking cold covers my skin. I reach the surface, gasping for breath, and hear another splash. I jerk forward, coughing up the water caught in my throat and nose. When I finally manage to blink the water out of my eyes, Eugene's body is dangerously close to mine.

I'm fine. Just startled. That must be why my heart is thudding out of my chest like I just ran a marathon.

"You jumped in after me?" I gasp, shivering from the cold. I steady myself on his shoulders, the fabric of my nightgown and bed jacket weighing me down in the water. He laughs, throwing his head back. His bright smile catches me off guard.

It's contagious. My lips crinkle up in a matching grin, and the two of us giggle like we had at the diner, only this time there's no orbiting french fry to blame it on.

A sharp blast of water sprays across my head, and soon, we're in an all-out splash war. I throw my hands up in the air to call a truce, trying to catch my breath.

When we're still, it's easier to see the sky reflecting around us. We're together in a pool of starlight. There's no one to see us—not the prying eyes of Anonymous, our classmates, or anyone else. We're completely alone. Suddenly, neither of us are laughing anymore, and I'm aware of the closing distance between us. When we're back at school, I wonder if he'll so much as smile at me in the hallway. He's worked hard to cultivate his tough guy image. Just because we're friends doesn't mean he's going to want the whole school to see this side of him.

The sudden thought pulls me away.

"W-what?" he asks. He has that look on his face again. His eyes are big and worried, and wet strands of hair stick to his forehead. It's so different from his cool, indifferent stare.

I don't want to go back to the way things used to be. I like this too much. How am I supposed to tell him that?

"I was just thinking..." I begin, unable to meet his eyes. "What happens when we go back to school?"

He stares at me. I don't know how else to say it besides just spelling it out.

"Is us, um … being friends going to hurt your image?"

"Huh?" He looks completely taken aback until he tilts his head back and starts to laugh. "Are you w-w-worried?"

About what? *My* image? I don't exactly have one to be concerned about. Am I worried about being seen in public with Eugene? No. Not in the slightest. I shake my head.

I float backward in the pool of stars. No one talks about me. Not unless they're calling me a square or a goody-goody. Who knows? Hanging out with Eugene might make me seem more interesting by proxy. Watch out Galaxy High: a new Susie is coming to town, and she isn't scared of detention! I picture myself walking into class wearing a leather jacket and stifle a laugh.

Eugene swims forward. His freckles reflect on the water. "People like you." He lowers his eyes and swallows hard.

"They'd like you if you let them get to know you," I say, keeping my eyes fixed on the glittering stars above us. "And you're wrong. People don't even think about me. "

"Impossible," he grumbles under his breath.

"Impossible?" I gasp. "When I walk down the hallway, there just isn't anything special. I blend right into the background!" My hands fly out of the water with a loud splash. "No one ever asks me out." I turn away from him. The water ripples, and I sink low into it, feeling the cold wrap around me.

He raises his eyebrows, his hands resting firmly on his hips.

"They don't!" I have no idea why he's giving me such a condescending look.

"W-we're going to Lester's after school," he says in a sing-song tone. I pause, I mean sure, I get invited to stop by the diner after school all the time, but that's just people being friendly. And since when is he paying attention to my social calendar?

"Want to come catch a movie or see the fireworks or—"

Eugene continues to bring up a slew of invitations made in pity or obligation. Conversations I wasn't aware he was listening to, and he certainly hadn't been a part of. Each comment stings more than the last. Most of those invitations had come from Skip, and he certainly wasn't asking me out. It's always been a group setting or study session. Eugene doesn't know what he's talking about.

"None of those are dates!" I shout, springing out of the water. We're face to face now, and his eyes finally soften.

I draw in a deep breath. I need to set the record straight. "As stated on page twelve of *The Space Age Ladies' Guide to Romance and Social Affairs*, a date must be made in a clear, unmistakable fashion."

"I-I'm sorry..." He swallows hard. "I just... I thought you... I thought... I..." His fingers brush through his wet hair.

He's mistaken. He must be. I remember all those little moments. It was mostly invitations with large groups after school. None of them like me—least of all Skip. Not like that. Skip's gold eyes flash through my mind, and I lower my head. "You're wrong," I say. I hate how quiet I sound.

He lets out a deep sigh. "P-people like you."

"Not like that," I argue.

He starts to reach out for me, then pulls back and shakes his head. "They do..."

"Can you please stop teasing me?"

He opens his mouth, then clamps it shut, biting his bottom lip to keep the words from escaping. Just like he always does.

But he's quiet now, and the mood is heavy. Gears won't stop turning in my head. I know why he rejects every girl at school. He doesn't want them to know about his stutter. But he's so certain… I need to ask.

"Is that how you'd ask a girl out? With a vague invitation?" I huff, my arms crossed over my chest.

He shakes his head. It seems like he's thinking. He hasn't spoken about it before, but he must have a crush on someone.

"Eugene," I begin, "is there someone at school you like?"

I look into his deep eyes. They're filled with wonder and stardust, deep blue and green swirling around each other. For as long as I've sat next to him, I can't believe I'm just noticing he has eyes that hold entire galaxies. I don't know what came over me. The question just slipped out. He always seemed too good for everyone at Galaxy High, but now I know better. He was just scared. And now, silhouetted by darkness and bathed in starlight, he nods.

"Yes." His voice wraps around me, and I wish it was his arms drawing me closer. I know in that instant. I want him to be talking about me.

It's selfish.

I already have someone on paper.

But Eugene is right in front of me. Our bodies drift closer. I look up, and the way he's gazing down at me makes every reasonable thought fall away.

"We should probably get back," I say softly, but my body doesn't move. I fight every urge to move closer and instead break away, taking heavy steps toward the ladder. The fabric of my pajamas clings to my body the moment I step out of the water.

My robe is heavy and sopping wet. I take it off and wring it out, watching water squeeze out of the thick, quilted fabric.

Eugene hasn't fared much better. His silky pajamas are stuck to his body like a second skin. Why am I not looking away? This is bad. But when I look up, I realize he's staring right back. My face glows as I quickly turn away and put on my dripping robe.

But even after I'm sufficiently covered, he's still looking at me funny. If I look half as silly as he does, I guess I can understand why. Still, I must admit, there's a sort of a charm to him with his matching striped pajama set clinging to his thin body.

My heart is going to explode.

We walk in silence, leaving droplets of water in our wake. I walk ahead for a few minutes, catching my breath. I remind myself that no matter how much I want him to be, he's not Anonymous, and despite the way his stars are glowing under the moon, we're just friends. We need to just be friends.

I reach the door. It's quiet, which means either Olivia or Wallace must have stormed off. As long as someone is there to answer it, I'm happy. I can't be alone with Eugene for another second.

To my surprise, the two of them open the door together. Their eyebrows are narrowed almost comically, like a pair of disapproving parents. "You kids have some explaining to do," Olivia says in a tone so stern I can't tell if she's joking.

I look past them at the clock on the wall. It's 1:45 a.m. When did it get so late?

"Time flies when you're young and falling in love." The quote from my book rings in my ears. I push it down as Olivia and Wallace tease us like worried parents for the rest of the night. But Eugene was right—they seem surprisingly better. Not perfect. But whatever conversation needed to happen, they had it. And it didn't matter if I was in the room or not.

That somehow doesn't make me feel any better.

I thought when the moment came for them to settle their differences, I'd be necessary, but it turns out I wasn't even needed. Maybe that's for the best, but still. I thought that

The Guide and I would be useful. If they're getting along, why should it matter? It's probably better that they worked it out themselves. Eugene's right. Maybe it's only my job to solve problems on paper.

I pull my hair up in a ponytail, too tired to bother with my usual beauty regimen. Tomorrow is our last adventure, and I don't know what's going to happen next. But I can't sleep.

The feeling doesn't go away. Not when I take a shower. Not when I hop under the covers. And not when everyone else is fast asleep. I roll over again.

At least Wallace and Olivia aren't snoring tonight.

I close my eyes tight but end up just looking at the ceiling. My wrist vibrates. Shoot! I was sure I sent Mom a check-in message before bed. I pick up my communicator.

[Eugene: Are you still awake over there?]

I guess he can't sleep either.

[Susie: How'd you know?]

[Eugene: The heavy sighs might have given you away. Are you okay?]

[Susie: Just thinking … about all of this.]

[Eugene: It's been an adventure.]

[Susie: But why bother to send me on it? I mean, why bother to send Miss Galaxy? What is it about her that would make someone want to do this?]

[Eugene: You're the expert... But a crush can make people do extravagant things].

[Susie: In that case, maybe I'm worrying about nothing. It's just … I don't know. It's silly.]

[Eugene: You? Silly? I don't buy it.]

I stifle a snicker and prop myself up on my elbows to see a sneaky smile on Eugene's face.

[Susie: I CAN be silly, thank you very much!]

[Eugene: That has yet to be seen.]

I type and erase, then type and erase again.

[Eugene: You're trying to think of something silly to say, aren't you?]

How dare he!

[Susie: You're an absolute fiend!]

[Eugene: You spelled "friend" wrong.]

My face brightens, and I cover my cheeks before Eugene notices I'm glowing. At the beginning of this trip, I would never have imagined that Eugene and I would have gotten this close.

[Eugene: Sorry, that was really nerdy.]

[Susie: I liked it.]

I hear him type and delete and type and delete again.

[Eugene: You don't have anything to worry about. I'm sure Anonymous thinks you're wonderful. I mean, who wouldn't?]

[Susie: I just hope Susie lives up to Miss Galaxy. On paper, I'm confident and knowledgeable, but in person...]

[Eugene: You're even better.]

I throw the blanket over my face to try to dampen the glow.

[Susie: You really are a good friend.]

[Susie: We should probably get some sleep, huh?]

[Eugene: Night, Susie. Sleep well.]

[Susie: You too, Eugene. XO]

I send the "XO" before I even realize what I've done. I hold my breath. Will he notice? And if he does, will he say anything?

Maybe it's not as big a deal as I'm thinking. I mean, I text Olivia that way all the time. But from the way my chest is thumping, I know it's more complicated than that.

Dear Anonymous,

What would you say if you knew that sending me on this adventure would draw me closer than ever to the wrong person? Even if they are just a friend.

XO,
Miss Galaxy

And that's a message I'll never hit send on.

16.

Glacies is a few hours away, not far enough that we'll need another hotel until the evening. Budget-wise, I'm glad we're catching a break. I shudder to think of what kind of dives we'll be sleeping in for the final two nights of our trip.

We've only been on this trip for a matter of days, but the four of us are different now. Sure, Olivia and Wallace still aren't on the best of terms, but things feel better now.

I guess my mom was right: a lot can happen on a road trip.

I settle into the backseat, and once we get into a major starway, Olivia sets her cruiser on autopilot for the first time. It's odd. We swivel the chairs around and play a short game of cards while the cruiser takes care of itself.

An hour ticks by. Olivia is the first to fall asleep, and Wallace goes next. Sugar courses through my veins. I don't think I'll sleep for days. My wrist vibrates. I look down, expecting a message from my mom—I've been good about checking in every so often—but it's not her. Eugene's name blinks across the display screen.

[Eugene: Is it weirding you out that no one is driving this thing?]

[Susie: YES!]

I type my answer without hesitation, looking at the steering wheel abandoned behind Olivia's turned chair. She's slumped over, snoring softly.

We snicker, the sounds of our muted laughs causing our sleeping companions to stir. I turn my attention back to our silent conversation.

[Eugene: Have you ever been to Glacies?]

[Susie: No, to be honest, I've never really been anywhere.]

[Eugene: Not even on family vacations?]

[Susie: My mom is on call seven days a week working on the dome. We're lucky if we can catch a movie together at the drive-in, much less a vacation.]

[Eugene: Oh... I'm sorry.]

I hadn't been trying to complain. But there's something about writing that feels more fluid. I should be able to edit my thoughts better on screen, but I'm not. Everything just spills out.

[Susie: I wasn't trying to complain. Sorry if it seemed that way.]

I correct myself before the conversation can go any further. But I'm left with a strange, awkward feeling.

[Eugene: It's okay. I mean... I don't really know all that much about you.]

I pause. The same can be said for how much I know about him. And after the recent revelation, I feel like I know even less.

[Susie: What did you want to know?]

[Eugene: What's your favorite breakfast food?]

I muffle a laugh. What a strange question!

[Susie: My dad's pancakes. He makes them as a surprise on weekdays.]

[Eugene: Me too! Except on weekends.]

[Susie: Ah, so that's where Dad disappears to on the weekends...]

He cracks a smile and shakes his head. I think he mouths the word "dork," but I can't be sure. And with the way he's smiling, I'm not sure I mind.

[Susie: Do you play any instruments?]

[Eugene: I could maybe manage the xylophone, but no. I don't play the guitar or anything cool like that.]

The guitar? A pit forms in my stomach. Is he referring to Skip? Another message pings on my wrist.

[Eugene: I sing a little bit. But not really in public. I tried to join the choir at my last school, but it didn't go so hot.]

[Susie: You sounded really nice yesterday.]

I watch his entire face illuminate.

[Eugene: So, did you.]

And now I can feel myself glowing too.

We chat idly. I learn that his favorite color is blue, and that his least favorite ice cream flavor is Tutti Frutti. That he's a total wimp when it comes to horror movies. And he learns that I have a different day planner for each season, color-code my closet, and when I catch a cold, all I want to do is lie on the couch while eating soup and watching terrible musicals. The latter seems like the only fun fact that surprises him. It takes only seconds before I've sent him an entire list of my favorites.

[Eugene: When we get back, the four of us could do a movie night.]

"Destination ahead! Ten minutes!" the navigation system reads aloud before I have a chance to reply.

Olivia snaps up and clicks the button for her seat to rotate, and mine rotates right along with it. I shoot Eugene a small smile before our seats pull us away from each other. We'll have to plan our movie night another time.

The starway veers, sending us into the planet's orbit. Olivia takes control of the cruiser, and we draw closer. The gleaming surface of Glacies comes into view, and it's almost too bright to look at. I expected an ice planet to be dull and blue. I rummage through my bag to find sunglasses.

"I didn't realize we were traveling to the surface of the sun!" Wallace exclaims from the backseat.

"I think that would be preferable," Olivia grumbles. I guess she hasn't warmed up to the idea of being in the cold.

Instead of parking by the lodge with the rest of the tourists, we make a quick stop to pick up our gear and the first of what I assume will be many of Olivia's hot chocolates. Then, we head off the beaten path. It's a half-hour more; I wasn't expecting that. I try to stretch out my legs in front of me. All this sitting has them feeling stiff and achy. I can't wait to get outside and skate.

By the time we reach our destination, we're on the other side of the planet. The sky is still dark in this hemisphere, which means we're going to see our first sunrise together! I've never done anything like this with friends before, and it makes me feel giddy. In our insulated suits, Eugene, Wallace, and I sit on the trunk of the cruiser in darkness. Olivia sips her cocoa with the heat on inside the cruiser. It's a good compromise, even though she's behind glass. At least she's still here.

It's dark for a while until a soft light hits the surface of the ice. It sparks, casting a violet hue across the planet's untouched surface.

I peer inside the cruiser. Olivia's amber eyes are bright, the light of the sun reflecting in them. She looks mesmerized. When we arrived, I thought she would have been happier sipping cocoa up in the lodge. But looking at her now, I'm not so sure she wants to be anywhere else.

I lean back happily, and my shoulders bump into Eugene's side. I allow my sleepiness to take over and lean against him for a moment before moving away. "It's beautiful," I whisper, turning my head toward him. It's hard to get used to the way my voice echoes inside the helmet.

"Yeah," Eugene says.

"I ... wow" is all Wallace can get out. Wallace, speechless! This is the one time there doesn't *actually* need to be a glass wall between him and Olivia!

We sit there for a long while until the sky is lavender and white, and the ice mirrors the sky above. It looks like the lid of a freshly opened carton of ice cream. It swirls with color, and each little ice crystal gleams.

I get back to the passenger seat while the boys lace up their skates outside. "What did you think?" I ask.

Olivia shakes her head. "I can't believe I almost asked to stay at the hotel." Her voice is small. It's strange. I'm not used to hearing her with this tone.

"I'm glad you're here."

She smiles, lifting her cocoa cup in a salute. "Me too. Let's get out on the ice!"

My heart leaps. "Wait, really?"

"Why not?" She stretches her arms out. "This is probably the only time we'll be here together."

We step outside, helmets secure and suits zipped up tight.

"Nope! I hate this," Olivia exclaims the minute the first gust of wind hits her. I can't help but laugh. We help each other with our skates and start small with a loop around the cruiser. She picks it up faster than I do, but then again, she has gone to the roller rink on quite a few dates. Maybe it's similar.

With her help, we glide together across the slick, icy surface.

"Does Eugene look different somehow?" I whisper, studying his frame from across the ice.

Eugene and Wallace race each other back and forth . Eugene throws his head back, and I hear muffled laughter echo back to us. I don't think I've ever seen him have this much fun.

"Different how?"

"I don't know. Since the start of the trip?"

"I mean, sure, personality-wise, but he looks about the same to me." She shrugs, and then a goofy grin crosses her lips. "Must just be you." Before I can ask what the smile is about, she skates off, surprisingly graceful despite her protests about even coming here.

I, on the other hand, wobble as soon as she lets go of my hand. Eugene skates by, and without thinking, I reach for him, grasping at the back of his space suit.

He squeezes my hand, and the two of us glide along together.

My heart bubbles, rising and popping at the top of my chest, like a soda bottle under pressure. It's because I'm embarrassed, I assure myself. If I wasn't so wobbly, I'm sure my heart wouldn't be pounding like this. It's not like Eugene and I haven't been this close before.

He says something, but the words are quiet and muffled, I turn, unsure if I should ask him to repeat himself, spinning back on my skates so that we're facing each other—I try to, at least.

"Whoa!" I slip forward laughing, only to be caught in his arms; the two of us slide backward as if we're dancing. Laughter trails from our lips as our legs cartoonishly try to keep our bodies from crashing into the ice.

I fumble forward again; Eugene catches me a second time. We giggle the same way we had the night before after falling into the pool.

"Sorry! I'm a total klutz, aren't I?"

We're steady on the ice now, but his arms are still tightly wrapped around my waist. I'm suddenly staring up at his dark blue eyes. The puffy fabric of our spacesuits keeps us from getting too close. The light makes the purple flecks in his indigo eyes look even brighter.

"Susie," he whispers and I'm weak at the knees at the sound of his name on my lips.

My eyes flicker down to his lips. My heart races. I know I'm supposed to be looking for Anonymous, but right now, I feel like I've found everything I need. I start to lean forward. Our faces are getting closer together, but neither of us back away.

Clang!

The dizzying sound of our helmets clashing together makes my ears ring violently. What were we just going to do? I stumble and pick myself up before Eugene can offer to help.

I'm not here for him. What was he thinking? What was *I* thinking? Am I misunderstanding? No... no, I can't be.

He was going to kiss me.

I was going to kiss him!

Oh, my stars.

Oh, my stars!

No. No, I must be mistaken. He was falling. That's all. He was falling onto my lips, and I was falling too. Oh, *no...*

"Susie! Susie! I found the clue!" Wallace's voice shakes me out of the moment. I'm both thankful and irritated. If our helmets hadn't been in the way... The thought of Eugene's lips, soft and warm, gently pressed against mine rushes through me. I imagine his hands brushing through my hair, pulling me close. My stars are glowing so bright they're casting a glare inside my helmet. I can't think about this right now.

My thoughts won't stop. I can't focus. I skate forward, falling all over myself in the process, but I don't slow down. I need to get away. I need to pretend that none of this happened. I need to get back to the cruiser, back to Olivia, and most importantly, back to *The Guide*! *The Guide* will know how to fix this. I don't *like* Eugene like that; we've just became friends, and I was about to ruin it. I know what this is. I'm using him as my stand-in. Anonymous isn't here, and he's the closest thing I have.

Wallace waves the note at me, and I take it with my gloved hand, struggling to open the envelope. With my frantic movements, the note spills onto the ice. The plain sheet of paper almost blends into the bleached surface, save for the black strokes of the pen.

Dear Miss Galaxy,

How does it feel to be in the "coolest" part of the galaxy?

Ceres is up there on the list too, but you can't exactly skate down an ice volcano. I wish I was saying these words to you in person.

The more we write, the more I'm anxious to meet each other. I like the person I'm writing to in these letters, and I hope when we meet, you'll like me too.

I'm glad you enjoyed the diner and the library, but there's one more place I want to show you.

Markets with endless rows, food from around the stars—this city on Valdrien is filled with tourists, day and night. Maybe I'll be one of them hiding in the crowd, looking out for you.

The next letter will be in the darkest place on the brightest city.

Xoxo,

Anonymous

P.S. I hope you don't mind, but I've tried over and over to make this one a poem, and it really isn't working. What are you supposed to rhyme with a word like "market" and "volcano"?

The beautiful words create a pain in my chest. It's so much more casual but still has the same impact. I can't believe I almost made this more complicated. Every word makes me like Anonymous even more. I don't want to throw that away before we even have a chance to meet in person. Without hesitation, I start to type.

Anonymous,

The glittering surface of this planet is more beautiful than I could have ever imagined. I hope you won't be disappointed, but it turns out I'm not very good at ice skating.

After all these adventures, alone but somehow together, I can't believe we're almost at the end. The darkest part of the brightest city, huh? If you really are lurking in the crowd of tourists, don't feel like you have to wait to reveal yourself.

I really want to know who you are.

Xoxo,

Miss Galaxy

I swallow hard. I'll have Wallace edit out the locations back in the cruiser, and we'll send it out as soon as possible.

My ears are still ringing from the sound of Eugene's helmet clanging against mine. I take a deep breath, and then another. But it doesn't seem to work. I almost kissed Eugene. I need to figure this out.

What does my trusted guidebook say about this? I try to remember and reason with myself. The only thing that makes sense is that I'm projecting.

I have a crush on Anonymous. Someone I can't see, hold, talk to, or ... kiss. Eugene, who I've recently become closer friends with, is right here in front of me, filling a void inside my heart.

A void I won't have any longer as soon as I meet Anonymous.

Eugene is too good to be a stand in.

I need to find out who I'm really falling for, and fast.

17.

*I*n the morning, the boys go out to gather coffee and treats from the vending machines, leaving Olivia and me to get ready for our last adventure. She helps me pull my straight hair up into a twist. I look in the mirror at the blue strands pinned artfully away from my face.

Soon, we'll be on our way back home. The thought makes a pit form in my stomach.

"I wish this week could last forever," I say and then realize if we stayed here forever, I'd never meet Anonymous. I swallow hard. I have to stop letting myself get distracted. Anonymous and I could really have something together. I don't want to mess it up by pinning those feelings onto Eugene.

Olivia shrugs. "Something tells me you'd get sick of living on gas station pastries in the next few days." She laughs. "But I have to admit, even with some of our present company being less than ideal, this has been ... nice." It's a change of tone since the beginning of the trip.

"So, are you two good?" I ask, obviously referring to Wallace.

"We've reached an understanding," she says, nodding her head. "He apologized, and I forgave him. Mostly, I guess. What he said to me still hurts. Like, I'm mad every time I think about it." She shrugs. "But it is what it is. I mean, he really apologized. And I know it was a long time ago. But with every article I wrote, every idea I pitch to Ms. Loretta, I keep it with me. The thing is, I'm kind of feeling sick of it all."

"What do you mean?" She's made it clear she's sick of Wallace every chance she gets, but is she tired of the paper too?

"I don't want to upset you."

What could she possibly say that would upset me? "You can always talk to me about anything." I take her hand and squeeze it lightly.

She draws in a deep breath. "Okay. I worked so hard to get into the newspaper, right?"

I nod. It took her a few tries to get past Wallace, though I never knew the scope of the negative reviews until the other night.

"I kind of feel like I don't want to do it anymore." Orange hair falls in front of her face as she hangs her head. "I just... I don't know, the idea of being in a club together felt like it would be so fun. I feel like there's something else I could be doing."

My jaw hits the floor. I assumed Olivia had been having just as much fun as I had. She gets a rise out of everyone at school and seems to love doing it. Her column is engaging, loud, and pure entertainment, just like her.

"Auditions for the school play are coming up," she continues in a low voice.

"Oh, you HAVE to try out!" I gasp. She would be perfect on stage.

"I don't know. I mean, it took me forever to even get into the paper." She flops back onto the bed.

"When an opportunity presents itself, you always need to ask, 'What do I have to lose'?" I quote *The Guide's* section on trying new things and saying yes to new experiences.

Olivia grumbles in response. She sits up in bed, her amber eyes meeting mine. I expect them to flicker with determination, but instead they are soft and dewy.

"See," she begins, shaking her head, "I hate that. Rejection hurts. Wallace's awful comments have eaten away at me the entire time I've been at the paper. What if they all think I'm pedestrian too?"

I pause. I never thought about it like that. *The Guide* touts peppy lines about trying and trying again.

There isn't a chapter, much less a paragraph, about how bad it hurts to not get something you really want.

"You'll never know until you try though, right?" I offer, but it feels hollow. I don't think it's what I'm supposed to be saying, even if it is the right thing.

"I just wonder if I'd rather not know at all." Olivia slumps forward, running her fingers through her long orange and red hair.

"Well, whatever you decide, you know I'm here." It's not what *The Guide* would tell me to say, but it's honest, and with the way she smiles back, I think maybe I might have finally gotten it right.

She gets up, literally shaking off the feelings with a toss of her arms and legs. "What about you?" Olivia asks. "Are you doing, okay?"

I think about how Eugene and I have almost kissed twice now. The way my heart pounded when I opened my eyes and saw him asleep in the other bed just a few feet away. Olivia might be able to help me sort through all my feelings about this. "Alright, so…" I take a deep breath.

The door swings open.

"Coffee delivery!" Wallace booms from the doorway. "Electric blue latte for Susie, cosmic coffee with cream for Olivia, and two Milky Way teas for Eugene and me."

Eugene lifts a brown paper bag. "Pastries," he says with less gusto. With the bags under his eyes, I'm sure it's about all he can manage.

The pastries are yellow and cut out to look like stars. Wallace explains that the entire hotel cafe was themed with a dark blue and gold mural on the wall. He snaps a shot of the treats splayed out on our bed with the camera hanging around his neck.

"I can't wait to see all the pictures," I tell Wallace. I know he's still not the most confident with his photography, but he's been snapping a scrapbook's worth the entire trip. "Too bad they're stale." Olivia grimaces. I shoot her a look and realize she's talking about the pastries—not Wallace's photos. Still, it's not enough to deter her from taking another bite. She's right though. The bready crust is dry, but kind of nice once you dunk it into your coffee.

"I was thinking about doing a parallel column to Eugene's this next issue." She shifts her gaze away from the rest of the group. "He's doing an article on the best road trip snacks. I'm going to do the worst. Maybe I could use some of your photos."

"Really?" Wallace and I gasp at the same time.

"I said *maybe*." She flips her ponytail away from her face, holding the half-eaten pastry. "Just get my good side," she instructs, putting on her best glower and striking a matching angsty pose.

Wallace snaps a few photos of her looking disgruntled. The next issue of the paper is going to be travel and spring break themed, so it should ease any suspicion over which staff member is secretly Miss Galaxy. Half the school is on vacation with friends or family, and the other half is busy daydreaming about where they wish they could go, given the chance.

Wallace stretches his arm out, and the four of us gather close for a group photo. I can't believe I'm—no, *we're*—here. I just wish it didn't have to end so soon.

We cram back into Olivia's cruiser and cruise off to Neo Viridis, a place I've only ever seen in pictures. Apart from the strange, glowing core of the planet, the food seems to be the main attraction. I doze off in the backseat and don't wake up until Olivia has parked on the surface. I was hoping to see the glowing green hue from a distance, but I guess I'll have to settle for it on the way back.

I hop out of the cruiser with my eyes half-open. When I glance down, my head spins. I feel my body rush forward; I'm about to fall. This is worse than I felt on ice skates! I steady myself on the closest thing I can find, but my cheeks flush when I realize that happens to be Eugene's arm.

Great. I'm clinging to him *again*.

You can clutch onto friends, right? Right. Yes. *No.*

His eyes widen with concern, two blue pools deeper than the oceans of Nimzar and bluer than the sands on Ceres.

Struck with a feeling that's somewhere between nervous and excited and happy and terrified, I look up at him. And suddenly, I worry it's not the planet that's making me dizzy.

It's him. I immediately let my hands fall away from his body, but he offers his arm to me like a lifeline, just like he had done while we were skating. Electricity pulses through me, and against my better judgment, I take his arm in the way a friend would—*not* a potential love interest. Just two chums strolling around the market. There's nothing odd or suspicious about that.

Walking around arm and arm, I think people will definitely think we are a couple. Heat rises on my cheeks. It's just nerves. *Just* nerves. But no shallow excuse can help me dismiss the fact that when my shoulder accidentally bumps into his, I'm left with goosebumps.

I turn my attention to the market. A soft neon green glow flickers across the different food stalls. I'm not sure where to head first, but Eugene seems to stroll with confidence. Even as my dizziness fades, I'm glad I still have my arm linked in his.

Olivia and Wallace are already a few shops ahead. Olivia's head tilts back, and I can hear her laugh echo all the way back to us. Wallace must be being self-deprecating again. Either that, or maybe the conversation they had last night really did help.

They keep looking back at us and laughing. I don't know what to make of the expressions on their faces. But I think they suspect something is going on. Ugh. I need to sort out my feelings and do it fast.

I look away from Eugene, focusing on the way Olivia and Wallace are walking next to each other and—wait a second, are they laughing? Stars, if I'd told her a couple days ago she'd do anything but cringe at Wallace's jokes, she would never have believed me. But then again, so much has changed on this trip. When our shoulders bump again, Eugene turns and offers me a small smile.

"Hey, slowpokes, come on!" Olivia shouts, her waving arm popping up above the rest of the crowd milling around the narrow street. "Please don't make me hang out with Wallace all day!"

"I guess we did get a little far behind."

"I—uh, d-don't mind," Eugene whispers, and the hair on the back of my neck stands on end. I do mind. If the last few days have taught me anything, it's that I need a chaperone.

"We're coming!" I shout. If I stand next to Eugene for one more moment, I'll explode. I rush toward Olivia and Eugene, my face flushed.

"I'll trade you!" Olivia offers, looping her arm in mine. I'm not ready to give up Eugene's arm yet, but I need to. The distance will help me catch my breath.

"There should be some consignment shops around here somewhere," she says, squinting past the crowd of tourists. "Let's blow the rest of the budget on dresses!"

"As junior editor, I can't—" Wallace stops himself short. "I mean, I can't let us leave without having some fun." His smile is tight and uneasy. He's trying so hard to be cool in front of Olivia right now, and it's painful.

"Wallace, she's joking!" I lean over to Olivia's ear. "You are joking, right?"

"Probably." She winks. "We'll meet back up later!"

"Rude!" Wallace shouts, but we've already whisked away into the crowd. She pulls me toward a small shop with secondhand clothes in the window. It looks like the perfect place to enact her threat of blowing the budget. A shopkeeper with light green hair gives us a lazy wave from the counter before the two of us find ourselves lost in the maze of racks.

"You and Eugene seem to have gotten ... cozy?" she says, flipping through the clothing racks.

"He's nice, isn't he?"

She nods. "I approve."

"Yes. It's a good *friend*ship." I stress the word, and she giggles.

"Uh-huh."

"Oh! Try this on!" I pull a yellow day dress out of the discount rack. It has a sailor collar and orange buttons up the front. A little girlier than her usual style, but it looks like it's about her size.

Olivia pulls out a teal swing dress with silver bows on the sleeves. It's so pretty, my heart aches. "Found one for you."

There aren't too many shops on Ceres, and with her mom being a seamstress, we barely ever go out shopping together. Not like this, at least.

We cram into the fitting room with more pretty things than we could possibly fit in our suitcases, much less afford, and come out with those first two dresses we found on the sale rack. Mom and Dad *did* say to bring home a souvenir.

"I wonder if my brother will be back at school when we get home," Olivia says suddenly once we leave the shop. It seems like the reality of it being the last day of vacation is setting in for both of us. "It's been a week. I know it's kind of selfish, but I hope everything has just blown over."

"I was surprised I didn't see him when we left." I sigh. It would be nice to see Rex. As much trouble as he brings, he's also pretty fun.

"My brother? At seven a.m.?" She laughs, shaking her head. "This might sound selfish, but I was really happy to get away. Not just to help you chase down this admirer."

I sling my arm around her shoulder, careful to not look down at the planet's core. "You can come over to my house any time."

"Susie, if I'm over at your house anymore, I'll have moved in."

"You know my dad always cooks too much anyway."

"Something I already take full advantage of." She sticks her tongue out. "There's an upside of getting home. Hey, speaking of home, isn't that Skip Stone?" She points at a familiar-looking tuft of silver hair.

Sure enough, he's standing in line with a few people I think I recognize from the beach.

It's a strange coincidence to run into each other twice on a trip like this.

"What are the odds that he'd be here?" Olivia asks, squinting. "You don't think..."

I shake my head. "No way. We're only two hours from home. He's got to just be doing a last-minute trip, probably."

I think about all the time I've spent with Skip.

"Something tells me he's just not the love letter type." I shrug. I think all he'd need to do is simply stand alone in the hallway for five minutes, and someone would come along and ask him out on a date.

"But he does seem like the type to let us jump the line to get closer to those snacks." She takes a step toward the giant line he's waiting in.

"Olivia Oren, that's cutting!"

"Is it?" she asks innocently, tilting her head and blinking her big amber eyes.

"Unless it's a line for saltine crackers and ginger soda, I'm not sure I can stomach anything else."

Her face softens. "Ah, okay. Well, we can find something else. Or I can just grab a snack if you don't mind, and then we can all eat later?" Olivia suggests, tearing her eyes away from the stall.

I look over. It appears we're in line for what looks like large silver candies shaped like coins. The sight of them makes my stomach turn. I imagine they would feel like a rock sitting at the bottom of my stomach.

"Hey, Susie!" Skip calls. I turn to see him waving us over. We should at least say a quick "hello."

As we approach, Skip opens up a gap in line just big enough for the two of us to slip in. Skip dazzles the rest of the line with his smile, and if anyone minds, no one says a word. Olivia looks happy enough. I focus on small talk and keeping myself from looking at the shining abyss of the planet's core. I was fine in the shop earlier. Once we curve around and are inside again, I'll be fine—I hope so, at least.

"What brings you all out this way?" I ask, then realize they could ask me the same question and really hope they don't.

"Making the most of the last day of break," Arleen says with a hair flip. She locks eyes on me. "It's funny how we keep meeting."

"Now our first and last days of vacation are like book-ends," Skip says. I'm taken aback by the surprisingly poetic statement.

"I almost didn't recognize you with your hair," he says, swooping around in line so that we're standing next to each other. Golly, he looks handsome today. He's dressed in a pair of light denim jeans and a cream and blue striped short sleeved button down that shows off the muscular cuts of his arms.

"Oh, I know. I got lazy and didn't curl it last night, so it probably looks like a mess." I can feel the short strands starting to escape from the up do, scattering across my forehead. I brush them away self-consciously.

He opens his mouth to say something, and the line surges forward. Whatever words he meant to tease me with get lost in the crowd. With every step, I'm uneasy. I'm supposed to love it here, but the glowing light is making me feel sick. I need to get inside again or at least find a bench to sit at. Skip's here with friends; it's not like he'll mind if I slip away.

I tap Olivia on the shoulder. "I'm going to find somewhere to sit down."

She nods. "I'll come with you."

I shake my head and tell her it's okay. She shouldn't have to miss out just because I'm feeling sick. I quickly excuse myself and spot a free seat in a courtyard. Maybe if I just don't look down for a while...

"Hey, Susie, wait!" I turn back and see Skip sliding through the crowd. He holds out his hand, which has something coiled around it. I reach out and he drops something into my palm.

"Olivia said you're not feeling great." I look down to find a small plastic package of something called "tummy fizz." There's a cartoon of a man in a spacesuit with a ray gun printed on the label. Why is Skip carrying around something like this?

"I'm sorry for just leaving like that," I start, easing myself down into the chair. "I didn't realize this planet would make me feel so strange."

"Maybe you just need someone to hold onto." He winks at me, and I immediately look away.

I think about the way Eugene looped his arm through mine and guided me from the cruiser, how calm and steady it felt to let myself cling to him, if only for a moment.

"Anyway, it's for dizziness and stomachaches. I used to get that way all the time on trips, and my mom still puts them in my bag when I go away. It's a little embarrassing," he continues, brushing his fingers through his hair.

"I think it's sweet!" I don't know much about Skip's family, but it sounds like something my dad would do, and that makes me happy.

He glows and closes my fingers over the tablet. "Normally, I'd think it was silly to be carrying something like this around, but today, I'm glad she did."

"Are you sure you don't need it?" I ask, looking down at the cute packaging.

He shakes his head. "It's all yours, Starlight."

"Thanks." I open the package and pop one in my mouth.

The chalky consistency makes my tongue feel dry, but after a few moments, I'm already I'm feeling a lot better. He takes a seat next to me.

"Don't you want to get one of those fancy candies?" I ask, gesturing over to the line.

"Arleen is going to grab an extra for me." He shrugs, stretching his arms up to the sky. "And I wanted to see if you were okay."

"It's just embarrassing," I admit. "Everyone else is walking around totally fine. But if I try to walk around for a few minutes without holding onto someone's arm, I'm completely dizzy."

Skip raises an eyebrow. "In case you didn't realize, you're not like everyone else."

My stomach might be recovering, but my heart could burst. It aches deep down in my chest with feelings built up over years of pining. I'd always assumed things with Skip were and would always be one-sided. But there's a spark in Skip Stone's eyes. It's hard not to notice it as soon as you look at him. I just assumed that spark was for everyone. Sitting together in this crowded market, a green glow covering our skin, I wonder if that look could just be for me.

He tilts his head to the side and looks at my arm. "Do you have anyone to hold onto?"

"Well, I..." My entire face is hot. I think of the letters tucked inside my purse. I can't hold onto pen and ink, which is what's been drawing me to Eugene. I don't want to make the same mistake twice. I can't let myself use Skip as another

Anonymous stand in. But this is different, isn't it? I've liked Skip ever since I can remember.

Anonymous or not, holding onto him and walking though the market should be a dream, so why am I so hesitant?

I hear footsteps coming up from behind me.

"Mostly me," Olivia says. I sigh. I wasn't sure who it would be. I turn, and she flashes four silver candies in front of my eyes. I smile. She's the one friend I am, under any circumstance, allowed to cling to.

I carefully stand, realizing the dizziness has faded, and turn back to Skip. "I think it worked!"

"Good!" He laughs and looks over at his group of friends, who are waving him over to a table. "I should go."

Olivia nods, tucking the candies into her purse. "And we should meet up with Wallace and Eugene before it gets too late."

Skip's expression changes at the mention of Eugene's name. "Be careful, would you?"

Odd. I know Eugene is the school "bad boy" to most of the population of Galaxy High, but it's not like he's dangerous or anything. What does Skip think he's doing loitering outside a dime store while wearing leather jacket?

Olivia and I walk a few feet, and I realize it'll be easier to locate the boys if we at least know their general location. They could be anywhere at this point. I tap on my communicator.

[Susie: Where are you two?]

[Wallace: Over by the train station! There's a HUGE festival. Find the last letter?]

Oh my stars! We haven't even been looking.

[Susie: Not yet! Be there soon.]

When I turn around, Olivia has her hands full of free samples.

"I wuv it hur," she says with a full mouth. It turns out the giant silver coins are a crunchy cookie filled with a sweet fruit filling and coated in white chocolate.

My appetite isn't back, but at least the thought of food isn't making me queasy anymore. I don't have to avert my eyes every time she flutters to a new stand and comes running back with something brightly colored on a toothpick.

We're still a block away from the train station when the sound of bright festive drums fills our ears. We can barely hold a conversation over the sound; it builds louder and louder along with my anticipation for the festival.

A festival of what, I'm not sure.

Music? Food? There's plenty of each in this dense area of people. And there also seems to be a dance floor with a collection of people of all ages side-stepping, doing a clap, a jump, and a box step along with live music. I wonder if Anonymous knew this would be happening.

I scan the sidelines, expecting to see Wallace and Eugene somewhere away from the crowd with just as many snacks as Olivia—or more.

Laughing, Olivia points. I follow the line of her extended finger and see them.

They're not in the middle of the dance floor, but they're not on the sidelines either. I wonder whose idea it was to get them out there.

Wallace is smiling bigger than I've seen him smile on this entire trip, and then I see why. His boyfriend Teddy is doing a slide, hop, and jump in between the two of them.

Is everyone spending their last day of vacation on Neo Viridis? Maybe running into Skip isn't so strange after all.

"If they spot us, they're going to drag us out there, aren't they?" Olivia shouts.

"No... no, I don't think so," I argue, hoisting my shopping bag over my shoulder.

"What makes you say that?"

My stomach is feeling settled.

I'm not dizzy anymore.

I take her hand and pull her onto the dance floor. "Because I'm going to do it first!"

We weave through the dense crowd until we've rejoined our group.

"Susie! Hi!" Teddy greets me, giving me a hug. "Wally told me you've been having so much fun! I'm jelly donuts over here."

No wonder they're all smiling. Teddy is a beam of sunshine and has the appearance to match. Yellow light radiates from his face and hair. When Wallace wraps his arms around him, they're a perfect pastel prism.

Wallace's pale pink hair has fallen into his face. The stiff "junior editor" aura that normally surrounds him has mellowed. I exchange glances with Olivia. We need Teddy to join the newspaper.

"Okay, it's a hop here, and then we *sliiiide,*" Teddy instructs, directing our attention to his movements.

The song is familiar. I think I've heard it on the jukebox before. But it's a step back ... forward. Back, lean, forward, backward, hop, slide...

Or was it slide, then hop? I crash into Wallace, and the two of us burst into laughter. By the next chorus, we have it almost mastered, and then the music changes and we're lost again.

It's a slow song. We singles vacate the dance floor while Wallace and Teddy stay.

Eugene says something, but he's too quiet. I shake my head, unable to hear him at all.

"It's too loud!" he shouts over the music, then bends close, his breath on my ear. A shiver runs up my spine. "Teddy. H-his family's ca-h-ruise. It's ... um ... it's their last stop."

That explains it. There is a port here. I notice an older couple smiling on the sidelines with the same sunny complexion as Teddy. At least, I hope they are with the way they seem to be cooing over Teddy and Wallace and snapping photos. Watching their son dance with his high school sweetheart must feel like the ultimate scrapbook moment.

"That's precious," I sigh, soaking in the sight of the two of them swaying on the dance floor, arms wrapped around each other, gazing into each other's eyes. Teddy waves at his parents. Wallace blushes. He must have forgotten he has an audience. I wonder what it feels like to be so lost in someone's eyes that the entire world just falls away.

"Find the last letter?" Eugene asks.

I shake my head. "As soon as I do, all of this will be over."

He looks at me intently, then down at the ground. "Don't y-you want something new?"

I look out at the crowd. Wallace, Teddy, and now Olivia are all dancing together. Eugene is actually talking to me. I'll be coming home from this trip with a box of new memories. Of course, I want to know who's been sending the letters, but at the same time, standing next to Eugene and gazing out onto the crowded planet, I'm not sure I want this adventure to end at all.

I shake off my hesitation. Everyone is here to help me chase down my secret admirer, and that is exactly what we need to start doing. "We should start looking," I say, typing out a message for Wallace. I don't exactly want to interrupt them.

[Susie: Meet us back at the cruiser at 10:30. Enjoy some more dances together!]

Olivia glances down at her communicator and decides to join us. As we walk, my hand brushes against Eugene's. For a moment, I wish he'd lace his fingers in mine and hold tight.

"Sorry," I whisper, snatching my hand away as fast as I can.

Olivia snickers, and I walk faster. *Focus, Susie, focus!*

What was the last clue? What did the last letter say? I almost can't remember.

"'The darkest place on the glowing planet...'" There's a map off to the side of the festival's entrance. I notice a small park right off Main Street that looks like it's covered in AstroTurf. The planet's core won't be able to shine through there.

Starting in a park. Ending in a park. What was it that Skip said? The perfect bookends?

We search until we find a small patch of grass with a statue of a rocket-style spaceship in the center. I can see the note tucked under it as we approach with *"Dear Miss Galaxy"* perfectly scrawled on the front.

My hands shake as I reach out and take the small envelope into my hands, slowly ripping it open. This is what this whole trip has been leading up to. *"Dear Miss Galaxy,"* I read softly.

Wow. We've certainly had an adventure. I just wish you knew who I was. But I want the timing to be just right. I hope you don't mind waiting just a little longer. I've hidden clues high and low, near and far. I've held my breath wondering if this was all too much or not enough. I hope you like the real me, just as much as you've liked these letters.

Our next destination is Galaxy High.

Until Monday,

Anonymous

Olivia slams her foot down on the ground so hard that I jump. "What do you *mean* we have to wait until Monday?" she shouts. "I'm mad."

"Don't be mad—"

"Well, I am!"

I laugh at her sour expression. "What did you expect? Anonymous to pop out of the bushes?"

"I don't know!" she huffs, crossing her arms. "But I thought we'd get something else!"

"So, Monday I'll know for sure..." I trail off, looking up at the night sky.

"Monday..." Eugene repeats, bitterness in his voice. His hand grazes mine lightly. This time I'm not so sure it's an accident.

We can still be friends, no matter what happens. That's all I want.

This time I don't edit out our next destination. Everyone at school could guess the Anonymous would be revealing himself at school. They'll be right there in class with us, so there's no use worrying they'll hunt down the last letter before I can get to it.

I picture a plain white envelope waiting on my desk for me. It doesn't fill me with the same feeling of excitement as before—something is off. I'm nervous; that's all it is. I reach down and type out the letter and my response on my communicator. What do I want to say to him in this last letter?

And beyond that, what are my readers expecting?

Dear Anonymous,

Is it terrible to say I'm disappointed? As much as I'm looking forward to meeting you in the halls of Galaxy High, I wish you were here with me right now, lying on AstroTurf and looking up at the sky. You've planned this entire scavenger hunt for me and haven't gotten to experience any of it. I wonder if you're already back home on Ceres, worried about what Monday will bring. If you're half as charming as these letters, and half as exciting as all these destinations, I'm sure we'll get along fine.

I'm honestly more worried you'll find me boring. You—and my readers—might be disappointed to know this is this biggest adventure I've ever had. But with you, it won't be my last, at least I hope not.

Whether we come out of this as friends or more, I can't wait to see who I've been talking with this whole time.

'Til Monday,

Miss Galaxy

I pass it off to Olivia and Eugene before sending, and the two nod approvingly. Olivia still thinks I sound old-fashioned. She wants me to gush and swoon, but for some reason, this reply is all I can muster. I must be too tired to be romantic.

The three of us lie back on the grass, looking up at the stars. Olivia passes out the candies she's had in her purse. I'm surprised they're not completely melted. They're not as good as the pastries from breakfast, but they're good enough to make my stomach grumble.

"Shoot! Susie, have you eaten anything today?" Olivia asks.

I'd felt sick for most of it, so I shake my head.

Eugene looks personally offended. His mouth hangs open for half a second before he sprints in the direction of the city center.

"Eugene, you don't need to go anywhere—"

But he does. He's gone for about twenty minutes, and when he reappears, it's with pizza, Teddy, and Wallace. Teddy gushes about the budding romance between Miss Galaxy and Anonymous while I shove pizza in my mouth to avoid letting any details slip. Wallace is doing the same. I can't imagine how hard it is to keep a secret like this from your boyfriend.

We eat together, camped out in front of the giant statue. I look at the stone ship pointed at the sky. Of all the paths this road trip could have led us to, I never dreamed that, at the end, we'd be lying on the grass together like friends who have known each other for years.

Sure, Wallace and Olivia are still debating, but this time it's about which pizza topping is the best. Eugene joins in here and there while I sit back and listen. The two of them didn't need Miss Galaxy to solve their problems—*The Guide* didn't end up helping at all.

Things are going to change when we get home. Olivia is leaving the paper, her feud with Wallace finally over. And I—well, if everything goes right with Anonymous, I might have my first boyfriend.

Eugene's shoulder brushes against mine as he adjusts his lanky frame atop the tall shaggy plastic. A jolt shoots though my chest at our proximity. We're all in a circle looking up at the stars, but Eugene and I seem to be drifting closer, and unlike the time in the space pod, lack of gravity isn't an excuse. Our fingers touch. When I turn my head to apologize, I meet his deep indigo eyes.

His smile gleams through the night, piercing through my heart. I was supposed to come home from this trip with a lead on my first ever high school romance, and the thing is, I am. It's just not the person I was supposed to fall for.

I lied in my last reply to Anonymous. The truth is, I can wait. I never want to find out who sent us out on this journey. I'm just glad I'm here—with him.

Hidden in the dark of the night, our fingers coil around each other's. He's warm down to his fingertips. I resist the urge to move in closer.

Right now, the star that's shining the brightest is the one who just bought everyone pizza. I *like* Eugene, and I think he likes me too.

I don't think what happens on Monday can change that.

18.

We drag our feet getting home. All of us have something to avoid: fighting parents, a trouble-making brother, a secret admirer, turning in a first article. People in general, in Eugene's case.

We walk slowly. Drive slower, stopping every chance we get. We idle at every tourist trap, every rest stop. But it doesn't change the fact that we have to go home; it just changes how late we get there. Dinner has long gone cold, and my parents are already off to bed. There's a plate waiting for me in the fridge with a note.

Hope your first big trip was everything you hoped it would be!
—Mom and Dad

I smile. I guess they missed me. It makes me feel like maybe I should have missed them more during my trip. I can't eat, not now. I'll pack it for lunch tomorrow.

On the counter, there's a giant batch of cookies. I break one in half and let the sweetness melt in my mouth. That's one thing I can always stomach just a little of.

I wash up before climbing into bed. I'm stricken by how quiet my bedroom is. It's always been this way, but after being crammed in such tight quarters with everyone, I feel totally alone.

[Susie: Night everyone.]

[Olivia: Night! Returned to literally everyone fighting. Should have spent the night at your place. Bleh!]

I let out a small sigh. I'd hoped everything with Rex had been at least partially resolved by now.

[Wallace: Goodnight, guys—sorry, Olivia.]

[Olivia: It's fine… I forgot this was the group chat for a minute. But thanks.]

[Wallace: If it makes you feel any better, my parents asked me about homework the minute I got through the door. They're convinced we're going to have a surprise pop quiz right after break or something.]

[Olivia: Welcome home, Son. START ON YOUR BOOK REPORT!]

[Wallace: Literally.]

The two chat for a minute. This would never have happened before. The magic of a good road trip, I guess. The only one who doesn't respond is Eugene. My heart aches deep in my chest, and I know it shouldn't. But what should and shouldn't be doesn't change the fact that I really wanted to hear from him again. I wonder if he's already asleep.

I think about how he looked curled up in the corner of the bed the last morning at the motel, blankets tucked around him. Or the time when his sleeping face was floating not even inches away from mine. I know what *The Guide* says about people who look at you in that way.

But something aches inside me at the thought of the unknown.

Something tells me Anonymous would have sent a text back right away. If his number was plugged into my communicator, I bet we'd be talking nonstop. Then would the loneliness I'm feeling be filled?

Or is this void something only another road trip, or smile from the boy I like, can fix? Maybe it's silly not to follow up on the last lead. Miss Galaxy and Anonymous are the story I've been waiting for ever since I started at the paper. I toss and turn all night, dreaming of the faces my admirer might wear.

I wake up in the middle of the night and see my communicator blinking green with an unread message.

[Eugene: Sleep well, Susie.]

My heart races for the rest of the night, erasing whatever doubt I had left. I'll tell Eugene tomorrow.

I've never faked sick or even been late, but in those small moments where I'm barely conscious, I'm tempted to roll over and go back to sleep. I'm sure everyone feels the same. We've all had quiet the adventure.

"Morning," I say quietly, expecting to feel Olivia stir next to me. But there's no movement. The room is quiet and still, and then I remember—it's mine.

I sit up in bed. I'd completely forgotten we got back last night. My communicator is next to the bed, and when I pick it up, it's blinking with good morning messages from everyone.

[Olivia: Morning.]

[Wallace: Is it weird that I'm missing vending machine pastries?]

[Eugene: Yes.]

I giggle to myself, holding the phone to my chest.

Mom throws my door open. "If you sleep any longer, you'll miss breakfast." She's smiling, but she sounds annoyed. It's too early to navigate the different signals I'm getting, still, I resist every urge to pull the pillow on top of my head and hide from the day. Instead, I roll over and take a closer look at the clock. Oh, no! I must have hit snooze a few times without realizing it. I have just thirty minutes to get dressed, have breakfast, and get off to school. I *never* hit snooze! I leap up and pull out my curlers, frantically styling my hair.

Today needs to be perfect. I'm going to tell Eugene how I feel about him once and for all.

But I don't think I've ever been this tired. Powder dampens the glow of my freckles and circles under my eyes. Now I don't look quite as sleepy, and no one will be able to tell if I'm glowing. It's surprising—all we did was drive most of the day yesterday, but my body has never been so sore.

I take one last look at myself in the mirror, smoothing out the blouse and circle skirt I laid out last night. It's mint with little pink diamonds across the hemline. I complete the look with bobby socks and saddle shoes. Nothing too showy. I don't want to look like I'm trying too hard. But after our week together, Eugene's seen me in all sorts of looks, even with face cream and curlers in my hair. Still, we're home now. I need this to be perfect.

I quickly apply a swipe of lipstick and brush out my curls, then bound down the stairs to find Dad's gone totally overboard with the family breakfast.

There are pancakes, eggs, sausage, toast, juice in my favorite cup, and he's even made coffee. I glance at the back door. Olivia is going to be sad she missed this spread.

"This coffee is … for me?" I ask, hesitating before grasping the handle.

He winks. "I heard you hit snooze a few times. Thought you might need it."

Mom gives me a neutral shrug.

"As long as it's just a cup," she says, taking a sip from her own mug. A ring of red lipstick adorns the rim. "I don't want you getting addicted."

Thank goodness she has no idea how much coffee I guzzled over spring break. I happily take a few large sips and quickly dig in. Even with all the exciting dishes I tried on the trip, I missed Dad's cooking. The fluffy eggs are still warm, billowing with steam before they melt in my mouth. The toast has gone soggy with butter, but it's comforting.

I take a bite, then another. I'm not sure if I'm eating too fast or my nerves are just catching up with me, but by the time I'm halfway through my second slice of toast, my stomach feels sick. I slow down. My expression must have visibly changed because Dad's hand is delicately placed on my shoulder.

"Someone has the Spring Break blues," he begins. "Anything you need to talk about?"

"Huh? Oh no—no everything's okay."

The sudden sound of my communicator makes my heart jump out of my chest. Frantically, I look down at the screen, then sigh. Olivia's name shines bright on the display screen. It's not who I was hoping to hear from.

I read the message. She wants to know if it's alright if we eat at the cafeteria today. Apparently, Wallace wants us to eat at his usual table with Teddy. I'm alright with it if she is.

It makes me a little sad that Eugene has lunch the following hour. He's the only one of us that will be alone.

"Dad, could I take a few extra cookies you made last night to school?" I ask.

"I already packed two for Olivia."

"Oh, um..." I can feel the heat rising to my face. "It's actually for someone else."

The two exchange looks, and Mom smirks. I haven't told them anything, and it's like they can see right into my soul.

"Sure, honey," Dad says, gathering a few up into a bag. Maybe I shouldn't have said anything.

19.

"Why is everyone looking at us?" I whisper, my arm linked though Olivia's. She pulls me closer as we navigate the hallway, letting a small laugh escape her lips. I glance around the mint and rose-colored hallway. Nothing looks strange, apart from the echoing whispers that follow us with every step we take. No one ever paid much attention to me when I walked through the doors at school before, but now...

The one thing each student has in common is the paper held tightly in their hands. I read the headline printed in bold on the front: *"DEAR GALAXY, I LOVE YOU."* My stomach flips. I knew at least some people were following along with our live updates, but I didn't realize Wallace was planning on printing a full recap. He must have stayed up all night putting this together.

There it is, right there for everyone to see. My hopeful musings about Anonymous. Not hidden on the second page. Not a small footnote. Right on the front page.

I'm *never* on the front page.

"Oh no, oh no, oh no..." I whisper, leaning in close to Olivia, who has a wide smile spreading across her face.

"I think your article was a hit." Her shoulders shimmy from side to side, and she tosses her curls, flames flickering across her face. At least someone is excited. She really is meant for a stage.

"But no one knows who Miss Galaxy is—why are they whispering?" I demand through gritted teeth. Olivia twirls me toward homeroom and shakes her head.

"*That's* why they're whispering." Olivia can't stop laughing. "I bet they've all been poring over the staff photos from last year's yearbook."

A lump forms at the pit my stomach, I wonder if everyone else from *The Gazette* is getting this much attention. For the most part, the upper classmen are a low-profile bunch. They didn't even know I was chasing this story. Olivia, Wallace, and Eugene might have all signed up for this adventure with me, but the rest of the staff didn't. I hope everyone isn't too upset at me. It hadn't dawned on me before—the school hasn't had a scandal this big in, well ... I can't remember! Olivia's smiling from ear to ear, waving at the gawking groups.

"Glad you're enjoying yourself," I mumble, holding my books close to my chest. I certainly am not.

"What did you think was going to happen?" she whispers with a knowing look. "You gave them live updates!"

I didn't think—that was my first mistake. But now... now I want to shrink small enough to hide behind my heavy textbooks. I thought maybe we'd get a few pieces of confused mail. I thought people might even be disappointed! Miss Galaxy isn't supposed to go on adventures.

And Miss Galaxy is certainly not supposed to fall in love with someone other than the admirer she chased all over the cosmos during spring break!

"Okay! It's fine. It's fine. Just get through today, and we'll make a plan at *The Gazette* after school."

"What if that's not soon enough? What if..." I bury my head in my hands. "Olivia, if they're rooting for me and Anonymous, then I don't think they'll like the conclusion I have planned."

Olivia raises an eyebrow. It seems I don't have to explain myself any more than that. We've been friends long enough.

She looks happy.

With the way she practically cornered me at the dress shop, I thought she might approve.

"Oh, wow! Okay! Okay!" she says enthusiastically. The smile on her face has shifted to something more genuine. "Ignore any questions. Tell them you're not allowed to discuss it or something."

She seems confident, but the spark in her eyes wavers. She shakes her head. "I'm sure everything will be okay."

"You're right." I nod. "I'll be fine."

It's okay, but certainly not normal.

All day, conversation buzzes around me. Miss Galaxy and Anonymous—the school's most tantalizing love story.

And there he is—Eugene stands in front of me in the hallway, and for a moment, the swirl of thoughts keeping me in a haze stop. His navy hair is messy, and the deep bags under his eyes suggest he had a rough night of sleep. I wish I would have been there to sip coffee outside of a rundown motel with him this morning. But the two of us are home now, and mornings like that have come to an end.

We stand a few feet apart. That night in the pool he said he'd be my friend when all of this was over. How will he feel when he finds out I want more? As he approaches, his face lights up and his pursed lips curve into a smile. He waves at me, garnering a few curious looks. I can feel my skin glow before I even have a chance to get too close. It feels like I haven't seen him in a week, and it's only been a night.

"I wh-wwant to talk to you..." His voice curls around my ear in a whisper. I nod. I want to talk to him too.

The bell cuts us off before we have a chance to say anything else.

"After school," I suggest.

"Yeah..."

"Oh! I almost forgot." I take the paper bag of cookies out of my purse and place them in his hands. "See you later!"

In between classes, I sneak off to the *Gazette* room. It's empty. I look at the title of the paper displayed proudly on my desk. I should have pulled the article. As soon as I knew how I felt about Eugene, I should have changed every word.

I sulk in my desk chair, sinking down low. I'm not sure how I'm supposed to wait. Should I just send him a message? No, a confession like this should always be in person.

What if he wants to kiss me after I tell him? He can't kiss me through my communicator! And I'd really like to make those odds play in my favor.

I can't stay focused. How am I going to handle this for next week's letter? Do I correct myself? Do I tell everyone the truth—that while I was busy following the letters, I was falling for someone else? They'll never trust me for advice again!

I let my head fall onto the desk.

How is everyone going to feel when they realize the person I fell for wasn't the one who sent me out on this adventure, but someone who just happened to be along for the ride?

I force my head up.

I don't know how I missed it but propped up on the keys of my typewriter is another crisp envelope with *"Miss Galaxy"* scrawled on the front.

And for the first time, I don't want to open it. I pick the envelope up and walk to the corner of the room. I know what I want. Eugene and I have our last class together. I'll walk him to his locker, and I'll tell him then. With everything that's happened, I know he feels the same. There's no way I'm misunderstanding.

I don't even want to open it. So, I don't.

Loosening my grip, the thin envelope tumbles into the trash can.

The next thing that happens will be up to me and me alone.

I just have to make it 'til after school.

The day won't stop dragging on, and everyone keeps staring at me.

I'm practically hiding behind my lunch tray when I catch Olivia waving me over. She's seated next to Wallace and Teddy at the table in the center of the lunchroom. It's still so strange to see them together. With every step toward them, I hear "Miss Galaxy" whispered again and again. I repeat Olivia's advice in my head.

Just get through the day. Just get through the day. Finally, I grab a chair next to Olivia and sit with a hard thud. There's a wicked grin on Teddy's face that tells me he knows everything.

"How are you, Susie? You must have *so* much on your mind!" he says. He wants the juiciest details from the source herself.

"Wallace..." I say through gritted teeth, but it's anger I can't hold onto for long. I doubt I'd be able to keep a secret like this from my boyfriend either. So, I relax—or the closest thing I can manage, which looks like burying my head in my hands.

"Sorry, Susie. We don't keep secrets," Wallace whispers with an unapologetic smile. I suppose I should be glad his loyalty is to Teddy and not his coveted position as junior editor.

"Everyone's talking." My voice is a wisp that's drowned out by the noise of the cafeteria. Memories of the week rush through my mind, and at the top of my thoughts is Eugene.

"Tell me about it." Wallace laughs. "I feel like I've been under surveillance all day. I didn't think I'd be on the Miss Galaxy suspect list."

"Why? You give great advice!" Teddy assures him. The two of them continue in a mushy exchange that makes me want to see Eugene even more.

I'm going to burst if I don't talk to him soon. Waiting until after school would be best, but maybe I could try to catch him after math class...

A rush of movement distracts me. Two legs swoop onto the chair next to mine, a lunch tray bumping into my own. I straighten up my blouse and comb my fingers through my hair. I didn't expect to see him so soon.

"I thought you didn't have lunch until later." I turn, but it's not Eugene staring back at me.
Skip Stone wears a look on his face that's both wide-eyed and devastating.

"Did you get my note?" he asks.

Teddy and Wallace gasp, their jaws collectively hitting the table.

"I guess maybe you haven't seen it yet..." Skip continues, ignoring them. His eyes stay keenly focused on mine, waiting for a response. "I've been wanting to talk to you since we ran into each other on Neo Viridis actually. I kind of chickened out."

"Olivia, you owe me five dollars!" Wallace exclaims, slamming his hand onto the table.

"No way!"

"A bet's a bet!" Wallace crosses his arms with a triumphant grin.

"What are you two talking about?" I ask. Over the past week, what thing would the two of them have to bet on? And what would it have to do with Skip? Unless...

"This whole time?" My voice carries through the entire gym. Suddenly it's quiet enough to hear a pin drop.

Skip's lips spread into a crooked smile. This entire spring break, he was everywhere. The beach. At the market. *The perfect bookends.*

I've liked Skip since forever. But never in a million years did I think he'd feel the same way, and I never would have guessed he would have planned something like this just to tell me how he feels.

All he would have needed was to ask me out, and I would have said yes. Then again, maybe he did, and I never noticed. Eugene at the pool seemed to think I've been asked on countless dates and have been too stuck on property to notice.

But now, here he is, my lifelong crush—and secret admirer—sitting next to me, and I don't know what answer to give him.

It's not that my feelings have vanished. I just have them for Eugene too. And I'm not sure who makes my heart beat faster.

"Are you really that surprised?" He cocks an eyebrow.

"That you're FREAKING Anonymous!? Of course, she's surprised!" Teddy shouts before covering his mouth with a gasp.

In an instant, all eyes in the cafeteria are on us, and we're surrounded in whispers. I can't blame Teddy for his outburst. Skip Stone, the most likeable, handsome boy at school, has spent his spring break writing me—a virtual nobody—love letters. Even as he stands in front of me, it's hard to believe.

Skip gives me a sheepish grin. A break from his normal overtly confident air. "Maybe we should go somewhere more private?" he whispers.

The ping of communicators echoes across the lunchroom as students exchange glances, copies of *The Galaxy Gazette* hanging loose in their hands or falling off lunch tables.

"That's Miss Galaxy?"

"What's her name again?"

"Skip is Anonymous. I could die!"

"Just kiss already!" someone shouts, and then another, and another.

"Kiss! Kiss! Kiss!" A table of freshmen chant from the corner, and soon more and more people are joining in.

I try to keep my attention focused on Skip, but it's like I've suddenly transformed into the lead in a romantic comedy I never auditioned for. This is what answering the letter led me to. It's supposed to be the start of my dream. My longtime crush's head bobbles in an uneasy nod.

He's just as nervous as I am. I get the feeling neither of us wanted this confession to be quite so public, and that's something that's comforting at least.

Suddenly, his hand is in mine, and I'm unsure if he reached down and took it, or if I placed it there myself, or if I've been holding it the entire time. In a daze, I look at the entire school, and it feels like the world is spinning around us.

His eyes squint as he smiles.

"Susie?" he says gently, his golden eyes shining down on me like a million stars. I open my mouth, but words won't come out.

I don't know what I'm supposed to do. A romantic lead would lean in for a kiss, just like everyone is cheering for me to do. He tilts his head. His eyes are big and pleading.

I lean forward to whisper in his ear, to suggest we continue this conversation in private, but the minute I move toward him, his lips tenderly meet mine. His hand is at my waist, pulling me closer to his firm, muscular body.

My ears rush with the sound of cheers.

Anonymous and Miss Galaxy, together in the flesh. I pull away, looking him deep in the eyes. He's smiling from ear to ear, joy radiating off his face.

He's so happy. I don't know if I've ever seen him glow quite like this, it makes my own lips perk up into a smile.

"I've been wanting to do that for a long time." His whisper tickles my ear, and I'm weak. This is all happening so fast.

"Alright, kids, break it up!" Someone's stern voice cuts through the crowd. A teacher? I tense up. Can you get in trouble for kissing in the cafeteria? This is the first time I've ever done it—this is the first time I've ever even kissed anyone. The shock and excitement has robbed it of the feelings it's supposed to have. Skip's arm drapes around me, warm and comforting.

"Can we get out of here?" I shout, but my voice seems to get swallowed up by the crowd. Finally, I lock eyes with him and gesture to the door.

"Miss Galaxy and Anonymous," I say under my breath. "Maybe we should talk about things…"

He leans down, kissing me on the cheek, and there's a spark of warmth where his lips touch.

"I'm looking forward to being Skip and Susie." A sweet smile illuminates his face, and I feel my chest tighten. "Now! For our debut as a couple, how about we finally get that milkshake after school?"

A milkshake with the boy with moondust hair and silver freckles who I've liked ever since I can remember? How can I say no to that, and more importantly, why would I want to?

"I can't wait."

20.

The minute Skip and I separate after lunch, I remember the mission I set out for today. I woke up thinking I'd said goodbye to love letters and Anonymous, but I guess I wasn't ready to say goodbye to my crush on Skip.

When push came to shove, and I was looking up at him in the cafeteria, everything was a rush of feelings, and nerves—nerves that I'm still feeling as the two of us sit in Lester's diner. Today's the first time I've ever missed a meeting for *The Gazette*, but this is sort of club business.

This date wraps up the Anonymous and Miss Galaxy saga. My fingers tap against the milkshake glass when I look into Skip's sunshine eyes. Skip drapes his arm around me with ease. It's second nature, as if we've been dating for years, not hours. He's slipped into this relationship like a worn-out pair of slippers. I, on the other hand, feel like I'm walking in heels for the first time.

"Everything okay, Susie?" he asks, pulling me close. His lips nestle in my hair.

Is everything okay? I'm sitting next to the boy I've had a crush on since sixth grade. Everything should be perfect.

I'm sure there's a chapter on this, but I can't remember it. Why can't I remember it right now? Stars! How do I act if he kisses me again? I think I did a good job in the cafeteria, but it was such a rush of adrenaline, I can't even remember where I put my hands.

I've answered so many letters about the "First Date Jitters," but now that I'm here, I'm drawing a blank.

His fingertips brush through my hair, and a shiver curls up my spine. He cups my chin, tilting my face so our eyes meet.

"It seems like time slowed down since I kissed you for the first time," he says breathlessly. His lips brush up against mine.

I lean toward the milkshake at the same time Skip does, and we bump heads. The moment reminds me of Astro's Diner, the way the four of us knocked our heads together, the rotating fry orbiting the glass.

Suddenly, his fingertips brush a stray hair away from my forehead. Without warning, his soft lips graze the skin, kissing the exact spot he bumped.

I jolt up in my seat, laughing uncomfortably.

"How did you get the note in the bottom of the milkshake anyway?" I ask, unable to get the memory out of my head.

His sunset eyes crinkle at the edges when he laughs. "You want me to reveal my tricks, huh?"

I nod, playing with the paper straw wrapper. Maybe if I'd been making memories with him and not Eugene, the other things would feel different.

"It's not as exciting as you'd think. You can walk any-where if you walk with confidence," he says, knocking into my shoulders.

"I can't believe I missed seeing you there!" I shake my head. It feels like nervous chatter. I'm overwhelmed and uncomfortable.

"You just didn't know where to look." He looks down, and I realize how impossibly long his eyelashes are. The specks of amber in his eyes sparkle a little brighter under the lights of the diner.

I should be swooning. It's like we're acting out a scene in a movie where the leads are the only two people in the world. But we're not. While we're in a booth in the corner, no matter how obscured we are by propped-up menus, we're still surrounded by the peering eyes of our classmates. They're the audience in this theater, waiting for the big, swooping, romantic moment. A moment Skip is more than willing to give them.

He leans down, and I gulp as his lips close in on mine. He's going to try to kiss me right now.

"Everyone is watching," I whisper. I remember for certain that *The Guide* always said to be mindful of public affection, but now that I'm here, I'm not sure what I should do.

His hands run through my hair, lips trailing up to my earlobe. "Let them," he whispers back.

His lips meet mine in a quick kiss.

Oh, my stars, we're really doing this. His lips are soft; his strong hands linger on my shoulder. By all accounts, it should be perfect. But an awkward feeling creeps up through me until it forms an uncomfortable laugh. I have to break away. It's too strange.

"Why are you laughing?" He looks upset.

"I..." I shake my head, covering my face. "I think I'm embarrassed," I admit, unwilling to remove my hands to let him look at me. Why is this so hard?

"Embarrassed of ... me?"

I sit up straight, uncovering my face. Behind his confident charm, his eyes are big and uncertain. I flail my hands out in front of me. That's not it, but what is it?

"No, no, it's… I'm just…" I gasp, struggling to organize my thoughts. With my frantic movements, I knock the glass over, and our milkshake spills across the table.

Reaching across him, I grab as many napkins as I can to try to mop up the mess.

"Susie?" he begins slowly, a small grin creeping across his face.

I turn back, my hands filled with soggy napkins.

"Is this your first real date?" he asks, cocking his head.

"I…" Heat rises to my face, and his grin spreads up to his eyes.

"Oh my stars," he gasps, practically announcing it to the restaurant. "This is your first date!" He shakes his head as if he's unable to believe it.

The embarrassment within me grows, and the distance between us closes. Skip leans forward, taking the napkins out of my hands. Slowly, he raises each of my hands to his lips with a kiss while I stare, wide-eyed.

"I'm only good at this on paper." I look away. Maybe he'll see what a mistake he's made. Maybe he'll walk right out of the diner and never speak to me again.

He turns my chin toward him again, his bright gold eyes looking down at me like I'm something delicate and precious. "You're…"

A fraud.

A terrible potential girlfriend.

A liar.

In the silence, I think of every single horrible thing he could say to finish the sentence.

"…really, *really* cute."

That's not what I was expecting. But then again, none of this is. Sitting in a corner booth with Skip, I shouldn't have a care in the world. I search my brain. Oh, my stars! Dad is expecting me home.

"I'm sorry! I forgot to tell my folks I wouldn't be home," I say. It's a sudden shift in tone that I'm not sure Skip appreciates, but he smiles, the perfect understanding boyfriend. I take my communicator out of my bag, ready to punch in a quick message, only to find that that I have three unread ones and two missed calls.

They're all from Eugene.

"Susie?"

I'm about to explain that I was just about to message my dad when Skip's face twists up into a funny smile.

"Oh, Suze, that thing is ancient!" Skip teases, but he doesn't move away. Instead, he pulls me in closer and laughs, trying to get a closer look at it.

I turn away. I don't want him to see who's been calling me. I shake my head, absentmindedly running my fingers through my hair. "My mom made it for me before the trip. I mean, she restored it; it was hers in high school."

His eyes sparkle. I'd been waiting for him to look at me like this since I first ran into him in the hallway.

"That is very precious," he says in a tone that makes me feel childish. "But I, um ... can understand why it's at the bottom of your purse."

Something snaps inside me. It's unfamiliar but strong. I can't stop myself. I take the communicator out of my purse and clip it onto my wrist. It's just as big and clunky as it's always been. But the truth is, I've gotten used to it.

"Oh, I just forgot!" I lie, a big smile plastered on my face. I hold my wrist out in admiration. "It's one-of-a-kind, and that's pretty special, don't you think?"

Poor Skip. He sucks his teeth and I can tell he's trying not to react. Shaking his head, my long time crush lets out small sigh. "No, it's great. Just watch: everyone at Galaxy High is going to be wearing one of those next week," he says, a cocky smile back on his face.

Silence stretches between us for a moment. He just keeps *looking* at me.

What am I supposed to say? He's always just been a classmate, but now everything is supposed to be different.

"It was kind of a whirlwind today," I manage to get out. "I think I'm still in shock." It's the honest truth. I still can't wrap my head around everything. "How did you know it was me?" I ask. I've been wondering it ever since he confessed earlier today.

"I kind of had a feeling all along, to be honest. You're always at the newspaper. When we studied together, I always saw you with that beat-up old book. And you know, some of the advice makes sense now. Knowing you've never actually dated anyone."

"What do you mean?" I ask, sitting up straighter in my seat. Mentally I go through my list of past articles. All my advice is always sound and well-researched.

"I mean, you have to admit, some of the letters were pretty funny."

"Excuse me!" I exclaim, trying to keep my tone playful.

"The smudged lipstick," he says in a low voice.

Smudged lipstick? I run through each letter in my head until I recall the right one.

He clears his throat. "Let's see if I can remember. 'Dear Miss Galaxy, my girlfriend and I both are lipstick-wearers and keep coming home from our dates covered in lipstick. Taking off our makeup before kissing seems like a moodkiller. Any advice?"

Ah, I remember it now. I had written back. "'Simple, switch to the same shade, and be very precise.'" I still don't see the problem. "What isn't sensible about that?"

"You don't kiss with precision."

"Oh?" I arch an eyebrow, trying to ignore the thudding of my heart. "Then how do you kiss?" I ask, knowing I shouldn't.

He leans in, and his lips brush against my ear. "With *passion*."

I laugh nervously and move a little farther away. He furrows his brow. Clearly, this was not the response he was hoping for.

The romance expert of Galaxy High is too nervous to kiss her boyfriend. I bury my face in my hands, crunching up until the sound of his chuckling is muffled.

"We can take it slow," he assures me, and some of the weight lifts off my chest. I just need to stay calm and be myself. That's what I'd tell a reader, and it's what I need to remember. There's a reason Skip likes me, although right now I can't think of why. But still, he wouldn't have written all those letters otherwise.

I lace my fingers in his and nod.

We have all the time in the world to get to know each other better.

Skip walking me home would have been sweet and romantic. Except as soon as we get close, I notice a lanky figure looming on my porch.

Eugene is standing in front of my house.

Why is Eugene standing in front of my house? My palms become slick in Skip's hands. I slip them away before he notices, clasping them behind my back.

This morning all I could do was fantasize about seeing Eugene, but now it takes all I have not to run away.

"Oh…" Skip says, following my gaze. "Did you have plans?"

"Probably something to do with *The Gazette*. I did leave pretty abruptly today."

Skip leans down and plants a kiss on my cheek. I stiffen, keenly aware of our audience. When I walk through the gate, Eugene's eyes narrow as he watches Skip walk away.

This is going to be awkward at best.

"I called," he whispers, shoving his hands in his pockets.

"I know."

"Skip…"

"I know."

"I thought…" He trails off, avoiding my eyes at all costs. "This is what you want?"

"I'm sorry." Looking at Eugene makes me wonder if I've just made the biggest mistake of my life. But the truth is…

"It's always been Skip." I shake my head, feeling my fallen curls brush against the base of my neck. I wish I could pull it all in front of my face and hide from Eugene's grim expression.

"To be honest, half the time I was answering the letters, I was imagining they were from him." It's a little strange to admit out loud, especially to someone I have feelings for.

He's staring at me like I'm a jigsaw puzzle he can't quite solve until his lips finally part.

"You're lying." Eugene's words are careful and deliberate and hit me like an asteroid. *Lying?*

"I've had a crush on him forever!" I gasp, crossing my arms. How dare he accuse me of something like that? This crush has lasted more than just a week; when push comes to shove, that's got to mean something.

"And that m-makes—" He stops short, taking a deep breath to collect himself. "You're okay with this?"

"I don't know what you want me to say. I'm sorry."

"Me too." He breathes out a heavy sigh, gazing off toward the empty street.

"We're still friends, right?"

There's a long stretch of silence between us. I'm not sure he knows how or what to respond. I know I'm asking too much, but I just got Eugene in my life. I don't want to lose him.

A forced smile stretches across his face but begins to wane with the nod of his head. My heart twists in a knot. It might be selfish, but I'm glad he agreed.

The road trip made things confusing. Eugene was a classic spring break crush. I was projecting feelings because we lived in such close proximity. I'm sure now that we're back at home, and I have a boyfriend, things can be strictly platonic. As long as he's okay with that.

Stars, it's probably what he wants too.

"Yeah," he says in a low voice that makes me ache. "Friends."

He sticks out his hand. It's formal like I'm being offered a position at a job interview. We shake, and I pretend it doesn't make electricity jolt through my body.

A message pops up on my communicator.

[Skip: Party at Peggy Sue's tomorrow?]

A party on a school night? Miss Galaxy would heavily advise against that kind of behavior. But then again, Skip did say he wanted to just be "Skip and Susie."

And going to a party sounds like not only the perfect debut as a couple, but maybe just what I need to make the heavy feeling in my chest go away.

I watch Eugene shrink into the distance.

[Susie: Sounds like a date.]

Eugene Eris is going to be just a friend. That's the way it's meant to be.

21.

The Guide has some strict warnings about high school parties. Be wary of spinning bottles pointed in your direction, punch should be avoided at all costs, and when the lights turn low and the record player switches to romantic ballads only, it's best to make a swift exit unless you want to be surrounded by canoodling couples.

I've been to parties in the daytime. Classmates' birthdays, graduations, things like that. But never a real high school party—and never with a date.

I fiddle with the communicator on my wrist. Skip must sense my nerves because he catches my hand in his and brings it to his lips. His lips softly brush against the tips of my fingers, and he beams down at me.

"Babe, they're all going to love you." His voice is peppy and by all accounts should be reassuring, but besides this being my first high school party, it's also going to be my first time really hanging out with his friends. Miss Galaxy would say "just be yourself." It's fine advice on paper, but with every step toward Peggy Sue's house, I realize they could hate me.

"You think so?" I ask, trying to steady my breath.

"You're going to fit right in, I promise."

"Oooh, if it isn't Miss Galaxy!" Arleen coos as soon as we walk through the door. I sense a shift in Skip's energy; he fiddles with the strap of the guitar he has strapped to his back.

It probably doesn't feel great to be left out. I link my arm in his, pulling us forward together.

"And Anonymous!" I announce. The small crowd hanging by the door lets out a rambunctious cheer—just the recognition Skip deserves—before going back to their conversations.

There's a record playing rock'n'roll in the corner and a few people dancing. Just as I feared, there are no parents to be seen. Our host Peggy Sue waves us over to the refreshment table with an enthusiastic hello. There's a spread of chips, cookies, a pink gelatin mold that seems to be wiggling if its accord, and in the center, a big crystal bowl of lime green punch.

It's every warning sign I've been trained to look for—and yet, we just arrived. I can't suggest we leave so soon. I'll just have to keep my guard up. I don't want to be here if things start to get out of control.

"So, Susie," Arleen begins, sitting on the arm of the couch. She's looking down at me with an expression that suggests she's a girl on a mission. "I have a boyfriend, but it's long distance. He was supposed to come visit over spring break, just for a day, but at the last minute, his parents decided not to let him borrow the flying saucer."

"Oh, that's a shame." I frown. She must miss him a ton. From everything *The Guide* has taught me, I know long distance can be really challenging.

"Right, so that night—the night we were supposed to be on a date—he goes to the movies with a bunch of friends! I'm just sitting at home, hoping he'll call so that we can spend a few hours talking. But he makes other plans and doesn't even tell me!" she rants, crossing her arms. I notice a few keen eyes turn toward me when she pauses expectantly.

Oh.

She's not just loudly ranting about her love life to a new friend. She's looking for Miss Galaxy's advice—in the middle of a party.

"First of all, that's awful. I'm really sorry your plans didn't work out," I begin.

"Thank you!" She crosses her arms with a huff. "At least *someone* feels bad."

"When you two decided on doing a phone date instead, did you set a general time frame? It was rude of him to keep you waiting like that."

She bristles, smoothing her long purple hair behind her ear.

"Well, we didn't exactly plan a phone date." Her voice is quiet. "But he should have known I'd be sad. We were supposed to be together all day, and I just got a few lousy communicator messages after he canceled."

"If you two didn't actually make plans..."

"Are you seriously going to take his side!?" she shouts,

"Oh, no, I'm not—"

"Wow. Well, what if I told you his ex-girlfriend works at the movie theatre? Hmm?"

"I have a question!" A boy swoops in, taking a seat on the coffee table in front of Skip and me.

"Okay, so my best friend and I have been joking about going to the spring dance together, but I think that maybe I like her more than as just a friend. I'm worried if I tell her, it's going to ruin what we have. What should I do?" he asks in one breath, staring at me with eager eyes.

"Well, I think, uh, what do you have to lose by telling her?" I ask, clasping my hands together to keep from fidgeting.

"A friend! I'm worried she won't be my friend anymore," he clarifies, visible irritation crossing his face.

"Right, I mean—what I mean is—uh." I have no idea what I'm supposed to say here. In my letters, I always have time to think and plan out each careful response. In the center of the party, I'm entirely exposed.

"Okay, but what we all *really* want to know is about your new exciting adventure." Peggy Sue cuts through the crowd, a gleaming green punch glass in hand.

"I'm going to grab some refreshments," Skip excuses himself, abandoning me with a hand squeeze and a wink.

"Did you know it was Skip the whole time?" Peggy Sue asks, moving closer, her eyes as wide as saucers. "I mean, he's had a crush on you forever."

"He hasn't!" I shake my head.

They laugh in unison. I guess my swooning hasn't been as one-sided as I thought.

"I'm tutoring the cutest girl!" Arleen mocks, dramatically draping a hand across her forehead. "She just doesn't seem to be getting any of my hints. What should I do?"

"No!" I gasp. I have a hard time imagining him saying anything like that after last year's tutoring sessions. I was always so awkward. I could barely look him in the eyes for more than a minute without blushing until just recently, and even that some days seems touch and go.

"When he said he was going to write into Miss Galaxy for advice, I never thought he'd do something like this." Peggy Sue lets out a dreamy sigh.

A smile sneaks across my face. I don't try to hide it. The whole situation he created was pretty dreamy. Though, it would have been a lot less complicated if he would have been along for the entire journey. At least we had our moments on the beach and on Neo Viridis. That stomach medicine he gave me was a life saver. They prod me with a few more questions about the trip. What was my favorite stop? What was it like seeing it all published in the paper? And aren't I just the luckiest? It's all been so surreal, I'm not sure that I've processed any of it. I stammer a few responses that seem somewhat satisfactory, waiting for the conversation to move to something else.

"Anyways!" Peggy Sue gets up, dusting off her sundress. "I think I need to start setting up for our next activity."

I gulp, eyeing the collection of empty glass soda bottles on the counter. If I opt out of their "party games," are they going to think I'm a total square? I hope no one notices the way my face is burning. Play it cool, Susie, play it cool. No one here knows that this is your first party, and if you just act normal, they never have to find out. Skip reappears with two dainty crystal cups filled with green liquid.

"I got you some punch."

"No!" Reflexively, I push the cup away until it presses against his chest. "Ah, I mean, just water is fine. "

"Yeah, uh ...sure." He raises the small crystal cup to his lips and heads for the kitchen. "Water coming right up."

"Miss Galaxy!" a girl in my math class calls from across the living room. "Quick question for you."

I can't deal with another question right now. I offer a smile and try to plan an escape route. "Sure, but first, do you know where the restroom is?"

"Down the hall to the left."

"Perfect!" I say, sounding way too excited. "I will be right back."

The darkened hallway feels like a trap. One wrong door, one wrong move, and I could accidentally burst in on a couple making out.

I'm down the hall, I'm looking left, but every single door is closed. I close my eyes and try out the first knob.

A closet—thankfully just filled with linens, not entangled classmates.

The second door reveals a bedroom I'm assuming belongs to Peggy. It's empty aside from a few tasteful decorations—thank the stars.

And finally, a bathroom. A perfectly empty, quiet bathroom.

I reach for my communicator and begin to type.

[Susie: I'm at my first big party, and I think I'm going to be sick.]

[Olivia: Why? What happened?]

[Susie: I have been offered punch!]

[Olivia: I'm sorry?]

[Olivia: Clearly. Who would dare put you in a position like that?]

[Wallace: Absolute villains.]

I let out a deep sigh. They haven't read *The Guide*, and I don't think either of them have been to a party like this.

[Susie: You know exactly what I mean!!]

Little help they are! I straighten up my hair and try to steady myself in the mirror. I can do this. I can get through tonight. I need to remember that I'm not doing this alone. Only when I step back into the living room, I don't see Skip anywhere.

I'm immediately surrounded by questions I've only answered on paper and pressed for details on the trip. It's a loop of similar answers, and my forced smile starts to wane. If Skip was here to help talk about this, it would be so much more interesting. I want to hear more about his process for choosing locations too.

I want to know everything.

My communicator chimes again.

[Eugene: Are you okay?]

My heart twists into a knot.

[Susie: Honestly, it's weird. Everyone keeps asking me Miss Galaxy questions. It's harder in person than it is writing them out for *The Gazette*. I feel like I keep messing up.]

[Eugene: I'm sorry.]

[Olivia: Tell them you're off the clock!]

[Susie: That would be rude!]

[Olivia: Then BE RUDE.]

[Eugene: Or try to change the subject if that would be more comfortable.]

[Olivia: I vote for rude.]

[Susie: They also keep asking about our trip.]

[Olivia: Ah well yeah... that was bound to happen.]

[Wallace: I'll have all the pictures developed by tomorrow.]

That's a nice distracting thought. It was just a short time ago, but I'm already nostalgic for those moments on the road with each other.

[Susie: I can't wait to see!]

[Eugene: Let us know if you need anything.]

Okay. Just try to change the subject. I can do that. I make my way back out into the living room and an arm squeezes around my shoulders.

"Is that your folks?" Skip asks, a glass of water in hand. "You don't need to leave already, or anything, do you?"

I pause. He has presented me with the perfect out. We could leave right now and not have to deal with any of the activities Peggy Sue has planned. Faced with that soft expression and turned down smile, I can't lie. "I can stay."

"Good!" He cheers, steering me toward the hallway. "Pegs needed some help setting up in the other room, and I got caught up talking in the kitchen. Sorry for ditching you out here."

"No, it's okay."

By the time we make it down the back hallway, I've drained my cup of water. Skip once again disappears to help with "set up." Not wanting to risk getting bombarded again, I sink into the corner and bury my face in my communicator, trying to look busy.

[Olivia: Yeah, let us know if they offer to hydrate you again.]

[Wallace: Haha yeah.]

[Eugene: You two know she's talking about alcohol, right?]

[Olivia: ...]

[Wallace: ...]

[Eugene: Oh my stars. Punch responsibly, Susie.]

[Susie: Thanks, Eugene.]

[Susie: How's everyone's night? Distract me.]

[Eugene: Slow at the diner. Working on some writing in between orders. Dad's trying out a recipe for a new dessert].

[Susie: What is it?]

[Eugene: Honestly, I have no idea. The amount of random ingredients on the counter is ... concerning.]

[Susie: Time for one of your food articles!]

[Eugene: I can't review my family's restaurant. I'll get disowned.]

[Wallace: Hey! I like it at Lester's.]

[Eugene: Then YOU come try this dessert.]

[Wallace: Maybe I will.]

[Olivia: How much chocolate is in it, because honestly, I'm bored and hungry.]

[Susie: I wish I could come.]

[Olivia: Ditch the party!]

[Wallace: Ditch ditch ditch!]

[Susie: I really shouldn't...]

[Eugene: You won't be missing out.]

Somehow, I don't think that's true. A frown creases my lips at the thought of them all together without me. I've gotten kind of used to the idea of us as a foursome—but I guess with Teddy, and now Skip, we're a group of six. It feels too soon to force Eugene to have to be so exposed to us as a couple.

We need to get used to being friends first.

"Susie!" Peggy Sue's chipper voice breaks through my thoughts. "Can I get you anything else? Water, juice, some punch?" She cheers her cup of the atomic-looking liquid at me.

"What's in the punch?" I finally ask. People are drinking down cups like water, and I'm worried about when its effects are going to hit.

Skip is on his third cup, and from what I can tell, he's still walking in a straight line.

"Oh, it's just sherbet and lemon soda."

I raise an eyebrow. "That's all?"

Peggy Sue crumples in front of me. "Is it not fancy enough?" Hanging her head, she smooths out the creases in her blue gingham dress. "I'm sure you're used to nicer parties..."

"No, it's not that!" I shake my head and lean in closer to her ear. "I was worried there might be um ... some extra ingredients."

"Are you asking me to add booze to the punch?" Peggy Sue asks, wide-eyed. "Because if you are, I'm sure I can find some. I just, I mean... I want you to have a good time and—"

"No, no, no, this is perfect!" I put my hand on her shoulder, hoping to help ground her back to the present moment. "Sherbet and soda is exactly my speed."

A long exhale leaves her body. "Good, good, good," she sighs. For someone who hosts weekly parties, it seems like this is the first time she's ever hosted a group of people. I wonder what's making her so nervous. "To be honest, I was scared to invite you."

Well, here's my answer. I can feel my jaw hit the floor. Do I make her nervous?

"Not because I didn't want to! It's just you're—I mean Miss Galaxy—is the reason these parties exist."

"What do you mean?"

She opens the door to the backroom, a beautiful atrium with bioluminescent plants and blankets and pillows laid out. It looks like we're going to be having an indoor picnic. On the wall, there's a big white drape and Skip is helping rig what looks like a projector.

"I wrote into Miss Galaxy last year," she explains. "I didn't really have any friends, and you gave me the advice to share my passions and find people with similar interests. That's how I got the idea for my Movie Mixer Nights! My parents are always out on Tuesday to play bridge with the neighbors. They let me take over the house, as long as we don't make a mess. We all take turns picking out a movie each week to watch out here in the back."

"It's gorgeous."

"My dad's super into gardening." She smiles. "And now this room has more life in it than just his plants."

"I'm glad I could help."

The glow on her face is undeniable. For all the bad advice I've given tonight, for Peggy Sue, writing into Miss Galaxy really made a difference.

She hands me a glass of punch and laughs.

"By the way, it was Skip's turn to pick the movie tonight." She shakes her head. "You've been warned."

Peggy Sue's warning couldn't have prepared me for the tension I feel when the leads in the movie are about to enter the very house where the monster resides. With every scene I want to shout, *Don't go through the door! Go back!*

The actor on screen screams, and I reflexively turn away into Skip's shoulder. His arms tighten around me as I bury my head into his chest. His body vibrates with muffled laughter.

Wait a second.

I should have seen this before. Picking out a scary movie—a textbook excuse for getting close! He grins. "I see what's going on."

"I don't know how you can see anything from that angle," he teases, his face getting closer to mine. "You know I'll protect you from any of those big bad space monsters, right?"

"It's just a movie." Logically, I know nothing on screen is going to pop out and hurt me. He starts to laugh, and I realize I'm clutching his hand for dear life. His lips brush against mine.

A scream interrupts us, and when I look back at the screen, the monster is attacking the protagonists. I turn away.

"Maybe next time we can watch a romance," he chuckles, tightening his arm around me, a soft kiss landing on my forehead.

A buzz from my communicator draws my attention to my wrist.

[Eugene: Update: The dessert is a chocolate, cherry, pineapple upside down cake with ice cream.]

[Susie: I'm having a hard time figuring out if that's a good thing or a bad thing.]

[Eugene: Me too].

Laying back on a stolen couch cushion, I turn my attention back to the unfolding monster movie.

"You're having fun, right?" Skip whispers, his body tucking close to mine in the dim room.

"Of course," I whisper back. "The movie is scary but—"

"You've just been on your communicator a lot."

I freeze. We're not at a theater, but I still probably shouldn't be messaging during a movie. Especially not on what I *think* is supposed to be a date. "It's nothing."

I look back at the screen just in time for a giant sea-monster to pop out of the ocean. The jump scare lands me right back in Skip's arms. I hear a few chuckles echo around us. "That was terrifying!" I justify with a shout.

"You can literally see the zipper on the back of his costume!" Peggy Sue shouts, and the whole room bursts out laughing—Skip included.

I unclip my communicator and slip it in my purse, a promise that I'll be a less distracted girlfriend for the rest of the night.

And when I hear it buzzing from my purse, I don't want to look at the messages, not even a little bit.

Not at all.

22.

*I*always imagined dating Skip would be like dating a celebrity: everyone at school knowing your name, countless invites to parties, and stolen kisses at the drive-in. I just didn't think I'd be a part of the equation. And I certainly didn't think any party invitations would have my name on them.

But I'm not just Susie at school anymore. I'm Miss Galaxy, a supposed love and friendship expert. Now, instead of just writing letters, I'm getting cornered every time I dare to walk down the hallway.

People who have written to me in the past aren't shy about thanking me for good advice or berating me for advice that didn't go as planned. Which, to be fair, has only happened once or twice, but it hurts. I've traded the comfortable blanket of anonymity for Skip's letterman jacket loose around my shoulders. He says it's the perfect fit, but it clashes with most of my wardrobe.

It's only been two weeks since we started dating. Miss Loretta, Wallace, and the upperclassmen from *The Gazette* all assure me it will be old news soon. But the school has never seen anything like this. As much pressure as it is to be Miss Galaxy all the time, it is kind of fun, especially with the spring formal right around the corner. The dresses, dates, and drama make school dances one of my favorite events of the year, and I've always loved answering questions about them. This time, Miss Galaxy and Anonymous are slated to be the season's "It Couple."

Skip hates being asked about the letters though. He says it should just be between me and him, and he doesn't "want to give away his secrets." I think he's just embarrassed. We've both had our hearts open and on display for everyone to see. As hard of an adjustment as it's been for me, I can tell he's feeling the pressure too.

I know he wants to just be Skip and Susie, but I'm not sure that's possible right now. We both signed up for these roles, opened ourselves up for all the questions and critique. I just wish he seemed more willing to face it together instead of hiding from everything. He should be proud of the adventure he created for me, shouldn't he? It's what led us to walking down the hallway with our fingers laced together. His hand is warm in mine, and a confident stride makes me feel like he's ready to take on the whole world.

I manage to get through most of the day without putting my foot in my mouth when answering advice in real-time, but by the time I'm seated at my shared desk at *The Gazette*, I'm ready to use my overflowing stack of letters as pillow stuffing. Tuesday has rolled around again, and I'm not sure if I can summon the energy for another one of Peggy Sue's parties.

I stretch my arms up over my head, look around the *Gazette* office, and catch Olivia's eye.

"Olivia, will you come out with us tonight?" I ask, swiveling around in my chair toward her desk.

"Oh stars, Susie," she yawns, and I already know she's planning on saying no.

"But we haven't hung out in ages!" I don't want to pressure her, but besides *The Gazette*, I feel like we hardly ever see each other. She still comes over for breakfast half the days of the week, but then again, so does Skip. It feels like the two of us are never alone.

"And whose fault is that?" Wallace says under his breath.

"Hey!" I turn sharply around. He's normally so sweet, but it seems like Olivia's snark is rubbing off in a bad way. He huffs, setting down the stack of papers that he'd been looking through.

"Sorry, Susie! But you haven't exactly been around lately! You haven't even been responding to our group messages."

Oh.

I look down at my empty wrist. I guess now that I'm home from the trip, I haven't exactly been wearing my communicator as much. And now, when I check it, it's always overflowing with messages. The group chat sinks to the bottom, under questions, party reminders, and "good morning" messages from Skip. It's been a few days since I've even looked at our chat. We get to hangout every day at The Galaxy Gazette, and sure we're working during most of it, but I didn't think it was a big deal. But now that I think about it, Olivia has been coming over less and less for dinner each night—mainly because Skip's been taking me to Lester's Diner instead. Our walks to school have felt different ever since Skip started joining us. Olivia isn't the one that feels like a third wheel— it's Skip who seems to materialize during every moment of my free time.

In my attempts to figure out this whole girlfriend thing, I may have turned into a crappy friend.

"And by the way, as mentioned in a previous Miss Galaxy article, everyone gets distracted by their first boyfriend." Olivia offers me an understanding smile, but I can see sadness in her eyes. "We just miss you, that's all."

"Sorry, Susie," Wallace says with a sigh. "She's right. I guess we like you or something."

"I guess!" Olivia echoes, her arm now firmly around my shoulders. Another thing I haven't gotten used to is the two of them acting so friendly. The bickering hasn't stopped, but now they feel more like annoying siblings and less like bitter enemies.

And Olivia certainly wouldn't call them friends. But for better or worse, I think they're rubbing off on each other.

"It's board game night at Eugene's tonight if you want to join."

I pause. The way he says it makes it sound like a regular occurrence. It's only been a few weeks, and they already have a standing tradition without me? Stars, I need to get back in the loop.

"Oh. We, um ... started it after the trip, but you've been busy," Wallace explains, but he can't hide the guilt in his voice.

Skip hasn't technically made plans with me yet. It's all just assumed. But considering who's hosting, I pause. "Oh, I mean, is there still room for me? I wouldn't want to make the numbers uneven."

"Yes." The firm voice makes me jump. Looking up, I'm startled by the person I want to see most and consequently, the least. Eugene Eris has gotten more handsome since I almost confessed my feelings to him. And I keep telling myself that, despite the weirdness, he and I are still friends. But I know better than to believe it, as much as I want it to be true.

I've avoided Eugene at every possible cost, and you don't generally avoid friends. But it's the sensible thing to do, considering what I had planned on confessing to him. We'll be going back to normal soon. We just need time. The feelings of infatuation will fade now that I'm with Skip. Still, every time I see him, my chest flutters, which means not enough time has passed.

Still, when we pass each other in the hallway, I smile at him.

Except Eugene never smiles back. Not a real smile anyway. I saw enough of those on the trip to know when he's faking it.

"Great!" I chirp, turning away to hide my glowing face. I fumble in my bag for my communicator and start to ask Skip if he'd like to join. Just before I can hit send, Skip pops his head around the doorway—a greeting that's become a common occurrence. I've told him he's going to need to start brainstorming article ideas if he plans on spending so much time in here.

"Knock-knock!" he announces before striding over to my desk, his lips touching my cheek as his arm curves around me. He doesn't bother to look at anyone else in the room.

"You about wrapped up?" he asks, already checking the time on his communicator.

"Oh, I was just about to send you a message! I just made plans with everyone to go to game night at Eugene's if you want to join us."

He looks confused.

"Everyone who?" His voice is innocent, but I can hear a quiet groan from Wallace and Olivia. "Everyone is going to Peggy Sue's tonight."

Olivia clears her throat and gestures to the rest of the room. "Not *everyone.*" She places her hand on her hip. If looks could kill.

"Oh," he says slowly, his face falling. "I'm sorry, Suze. I already told her we'd be there."

My stomach twists into knots. I really wanted to go to board game night, but if he already promised, I'm not sure what else to do. A good girlfriend is supposed to be easy-going. But it doesn't feel good to cancel on plans I just made.

I mutter out an apology, and suddenly, the entire room feels awkward and stiff.

"Well, if it doesn't get out too late, you can drop by afterward. We normally cut it close to curfew," Olivia suggests, popping in between us.

"And Eugene's dad normally stops by and drops off leftovers from the diner!" Wallace adds.

That's really cute too. I've only ever seen his parents from a distance at the diner. His dad is normally in the back of house with Eugene. For all the times I've eaten at Lester's, I've never actually seen Eugene working there. He's like the phantom of the diner.

I wonder if he wears one of the cute uniforms. No. No, I don't. I have never once thought about that, especially not while standing next to my boyfriend.

"Sounds like a real party." *I* think so, but sarcasm hangs heavy at the edge of Skip's tone.

"We'll be there! After the movie," I exclaim. Maybe this is exactly what we all need to finally bond as a group of six.

We leave Peggy Sue's before the movie starts to make it over to Eugene's before curfew. Skip had me whirling around the room to one of Arleen's new records all night. It was hard to get him off the makeshift dance floor.

"Is it so bad that I want to dance with my girl on a Friday night?" he asks, spinning me around on the sidewalk.

"We'll dance plenty at the spring formal in two weeks!"

"Oh, yeah, got a date for that thing yet?" he asks with a cheeky grin. Playfully, I elbow him.

"My boyfriend hasn't asked me yet," I play along, ignoring how strange the word still feels on my tongue. But he *hasn't* asked. He just assumed we're going together. Today it seems like he assumes I'll be everywhere he goes.

"I'll have to have a talk with him." He winks. Under the starlight, he looks more handsome than ever.

Like most houses on Ceres, Eugene's is a mirror image to mine on the outside, but the inside has an entirely different feeling. There's the lingering smell of fried diner food, and photos scattered across the walls of their lives before they moved here to take over the family business.

A photo of Eugene at private school draws my attention as we walk toward the family room. Two shy eyes stare back at me. He hadn't adopted his cool/scary persona yet. He was just a nice, normal kid. The blue blazer he's wearing looks familiar and odd. A school uniform doesn't suit him as well as his leather jacket.

We turn the corner, and I see Oliva jump up from her spot on the couch. There are soda cans and snacks on every surface with a mess of cards and dice in the center of the coffee table.

"You made it!" Olivia exclaims. Within seconds, she's wrapping her arms around me. I relax into the tight hug. I missed this.

We laugh, and she guides me into the living room with such familiarity that it feels like she's right at home. Wallace looks the same way, flopped on the couch. He waves lazily, his arm around Teddy, who's snuggled up next to him.

"Galaxy High royalty has arrived!" Teddy greets us, raising his neon-colored soda in the air.

"Hi, everyone!" I wave.

More hugs are exchanged, but Skip seems stiffer than usual. I remind myself that they're still relatively new to him, then take his hand and squeeze it. Just then, Eugene walks into the room, a tray of snacks in his hand.

I loosen my grip on Skip's fingers, but Skip holds on tight, waving with the hand entangled in mine. I'm sure I've given him nothing to be jealous of, but it doesn't seem to matter. I'm his girl, and he wants to make sure everyone knows it.

"Hi," Eugene greets us quietly.

"Hi," I say back. "Uh, thanks for inviting us!"

Eugene nods and sets the tray down.

"Nice apron, beanpole!" Skip exclaims, giving Eugene a hearty slap on the back. Beanpole? I take a minute to study Eugene's lanky frame. I guess, without his jacket, he is pretty slender. His arms are lightly defined, just strong enough to hold someone tight or catch them if they fell.

I gulp. I'd been so focused on his face and his arms; I hadn't even noticed the plain blue and white polka-dotted apron tied around his waist. I try not to focus on how cute it looks on him.

"Thanks." Eugene's reply is serious and cold. His unchanging expression almost makes the entire interaction seem comical. Almost.

I always thought a boyfriend being jealous might feel flattering. In books, it's a perfectly normal emotion, and I'm sure that's true. It's just that when I look at the anger twisting in Skip's eyes, I'm not sure how to react. Can't we all just be friends?

"So, what are we playing?" I pipe up, eager to change the subject.

"Some game Teddy is making up all the rules for!" Olivia says, grabbing a fry off the tray and sitting next to me.

"How dare you!" Teddy gasps, and the four of them laugh like this is an ongoing joke. One that I was too distant to be a part of.

"It's simple, really: your dice roll just has to match up with one of the cards in your hand. If it doesn't, then you draw—"

"Nuh-uh! No way. We're playing something else," Olivia interjects.

"If you gave it a chance!" Teddy whines, throwing his head back.

"We've played four rounds, and you keep cheating!" Teddy holds his hand to his heart and looks toward Eugene for help. "Are you going to let me get viciously attacked like this in your home?"

"Yes," Eugene answers matter-of-factly. Again, they roar with laughter.

"Honestly, I'm surprised we could squeeze into the PR agenda for you two," Wallace says. He sounds just as annoyed as he was in the newspaper room. "You two have practically moved into that corner booth at Lester's."

"Well, not every night can be ice skating, night markets, and wild adventures around space," Skip counters, his arm curving around my shoulders and pulling me in close.

"Why?" Eugene mutters bitterly from his spot next to Teddy.

"Got a better suggestion for our next date?" Skip asks, raising his eyebrow.

"No." Eugene shakes his head. His eyes are impossibly dark. He looks down at the ground, and suddenly I very much regret coming over.

Skip pauses to look around at the rest of the room. "I guess this doesn't really compare to all the places you got to visit over spring break, huh? You should have said something. I thought you'd need a break from adventure, but if it's adventure you still want..." His soft lips curve into a smile when he looks at me. I'm not sure how I'm supposed to say no. I miss traveling around space more than anything. But where are we going to go this late?

"That is, if everyone wants to join us," Skip adds. It seems like he's singling out Eugene in particular.

Eugene nods while the rest of the room remains tense.

Skip hops off the couch, a plan clearly forming in his head. "Alright, everyone, grab your coats. Let's make tonight unforgettable." He winks at me and offers me his hand. Another situation where taking Skip's hand might lead me into more trouble than before.

"Wow, that sounds swell, but I have a science project due in the morning, and I should really get back home," Teddy says, springing to his feet. "I've already stayed out too late, and it seems my *very fun game* was unappreciated!" He's still stuck on that. With the rising tension, I almost forgot that everyone was laughing just a second ago.

Wallace swoops in and gives him a kiss on the cheek. "I appreciate you."

"Yeah, yeah! It was fun. Later, Teddy." Olivia sticks out her tongue, and Teddy mimics the expression. He waves to Eugene. "See you next week, neighbor!"

"I'll be back after I walk him home." Wallace winks.

Skip seems frazzled that his declaration wasn't met with more excitement. He promised to "make the night unforgettable," and here everyone is barely flinching and making small talk. His effect on people is normally more commanding in my experience.

He brushes the hair away from my face and leans in to give me a kiss. "I hope this little surprise is the sort of thing you've been looking for."

I don't know why he still feels like he needs to impress me. After all, with every letter on spring break, I was looking for him.

23.

"Are we sure this is a good idea?" Olivia whispers, leaning in close to my ear. For the first time, she's the one who looks worried.

"Anonymous hasn't led us off-track yet!" I exclaim, but even I have to admit this feels different.

I know that I need to be optimistic. Susie before Spring Break would have run at the first sign of anything dangerous, but after all the adventures we've had, I should know better. I have confidence in wherever Skip is leading us.

This is no different than another one of the stops of the road trip. Except instead of going to a roadside attraction, a beach, or a market, we've cut past "Do Not Cross" tape.

Despite what felt like wild adventures on the road, we never actually broke any rules. And now, we're walking closer and closer to the restricted area. The legendary ice volcanoes my mom is always warning me about. It's a big jump from markets and malt shops. There's a reason they're bubbled off from the rest of town. But still...

"He wouldn't suggest it if it wasn't safe..." I trail off at the end of my sentence and turn back to Olivia. "Right?"

Skip drapes his arm lazily around my shoulders. I jump. I wouldn't have been talking about him like that if I knew he was right next to me. He'd been walking ahead just before, but maybe I was too distracted to notice him slow down.

"I wouldn't do anything to put my best girl in harm's way." He laughs, pulling me closer to him. I wish it eased my nerves. Those are the sorts of little cliché sayings that used to make my heart race when I'd watch cheesy romance movies, so why am I not swooning?

I know it's silly to need reassurance. Every pit stop brought the four of us together. Me, Olivia, Wallace, and Eugene. But even though Skip was the one secretly leading us, I don't know where he fits in. Little tremors shake the ground beneath my feet with each step, warning signs to turn back that I pointedly ignore.

Eugene mumbles something inaudible, jamming his hands into his pockets.

"Say something, beanpole?" Skip turns his head sharply around.

"Maybe you shouldn't call him that." My tone is more passive than I mean for it to come out. Sometimes nicknames can be a cute way to bond with new friends, but I don't think that's what's happening here.

"Hey! I'm only teasing," Skip says, and that big grin spreads across his face. "Only a square would get bent out of shape by something like that, right?"

Eugene's silence says enough. He's not happy. What can I do to make this situation less awkward? Searching my mind, I can't think of anything. But nothing makes sense.

Maybe I should have just agreed to stay at Peggy Sue's party.

Wallace trails behind us. I'm not sure how he got stuck carrying the sled. Every time he gets in earshot, I hear him repeating over and over, "Oh my stars." I wonder if he thinks this is a bad idea too. This certainly doesn't seem befitting of the junior editor of *The Galaxy Gazette.*

We continue to walk closer and closer to the volcano. With every step, a bad feeling builds up inside me. I notice the way Eugene's large eyes bulge as he looks at the volcano and then back at me, clearing his throat. *We should go back,* he seems to signal, but still, he keeps walking. We all do.

"I'm right here. There's nothing to worry about." Skip's voice snaps me back. "Kids at school do this sort of thing all the time. No one ever gets caught, I promise."

Wallace hands the sled to Skip.

We're actually going to do this.

"You ready?" He turns to take my hand, his teeth glimmering in a dazzling smile. I take a deep breath and step forward, then feel another rumble beneath us.

"W-w-wait!" Eugene shouts, and I freeze, whirling around to see his wide-eyed expression.

"L-let's gh-g-go back..." he says quietly, and this time, he's only looking at me. Involuntarily, I step away from Skip. Another little tremor shakes the ground beneath us, and I look down at the path of snow and ice forming beneath us.

Stars. This was a really bad idea.

"W-w-why? Y-you s-s-scared?" Skip says mockingly, taking a step toward Eugene. Guilt and anger course through me. Is that what I sounded like when I made fun of him at the library?

"*Whoa!*" Wallace and Olivia exclaim angrily at the same time.

"That's not cool—"

"—don't you *dare*—"

I'm too startled to even find the right words to join in with them, but my sentiment is the same. What he did is *not* okay.

"Jeez! It's a joke!" Skip exclaims. "What is up with all of you? I'm just busting his chops—it's what friends do, right?"

"Not these friends," Wallace says firmly, stealing a glance at Olivia, who smiles a little proudly.

"Yeah," she agrees softly, "not anymore."

Tears pull at the corners of my eyes. It finally happened. They're finally friends! But I can't dwell on that right now, not when Eugene's honor is at stake. I glance between the two boys who make my heart beat faster before narrowing in on Skip. "You owe him an apology," I say.

"Okay, fine! I'm sorry!" It's not very genuine, and I'm disappointed. He's better than this; why isn't he showing it? The ground rumbles, and Skip sits on the sled with a thud, gesturing for me to get on.

I hesitate. I don't really want to be near him right now.

I step forward, and another rumble catches me off-guard. The pressure seems like it's building. The sled starts to slide off the hill, and Skip reaches out his hand just as I go to grab it. The ice cracks under my feet. I glance down and realize it's not just ice that I'm standing on top of—it's a geyser.

Before I have a chance to move, I can't see. There's freezing water all around me; I try to get out of the way, but the pressure of the water makes it feel like I'm frozen in place.

"*Susie!*" someone screams out, and a firm pair of hands grasps at my waist to pull me out from the sludge. But it's too late. I'm completely soaked.

"I got you, girl!"

Opening my eyes, I realize Olivia is the one saving me from the disaster. We're bolting forward with her pulling faster and faster down the hill.

I turn back to see Eugene practically carrying Wallace, who is unhurt, just slow. They're at the back of the pack while Skip got sent sliding down the hill on his sled. He's swerving away from the explosions of ice, and he'd almost look cool if I wasn't so terrified. We need to get out of here as fast as possible!

I grab Wallace's hand, adrenaline overriding my frozen muscles. Eugene can't drag him along by himself.

Wallace's cold hand grasps mine, and I hold it like a lifeline as we drag and pull each other out of harm's way. Everything feels like it's happening in slow motion, geysers of slush exploding from the ground while we pivot away from the explosions of ice. By the time we reach the bottom of the hill, Skip is already back at his mom's saucer, beckoning us inside.

"Come on!" Skip shouts, throwing the doors open. We're far enough away that the explosions have stopped, but the ground beneath us is still shaking. We pile inside, Skip in the front seat. I can see Olivia and Wallace, but—

"Where's Eugene?" I croak. My body won't stop shaking.

"Here," he says, and his hand reaches for mine from the backseat, cupping my fingers tight. I didn't see him get into the cruiser. Wallace berates Skip for his "awesome date idea" while Olivia complains that she is going to "move off this ice planet once and for all" but Eugene...

Eugene's eyes are locked firmly on mine. He clears his throat, loud enough to get everyone's attention.

I take another gasping breath. We're all here. I don't want him to let go, and he doesn't. His hand stays firmly attached to mine.

We're safe.

We just need to get out of here. Olivia looks at me, color returning to her face, but her lips are creased into a frown. Wallace struggles to catch his breath. For some reason, they're all looking at me.

"Susie! Are you okay?" Skip shouts from the front seat. "I'm so sorry!"

"We need to get her home now!" Olivia shouts, her voice frantic. I feel okay. I'm more worried about her. Her snowsuit is intact, but Olivia hates the cold.

"I'm just chilly," I get out through chattering teeth.

"You're turning blue!"

"I'm always blue..." And so is my vision. Blue. Blue everywhere.

And red...

Red and blue hues blind me. I blink, reaching out and clutching the first hand I find. The longer we sit here, the harder I shake. I grip Eugene's hand as he gazes down at me with worried eyes. It's the most upset I've ever seen him look, and the longer we stare at each other, the harder he squeezes my hand. Blue and red reflect off his face.

Olivia turns back to Skip. "Why aren't you driving?" she demands sharply.

"Because we have company."

Straining to sit up, I follow everyone's gaze to the window. Accompanied by two neighborhood watch bots, there's the dome repair team, with my mother at the front of the pack.

24.

"Have you kids lost your minds?" Mom shouts. I retreat further under the electric blanket we're all huddled under. Even with the heated vibrations permeating into my skin, I still feel as though I'm freezing.

I don't know how I hoped tonight would go, but this is not the way I wanted it to turn out. Considering that we could have had giant shards of ice shooting at us instead of just freezing slush (as my mother has now reminded us multiple times), I count my blessings that things hadn't been worse. Skip hangs his head, unable to meet my mom's gaze.

"It's my fault. I just wanted to take Susie on her biggest adventure yet," Skip confesses, draping his part of the electric blanket over me.

"As far as I'm concerned, you're all to blame," she continues, shaking her head. "I don't know about the rest of your parents, but I know we raised you better than this, Susie."

I nod, too embarrassed to speak. Couldn't she save the lecture for when we get home? I don't make eye contact with anyone; I just want this night to be over.

But I understand why she's upset. I've heard "if all your friends tried to climb up the ice volcanos, would you?" and it turns out that, when push comes to shove, I would. Skip shoots me an apologetic look. I know he means well, that he was just trying to impress me. After everything that happened over spring break, he's right. My expectations *were* high. It's my fault that I let it get this far. My stomach twists into knots.

Everyone's parents are called, and we're shuffled off to our respective homes. Dad barely says a word, and Mom won't stop shouting. I'm not grounded exactly, but my curfew is an hour earlier, and my communicator privileges have been taken away. Which is awful because all I want to do is call everyone and tell them how sorry I am.

Slipping into bed, I wrap myself in every blanket I can find around the house.

"After the stunt you pulled, you're lucky you just have a cold! You could be *dead*!" Mom reminds me for the fifth time the next morning. Saturday was supposed to be spent fabric shopping with Olivia and her mom, but I'm not even sure if I'll get to go to the dance anymore. Right now, I'm not even sure I want to.

I've been out sick all week. Sunday was supposed to be a movie date with Skip. But after spending all of Saturday in bed, a doctor's trip, and orders of hot liquids and rest, our plans were once again canceled. I hoped that I'd be better by Monday, but I'm not. Not Tuesday or Wednesday, either. By Thursday, I'm starting to feel like this is my karma and I'm never going to feel better again.

I've taken over our sofa in the living room with an endless stream of television. The songs and jingles blur together in a fever dream.

"Susie, you have company!" Dad calls from the front door. I turn, expecting to see Skip with a pile of homework and another apology. He really seems like he means it every time. Everyone makes mistakes. Sure, it was his idea, but I'm just as guilty for going along with it. Skip never stays long to visit. I don't think my parents will let him.

Instead, three sullen figures stand in the hallway. The road trip crew is in my living room, and I can't believe how much I've missed their faces.

"Oh, my stars!" I gasp, pulling the blankets around me tighter before remembering they've seen me in my pajamas already and relax. They're each carrying something: Eugene has a glass serving container with stars printed across it and what looks like a few movies tucked under his arm, Wallace carries a small basket, and Olivia has the biggest box of crackers I've ever seen.

"How are you feeling?" Olivia asks.

I shrug. "Okay."

She raises an eyebrow.

"Okay, I feel awful," I admit.

Eugene sets the container down on the table and waves shyly, his lips crinkling into a smile that makes my heart beat even faster.

"We all brought over something to make you feel better. I have those saltine crackers you like," Olivia begins.

"I brought the tea, and Teddy always brings this vapor stuff when I'm under the weather," Wallace chimes in.

"It's soup," Eugene says flatly, holding up the mint green glass dish.

"You made it?" I gasp. I know it's not the fever that's making my entire face hot. It makes sense that he knows his way around the kitchen. But soup? There's something else in his hands that catches my eye.

A bundle of old cheesy musicals. I can't believe he remembered.

"Way to show us all up, buddy." Olivia laughs, elbowing Eugene in the arm. He shyly grins at her, then me. "Anyway, rest up! Your public will be waiting for you at the dance, and my mom finished your dress. We went and got the fabric without you."

"Can we get ready together?" I ask.

"Obviously!"

They fill me in on what's been going on at school while plopped around me on the couch. It's small talk, but it's nice. I keep waiting for Dad to tell them it's time to go, but thankfully he doesn't. Maybe he knows the company is just what I need to get the rest of my pep back in my step.

The three of us sink onto the curved couch together. Olivia clears away the pile of messy blankets and replaces them with a soft knitted throw that covers all four of us. She takes the corner next to me, then it's Eugene on the other side and Wallace hugging the other corner.

We start out with "A Star Shines So Beautiful," an old movie in black and white about two stargazers who meet and fall in love. The plot is simple but the songs, the songs are so—

"Cheesy," Olivia says as if reading my thoughts. "I think this might be the worst one."

"How are they tap dancing if there isn't any gravity?" Wallace muses, leaning toward the screen. "I mean, the song is 'My heart is soaring, my feet are off the ground, yadda yadda.'"

"But their feet are on the ground," Olivia joins in on the criticism. "Thematically, it makes no sense!" The popcorn she helped herself to spills out of the bowl as she throws herself back against the couch.

Wallace points at the actors, who are in the middle of a mid-song dance break. "Is the love weighing them down, or are they floating through the sky?"

I can't with these two. I point at the set; the floor is literally decorated to look like they're dancing in the stars. So, what if it's low budget? The message comes across if you're paying attention.

"Back us up, Eugene." Olivia drags him in, chucking a few pieces of popcorn that land in the folds of his V-neck—which I am certainly not paying attention to. Without the bulk of the leather jacket, Eugene's body is warm and soft next to mine. I'm suddenly keenly aware of the distance—or lack thereof—between us. But it's fine. This whole couch is strictly platonic.

Eugene glares at Wallace and Olivia as if to say *just watch the movie.*

"They're almost worse now that they're friends," he sighs under his breath.

"Insufferable," I happily agree. Though, I'll take them bonding over their mutual hatred of my favorite movie over fighting any day. We manage to get through most of the movie without too much commentary. By the time the credits roll, my bowl of soup is drained and our popcorn bowls are empty. After a week of isolation, I'm grateful for the company but can feel my eyes getting heavy. Still, when Olivia suggests popping in the next title, I can't resist. We brew tea, warm more soup, and I sink deeper into a puddle on the couch.

"This is nice." I say the words without thinking and feel Eugene relax next to me.

"Yeah," he exhales. I wonder if he secretly thinks the movie was just as cheesy as everyone else.

"I didn't realize there was a party."

Skip is standing in the doorway. I must be so out of it that I didn't hear when Dad let him in. There's a can of soup clutched in his hand, and a sullen expression on his face.

"Hi," I call out. When he comes closer, I see his brow is pinched at the center, and the usually friendly smile is replaced with a scowl. I can't imagine why until I realize just how close Eugene and I have drifted together.

"This is sure cozy," he snips. There's something in Skip's tone that instantly makes me feel guilty, but we weren't doing anything wrong, were we?

It was just a movie.

"Can one of you help me with this soup?" Olivia shouts from the kitchen.

"Yup!" Eugene springs off the couch and hurries into the kitchen.

"Eugene made soup..." I explain, pointing to the two of them disappearing into the kitchen.

"Of course he did." Skip sighs, eyeing the can of soup he picked up from the store. Surely he can't feel jealous over soup; it's the thought that counts. His fingers lace together with my own.

"How are you feeling?" he asks, his expression softening into one that I recognize.

"I'm okay," I admit. "Just tired and a sore throat. I'm glad I'm the only one who got sick."

"I'm not." He reaches out and smooths a strand of hair off my forehead. "I wish it was me."

"You don't mean that." I shake my head.

"If it was me," he begins in a quiet voice, "I think you'd be the only one I'd want nursing me back to health."

"I'm sure you'd have a slew of friends bringing you soup and flowers." I laugh, knocking into his shoulders with my own.

He turns to me with an expression that stops the light-hearted feeling in my chest.

"But you'd be the only one I'd *want.*" He glances toward the kitchen and leans in, his voice suddenly low. "Weren't *we* supposed to have a movie date today?"

I had completely forgotten.

"This was very impromptu," I try to explain. "They all just stopped over to check on me."

"Sure, right..." He glances over at the kitchen where Wallace, Olivia and Eugene are gathering round two of our movie snacks, including a second cup of soup for me and a pile of crackers I'm not sure I'll be able to stomach.

"Oh, hey." Wallace has a hard time masking the disap-proval in his voice. I think he blames Skip for the whole incident. Anonymous didn't steer us wrong roaming around outer space, but here on Ceres, Skip sure floundered on our first adventure.

Maybe, in a way, it was easier just living out those fan-tasies on paper.

"There's enough popcorn for everyone," Wallace says, pushing the bowl in our direction. "You're staying for the next movie, right? Or has Susie made you sit through enough of these on your dates?"

"What's the movie?" Skip asks.

We haven't talked about my love for musicals yet. I wonder what his reaction will be. So far I've only heard him talk about action and horror movies. He and Olivia honestly have pretty similar tastes.

"*Dancing in Moonlight*," I say sinking deeper into the couch's soft cushions. "Or there's *Mysteries on the Orange Sun*, the Cara Cosmos musical."

"Bleh, no thanks." He laughs. I guess not all of the book's fans are keen on every adaptation, but I'm a little disappointed. The musical is underrated and has one of my favorite soundtracks. "But the other one, I think I remember watching it with my Granny."

"Susie is the grandma of our friend group soooo..." Olivia plops back on her corner of the couch, claiming a spot under the blanket.

"Am not!" I argue. I thought they had dropped this by now.

"You have hard candy in your purse!" the three reply in unison, Eugene shouting from the kitchen. They burst into laughter.

"Cough drops are not candy!" I huff, but the giggles catch me too.

The only person left out is Skip. A side effect of him being on the road trip, but not actually *on* the road trip with us. I start to explain, but he waves me away. "We all have inside jokes. It's fine."

But it doesn't *feel* fine.

Eugene is the last person to rejoin us, a clattering bowl of soup in hand. He places it in front of me.

"Thanks, Eugene." When I look up at him, his dark eyes swell as deep as the night sky. I'm lost for a moment.

"W-what are friends for?"

My smile is strained as he grabs a spot on the arm of the couch.

"I should have been the one doing that," Skip grumbles, glaring daggers at Eugene.

"Y-you didn't," Eugene says in a low growl, and just like that, he is the scary tough guy I'd been afraid at school. Now

I know he's much more, but there's something in his expression that makes me hope Skip will back down.

"Okay so! We're thinking *Dancing in Moonlight,* right?" Wallace's voice is loud and jumpy. He practically sprints to the television to get things set up, and Olivia takes large handfuls of popcorn while looking at me. It seems she's found a better source of entertainment. Eugene and Skip's eyes are fixed on the screen's static while Wallace scrambles to press play. Skip drapes his arm around me, but it feels more like a sign to Eugene to back off rather than genuine affection.

I always thought having a jealous boyfriend would be fun and flattering. It turns out being clutched like some kind of prize is *not cute* in real life. Eugene made soup from scratch, so what? We were sitting close on the couch, so what? Nothing happened and we're in a group setting. Maybe Skip feels intimidated somehow? Eugene and I have spent a lot of time together.

The movie ends as quickly as it started. I didn't close my eyes once, but I feel like I slept through the entire thing. My thoughts spin, my back ratcheted tight with tension. If Wallace hadn't jumped in, would Eugene and Skip have started clobbering each other in middle of my living room?

"We should probably get going soon." Olivia yawns, stretching her arms wide over her head.

"Yeah," Eugene agrees.

But no one bothers to move. In fact, their eyes drift toward Skip as if they're waiting for him to leave first.

"Everything alright in here, kids?"

Oh, thank the stars!

Dad's voice cuts through the mounting tension, and everyone jumps to their feet to start to tidy and gather their things. Olivia moves more slowly, unaffected by my dad's stern voice.

"We were all just leaving!" Wallace says, his voice jumping up a nervous octave. "You have a lovely home!"

"I'll come by in the morning!" Skip calls from the doorway. The door shuts, and I let out a sigh.

"He'll come by alright, and eat every single slice of toast," Dad grumbles under his breath, taking a seat on the couch next to me. "I thought Olivia was bad. Ah, but he brought you soup. That's a nice boyfriendly thing to do."

"It's from Eugene."

"Oh." Dad seems surprised by that.

"Yeah." I pick up the canned soup he'd left on the coffee table. "He did bring this though."

"Skip does seem more like the canned soup type." Dad sighs. I'm not sure what he's trying to say, but it seems like we're not talking about food anymore.

Skip is kind, considerate, smart, and has been checking in on me all week. So what if someone else made the soup he's delivering? He has shown how much he cares every single day. According to *The Guide,* he's a textbook "Perfect Boyfriend."

Exactly what I've been searching for.

"Well, that was very kind of Eugene," Dad continues with a tense smile. "You two got pretty close over spring break, huh?"

"We all have," I admit. Still, I wasn't sure where Skip fit into all this. With the letters, he created a tight-knit group, but the space that should have been saved for him had already been taken. Or maybe, deep down, I just didn't want to let him in. I stare up at the flecks of silver on the ceiling, my heart beating fast.

"It looks like your friend left his jacket," Dad says, slipping me my communicator. I don't hesitate to clip it onto my wrist.

I look up and catch a glimpse of the shiny leather, then shrink under the pile of blankets. I can't believe Eugene forgot something so important to him. I'm going to have to give it back to him, but I'm not sure if I can see him right now.

The communicator on my wrist vibrates.

I gulp, refusing to look at it, until finally, with both excitement and dread, I look down. Olivia's name is lit up in pale yellow.

I'm relieved, but at the same time, my chest feels heavier.

I really thought it might be him.

I wanted it to be.

I ignore the ache building in my chest when I glance at the familiar leather jacket. I'll give it back at school on Monday, and when I do, things will be totally normal.

25.

*I*finally reappear at school on Monday. My absence has been felt more than I realized it would be. *"Feel better, Miss Galaxy"* notes are posted all over my locker, and I'm getting a strange number of smiles everywhere I turn—but that might just be the lingering effect of being escorted by Skip.

In the week I was gone, I forgot how much of an event going to school with him can feel like.

"And you're sure you're doing alright?" he asks at lunch. "I still feel so bad about the entire thing."

"I'm really okay now." I'm still stuffy, but for the most part, I feel like a functional member of society again.

"I can't believe you ditched my party to go volcano sledding." Peggy-Sue shakes her head. I can't tell from her tone if she disapproves or if she's jealous she wasn't invited. Either way, it feels like a bad dream. "You're going to have to give us every single detail in that next article of yours."

I shake my head. There's no way I'm turning Dear Miss Galaxy into a date-recap. It would be like writing a tabloid about myself and Skip. I can't imagine how uncomfortable that would be for Skip, and it's definitely not something I want. Besides, who would really want to read the details of our love life? The journey to finding each other was one thing, but writing about how much I regret going volcano sledding? No thanks. Besides, Miss Galaxy would never have done something so dangerous.

"People are invested!" Peggy-Sue whines from her place across the lunch table.

"People can mind their business." Skip rolls his eyes "It was a goofy date idea, and I never should have suggested it. We're a house party and diner couple from now on."

Skip reaches out, his fingers entangling with mine. He leans forward until his soft lips brush against my ear, causing a chill to rush down my spine. "Don't let it get to you." His whisper is soft and sweet. The truth is it *has* been getting to me. For all the well wishes I've gotten, I've also noticed some strange looks in the hallway.

Not everyone has been happy with Miss Galaxy's advice over the past two years, and now that they know who I am, there's been more than just a random lewd drawing in the letterbox.

Once the day is over and I'm safely tucked away at *The Galaxy Gazette*, I crave normalcy. Diving into this week's pile of letters, a frown creases across my lips. Most people aren't bothering to write to Miss Galaxy anymore. Susie is scrawled across the front of each envelope; there's an intimacy to seeing my own name written out that I never expected or wanted. My heart hammering in my chest, I open the first letter.

> Dear Susie, is it true this is your first actual relationship? Why have you been pretending to be some kind of love expert for years?

It's the question I've been dreading but knew was inevitable. Judging from the size of this pile, I'm sure they're not the only one wondering.

What am I supposed to say? Everything you need to learn about romance you can learn from *The Guide*. It hasn't failed me yet. Well, no... I guess that's not true anymore.

But it's almost never failed, and that counts for something, I'm sure.

I gulp as I crack open the next one, silently hoping it's about which shoes to wear to the dance. Flats or Heels? The answer is always whatever you'll be comfortable in. You don't want to kick your shoes off by the middle of the night.

> Dear Susie, Now that I know who's actually behind Miss Galaxy, your ridiculous advice about coordinating a back-to-school wardrobe last fall makes a lot more sense. Your style is way too matchy-matchy, and you're never up on the trends.

My hands quake. Who wrote this? I look down at my outfit. Pink shoes that match my pearls, hair bow, and cardigan, and a pale-yellow dress. I mean, aren't your accessories supposed to match? Cultivating a convenient and stylish wardrobe is all about a limited color palette you can mix and match. I'm just being practical.

And proving their point completely.

My shoulders crunch forward. I reach for another envelope; I shouldn't do it. My name is written large and aggressively on the front. Whoever wrote it has a bone to pick with me. I can't seem to stop myself from tearing it open.

> Dear Susie, I checked out that book Anonymous sent you after at the library stop, and I can't believe it. PLEASE don't tell me this is the trash you've been using to tell people how to live their lives. I mean, it was bad enough

when I thought it was all your own ideas, but are you
seriously relying on tips that came out when our parents
were kids? Unbelievable...

The room feels like it's spinning. Some advice is just timeless, isn't it? If people really hate my column so much, why do they keep writing in? Has Miss Galaxy just been a joke this entire time? The next one is written in pink sparkly gel pen.

How could you put Skip in danger like that? You're lucky
he didn't get sick too! What a selfish date to make him
take you on.

Whatever the rumors are around that night, someone wants to blame me for all of it. Maybe a freshman with a crush on Skip? It doesn't matter.

That night was horrible.

I should have said no.

We should have just stayed at Eugene's, played board games, and eaten leftovers from the diner. That's all I wanted that night! Why did I let myself get swept away? I sigh, looking at the pile of letters spilling across my desk.

People seemed to love Miss Galaxy, but Susie? Susie they have mixed feelings on.

I don't feel like I'm *her* anymore. I've lost my title and whatever power came with it. Sure, my advice has helped people, but how many of my peers have I disappointed or hurt?

My fingers spring to the keys, and I start to type.

Dear Readers,

I regret to inform you that Miss Galaxy would never,
EVER go volcano sledding—but I, Susie, did. And because

of that, I am unfit for the job. I am unfit to answer your letters or give you guidance.

I yank out the paper and crumple it into a ball, letting my resignation fall to the floor with my dreams of being the perfect advice columnist.

I'm honestly not sure that I want to quit at all! I love to write, but looking down at the pile of letters demanding personal answers, I realize I don't think I'm willing to turn my articles into a diary. Sharing the sugar-coated good stuff was one thing. It always felt strange, but this is so much worse.

"Hey..." Eugene's voice calls from behind me.

I turn.

I wasn't even aware he was here. He's wearing a thick black cardigan. It's sweeter and softer than his usual look. And then I remember—I have his jacket.

"You left your jacket at my house," I blurt out. It's probably not the hello he was looking for, but he lets out a relieved sigh. The tension on his face! I bet he tore his room apart looking for it this morning. "I should have messaged you or brought it over. I don't know what I was thinking." But that's a lie. I liked seeing it draped around the chair in front of my vanity table. I knew I shouldn't. I knew I should give it back right away. But it was like stealing just a small piece of him.

"The cardigan looks nice," I admit.

His cheeks start to glow; his dark eyes brighten. I don't know what to say.

Finally, I settle on: "I can bring it to school tomorrow."

He looks like he wants to say something, but just nods. "Yeah... a-are you feeling better?" His dark blue eyes are filled with concern.

I frown, making a so-so gesture with my hand. "Still a little stuffy, but better than last week. I think the soup helped."

He smiles. "Good." He bites his bottom lip, and silence hangs between us. I follow the lines of his lips, watching them part as if there's something he wants to tell me before clamping shut again.

"Eugene?" I ask. Whatever he wants to say, I wish he would just say it, even if the words would be inconvenient to hear.

Stars, I want to hear him say them.

My face burns. This isn't fair. He can't keep looking at me like that. There's a name for the expression, the softness on his face, the way his deep-set cheekbones lead into his pouted lips. But I have a boyfriend.

He looks around the room. Olivia left early to get things set up for our dress-fitting later with her mom. Wallace is working quietly with his headphones on, and I think Ms. Loretta is asleep at her desk. With her sunglasses on, it's hard to tell. Everyone else is distracted, it might as well just be the two of us, and I can't take it for another second.

"Have a good day, everyone!" I say quickly, gathering up my things.

I don't say hello to my parents when I get home. I just bolt up the stairs and straight over to my dresser. How am I supposed to navigate this? In the past, there's one book I've always turned to for advice, a good resource I thought could never lead me astray.

Heaving a heavy sigh, I pull out my copy of *The Space Age Ladies' Guide to Romance and Social Affairs* and flip to the section on love triangles.

Never did I ever think I'd be in this situation. I flip to an illustration of a distraught girl surrounded by two boys. Boys who seem to bear an awfully strong resemblance to Skip and Eugene.

One, a bad boy in a leather jacket.

The other wearing a sweet smile.

Two paragraphs down, I find it.

"Q: Help! I think I like someone else, but I have a boyfriend!

A: Be faithful and true, and don't let pretty words tempt you from your special someone. Now, if you've developed a crush on this person, chances are it's a passing fancy. But if the feelings persist, you have to ask yourself: What's keeping you in your relationship? Are you as devoted to your beau as he is to you? Or is your newfound wandering eye a sign that you aren't quite as devoted as you used to be? Try to reignite the spark before doing anything drastic."

It's exactly what I would write back to someone if they wrote to Miss Galaxy. But... reignite the spark? I like Skip just fine.

Maybe this book *is* outdated. No, I can't let that silly hate mail letter get in my head.

If *The Guide* says to do it, I guess I'll have to try. After all, it's barely-almost-never steered me wrong so far.

By the time I reach Olivia's house, I've pulled myself together. Mostly. I carry Eugene's jacket with me. I'll have Olivia give it back to him tomorrow. Or maybe I'll just leave it at his door tonight. I'm not sure. I just can't keep it at home anymore, not when I need to focus on finding "the spark" with Skip again.

"Door's open!" Olivia calls. I open it up to find spools of shiny fabric billowing across the table.

I gasp, my hand reflexively grasping at my heart. Olivia stands on a stool in the kitchen with gold fabric spilling from her hips and cinched in waist on the form-fitting bias. She's shining like the sun itself.

"You look amazing!"

Mrs. Oren is perched on the floor, working on the hem, her bright red hair tied back into a bun. She offers me an absentminded wave and a tight-lipped smile, sewing pins sticking out from the side of her mouth.

"Well, if it isn't little Susie!" Rex leaps from his seat on the sofa, and before I can react, he pulls me into the kind of hug you'd expect from a doting big brother. I'm whirled around the living room in broad circles until my head is dizzy and my cheeks ache from laughter.

"Taking care of our sweet Olivia while I'm away at school?" he asks while I'm still mid-flight.

"I think it's been more the other way around." I frown. Lately, I haven't been the best friend, and she's been nothing but understanding.

"All grown up and going to school dances." Rex pretends to wipe a tear from his eye, and a sly smirk appears on his face. "Maybe I'll make an appearance, for old times' sake."

"You will do nothing of the sort!" Mrs. Oren calls from the kitchen.

"Mom, don't yell with pins in your mouth!" Olivia's says. "I don't even think they'd let Rex in, considering the whole explosion thing."

"Oh please, it was just a few fireworks in the school gym." He snickers, running his fingers through his bright red hair.

Olivia's older brother seems like he's gotten taller since the last time he came to visit. A holiday break—not another explosion. It's always strange to see the "delinquent" who's caused so much trouble in their household helping with the laundry, baking cookies, or spinning me around the house like I'm his own little sister, for that matter.

But I've been seeing more and more that people have multiple sides to them. His orange eyes crease up with his smile. I shake my head. That's the sort of charisma that could tempt even the most straight-laced student into drag racing.

Which, if I'm not mistaken, is at least *one* of the reasons he got kicked out of a previous school.

"If you don't come help me pin this fabric, you'll be expelled from this house!" Mrs. Oren shouts. The two of us head back into the kitchen.

"Susie will do it, right Susie?" Rex strides past his mom and opens the fridge, chuckling to himself.

Typical older brother, alright. Mrs. Oren opens her mouth and then shuts it. Clearly, this has been going on all day, and she's picking her battles. I hold the fabric in place.

"Sorry, Susie. My brother is the worst!" Olivia shouts behind her.

"Oh, no! Honestly, this is the least I can do. Considering all the hard work your mom is putting in for both of us."

Rex cocks his head, staring at me. "Have you gotten even more polite since the last time I saw you?"

"She is a perfectly adequate amount of polite. Maybe you should take notes," Mrs. Oren snaps. At least this time, she's taken the pins out of her mouth.

I feel a change in Olivia's posture and realize she's tensing up. They've been fighting with Rex nonstop since he came back home.

"Mom, once we're done, is it alright if Susie and I go to Lester's?" Olivia asks, either trying to lighten the tension or look for an escape—I'm not sure. All I know is that I don't want to go anywhere near Lester's tonight. I can't risk running into Eugene.

But Mrs. Oren doesn't know that, and therefore, can't provide me with an out. My stomach twists as she nods her head. "Just don't stay out too late."

Olivia's eyes sparkle and then fade when she looks at me. Clearly, my hesitation is right on my face.

"Unless, Suze, do you have boyfriend plans tonight?"

I shake my head. Skip pouted a little when I told him, but needing to finish my dress was as good an excuse as any. I open my mouth, but Rex slides across the kitchen floor toward us, nearly spilling milk all over the floor.

"Boyfriend?" he echoes, then eyes the leather jacket draped over the kitchen chair by the door. A smug smile crosses his face. "Ah, I was wondering who that jacket belonged to."

My face flushes.

"Oh, no... that's my friend Eugene's. He left it at my house, and I haven't given it back yet."

I haven't *wanted* to give it back yet is closer to the truth.

"Not Eugene Eris, is it?" A strange tone overtakes his voice.

I nod.

"We went on a club trip together with *The Galaxy Gazette*. He was supposed to be taking me to the dance as friends, but he's working the concessions stand for his parents, so they can keep the diner open. They're sponsoring the dance, did you hear?" Olivia gushes. A prickle of jealousy crawls down my skin.

I hadn't heard about any of it. They had plans to go to the dance together? Since when was that decided?

"Well, if he ended up with such nice friends as the pair of you, then I don't feel so bad. He earned it, after what he went through."

Mrs. Oren directs Olivia to hold still while she goes into her office to get more pins to finish the hem, instructing all of us to behave while she's gone. Her voice is muted as thoughts swirl around me. The school Rex just got expelled from—is it the same school Eugene transferred from? I can't believe I didn't put the pieces together.

The blue sports jacket. The navy and gold tie. The exact uniform Eugene was wearing in those photos on the wall at his house is the same uniform Rex wears whenever he comes home to visit.

"Did you try to stop him from getting picked on?" I ask in a small voice.

"No." He shrugs, a goofy smile creeping up his face. "But gosh, I remember this one time poor kid got shoved into a trashcan, and it was just these two spindly legs sticking out while they rolled him across the school. It was hilario—"

"Rex!" I gasp before he can say another word.

"I mean no—it was really awful. Not funny at all." He puts on a stoic expression I have a hard time believing. He shakes his head. "Other than that, I never saw anything with my own eyes. Well, there was one time…"

"What happened?" I ask. Eugene might not want us to hear this, but I can't help myself.

"I cut out early, and while I was heading back to the dorms, I heard this banging sound coming from inside a locker. It scared the crap out of me. I figured there was a kid stuck in there.

"Well, I got a pair of bolt cutters out of my locker and ran back, but the banging had stopped. So, I get worried, right? I break the lock open, and there he is, all crammed in there. His legs and arms were all pretzeled around him. I helped pull him out, and he collapsed onto the ground. Wouldn't let me take him to the nurse, couldn't explain to me what hap-pened. I was too late, and I just thought, how many times has this happened to this poor kid?"

"If you hadn't been too late, would you have stopped it?" I feel like I'm going to be sick. He smirks. It's an expression that makes him and Olivia look more alike than usual.

"Why do you think I keep getting kicked out of school?"

"Because you're the type that keeps bolt cutters in your locker," Olivia teases, shaking her head. "I'm glad you had them, though. Although, knowing you, if you hadn't, you would have ripped the lock off with your bare hands."

He sighs. "I remember when I was doing the shoving, not the rescuing." He turns his head, looking at the hallway Mrs. Oren disappeared down. "There's a reason joking about going back to Galaxy High didn't fare well with Mom," he says to Olivia. "I have a lot to make up for."

Mrs. Oren's footsteps click on the tile behind us. "You can start with cutting the organza for Susie's dress," she says, crossing her arms. I wonder how much she heard. "... and maybe give your mother a hug."

I smile. It looks like she heard enough.

"And bolt cutters? At your age, I could have done the job with a bobby pin *and* not caused any damage to school property."

My dress fitting takes longer than I thought it would, but we still have enough time for a trip to the diners. The thing is, I'm not sure that I want to go anywhere near Lester's.

"Olivia," I begin, "I don't want to get milkshakes."

"But you always want milkshakes."

"The thing is ... I think I might like milkshakes too much. I might need to stay away from milkshakes for a while because things are complicated between ... milkshakes and me." I let out a deep, prolonged sigh. We've been friends for long enough; I'm sure I don't need to say anything else.

I meet her sunset eyes. She's squinting at me like there's a small speck of something on my face, then suddenly goes completely deadpan. "What?"

I throw my hands up in the air. "Eugene is milkshakes!" I blurt out, my face glowing bright.

"Oh..." she replies, lying back in her chair in a relaxed manner, and then the information dawns on her. She sits up. "*Oh!*"

I crumple onto the floor next to her chair, tears filling my eyes.

"I think I still like him. I *know* I still like him," I confess. It feels good to finally talk to her about this, but it also makes it feel real, each word at a time.

"Wow... okay. I mean, I had a feeling. What are you going to do?" She sits back, trying to take all this in.

"I mean, what can I do?" I ask. "I have a boyfriend."

"Susie, I've been wanting to ask you this for a while." She slides onto the floor next to me, looking at me seriously. "Do you ... *like* Skip?"

"Of course, I do!" I answer too quickly, but my tone alone makes it clear to both of us I'm not telling the truth. "*The Space Age Ladies' Guide to Romance and Social Affairs* says he's the perfect candidate."

She narrows her eyes. "And is that what you think?"

What I think?

When we kiss, all I wonder is if I'm doing it right. I've heard that kissing gets better over time, and maybe we're just not there yet. But how am I supposed to tell Olivia that? I'm silent for a long moment, and finally Olivia reaches out and puts her hand on my knee.

"You and Eugene seemed to have something really special on the trip. I don't want you to miss out on that. If you're just going through the motions with Skip, then break up with him."

"After all the letters, I owe him a chance, don't I?" What would everyone think if I just broke up with him? Right before a school dance? I'd be an absolute monster. Instead of looking at me with admiration in the hallway, they'd look at me with scorn.

I wonder if that would feel any different.

"Don't you think you've given him that?" Olivia snaps. "It's been a month!"

"We're still getting to know each other." Another excuse tumbles out of my mouth. "Before I do anything drastic, I need to try to reignite any spark I had with him. I mean, you remember the crush I had on him in middle school…"

"But that was in middle school." Her reply is flat, and the look on her face is even worse.

"Olivia!"

"What?" Her amber eyes bore into mine. She's completely lost her patience, and I'm not sure if I blame her.

"I just… I do still really like Eugene," I admit, burying my head in my hands. My heart lights up every time I see him. "But I just… I'm not… maybe I like Skip too? I mean, he's nice. This is everything I've wanted for years. *The Guide* says I should keep trying, but Olivia—I'm scared."

"What do you have to be scared of?" She moves closer. "Eugene is crazy about you, and who cares what *The Guide* says or people at school think?"

"I do!" I shout, letting my hair fall in front of my face in messy curls. I've been letting that book run my life since I started high school—even before that I studied it endlessly. It's been my peek into what the "real world" was supposed to be like, my cheat sheet to everything I'd ever need to know. But I'm starting to realize love might not be as simple as a step-by-step guide. Maybe it's doing more harm than good.

"I did, at least." I curl up on her floor, letting out a dramatic moan.

Skip is a good guy. He's nice, he's funny, he cares, but I don't know if he's for me. We don't fit together the way we're supposed to. But with Eugene, since I've gotten to know him, we've felt like two puzzle pieces.

But breaking up with Skip before the dance? I can't do that to someone.

"He's already got a corsage that matches my dress. He'll be so upset." I bury my head in my hands. "Besides, maybe the dance will help us figure things out."

"I guess." Her shoulders rise and fall. "But do you really think it's okay to wait? I don't see how a dance is going to fix things."

"A night of music and dancing—that can set the mood for just about anyone." I nod to myself. Whatever my future is with Skip, we can figure it out after the dance.

As for where Eugene and I stand, I'm not sure.

"Thanks for finally telling me about this. Next time, don't wait so long." She sighs.

I drape my arm around her shoulders and pull her close. "I won't." And for both our sakes, I hope there isn't a next time. I never want to be in a love triangle again.

I look out at the sky, and the stars sparkle back in tones of silver and gold.

"What do you say to going to the dance together?"

"Won't your date be offended?"

"Well, we're already planning on getting ready at my place. Besides, who wouldn't want to escort not one but two beautiful girls to the hottest social event of the spring?"

"Are you sure you're not using me as some kind of buffer?" she teases, sticking her tongue out.

Am I? No... no, of course not. That would be ridiculous.

26.

"**G**irls! Skip is here!" Dad calls from downstairs. "Well, he'd better get ready for me to steal every dance with you!" Olivia takes my hand and twirls me around the room. My skirt billows out around me. The sequin stars are large at the hem and get smaller as they reach my waist. The whole design was Mrs. Oren's concept, and it turned out even more beautiful than the sketches.

We fill our purses with bobby pins and lipstick, then snap one last picture in the mirror. Our hair is styled in curls. Olivia wears a sunburst headpiece while I don a tiara of stars. The two of us are racing and giggling as we zoom down the steps to the living room.

Skip beams up at me the minute I come into view. He radiates joy and his soft gasp should make me weak in the knees.

"Wow," he whispers, just the reaction middle school Susie would have died for.

He doesn't look so bad himself. His slick blue tux is accented with a silver bow tie that matches the stars on my dress and his perfectly combed hair.

"Hi," I greet him, blushing the minute he catches my eye. Despite all my reservations, his brash nature, and everything Olivia's said, he's still just as handsome as the first time I ever saw him. He kisses me on the cheek.

Dad flutters around, taking a million photos of all of us. And though the heavy feeling doesn't lift from my chest, I'm having fun, I think.

We crowd together in the middle of the living room. Skip leans in close, his breath tingling on my ear. "I thought it'd just be the two of us," he whispers.

"I told you on Wednesday." I blink. It's not a lie. I did technically tell him. Sure, it was while we were watching a movie, and sure, it was during a loud action scene, but I did tell him. He even replied with a distracted "Mhmm." Is it really my fault he wasn't entirely paying attention?

"That's all for now, kids! Have fun!" Dad says, retreating into the kitchen with a proud *That's my girl* look on his face. "Your mom is going to love these."

"Oh! I left my instant camera upstairs! Be back in a jiff!" Olivia announces.

I wait until both she and Dad are out of sight before saying anything else to Skip. Guilt swells up inside me. I shouldn't have been so sneaky about wanting Olivia to come along with us. "Well, Olivia and I wanted to get ready together, and I'm sure we'll all be hanging around at the dance. I was sure you wouldn't mind."

The frown on his face doesn't budge, and the more I speak, the more uncertain I am of the words coming out of my mouth. His confusion and disappointment were by design, and yet, I feel so bad. "—and Olivia offered to help me with my hair." I spin around showing off the tight curls falling to my chin, knowing her handiwork can't be denied.

"I like the way you style it better." He sulks, clearly still bummed about the third wheel situation. I can tell he doesn't mean it; I saw the way he looked at me when I came down the stairs.

Still, a pain shoots through my chest. I know it was supposed to be a compliment, but I can feel the confidence I'd felt when Olivia and I gazed into the mirror together draining out of my body. "Oh" is all I can manage, slumping down onto the sofa.

"Besides, I only brought one of these." He leans down and slides a glittering silver corsage onto my wrist.

"It's beautiful."

He drinks in the sight of me until finally, he smiles. "*You're* beautiful." Taking the seat next to me, Skip kisses me—really kisses me this time. I wait for the world to fall away, but all I can focus on is the anxiety that lipstick is all over my face.

He breaks away, and the pink shade is decorating his lips. My boyfriend tilts his head back, letting out a sigh of satisfaction before I take out my compact, addressing the damage. His hand pats my leg.

"I guess it's fine. Giving her a ride, that is. As long as Beanpole doesn't get in the way."

"I thought I told you not to call him that." My voice is an awkward whisper, but after everything that happened with the volcano, we should be past this.

"Oh, it's not like he's here." He shrugs.

"Are you still upset about the soup?" I ask, lowering my gaze as I pull away from his arms.

"Do I have something to be upset about?" The question isn't said in anger, and I could tell him right now and ruin the entire night.

Before I can say anything, Skip breaks through the tension with that smooth signature smile. "I'm sorry. I know he's your friend, but I just don't trust him, okay?" He draws me in closer. His voice softens. "You two spent an awful lot of time together. I still remember the way you wore his jacket at the beach."

Another pain sears through my chest. He'd been paying attention even back then. But then again, I guess he'd been watching the whole time.

"It was a jacket."

"Like it was just soup?" Eyebrows raised, he stands and offers his hand. I gulp, hesitating before I take it. "It's funny. Peggy-Sue said she saw you out the other night wearing one that was similar. I told her she must have been mistaken. Why would my girl be wearing someone else's jacket, right?"

I took it back with me the night I went to Olivia's. When I was almost home, I slipped it over my shoulders. Just for a moment. Just to see what it felt like. I didn't think anyone was around to catch me. But I guess in small towns like this, there's always someone watching.

"Got it!" Olivia bounds down the staircase, camera in hand. She steps directly between us, as if sensing the tension. "We don't want to be late!"

Skip, who's normally concerned with appearances, wears the lipstick marks into the dance like a badge of honor.

It's so embarrassing that Olivia walks a few steps in front of us. I'd take a guess she's glaring at anyone who dares to whistle.

Silver and gold balloons float in the corners of the room. The photo backdrop is a giant shooting star. Skip looks less than enthused when, following our couple's photo, Olivia pulls me into her own, posing as if we're doing the tango.

It should be funny, but with the grim expression growing on his face, it's hard to laugh.

"Oh, there's Teddy and Wallace!" Olivia waves, pointing to the middle of the dance floor.

My jaw drops. Everyone had been talking about the zero-gravity dance floor, but I didn't expect it to be so … literal.

On the outskirts, everyone dances normally, but the closer you got to the center, the more couples flip and jump through the air as if in slow motion—which is exactly where Teddy and Wallace are.

Teddy wears a pink suit with holographic constellations sewn onto the collar and cuffs, with a shiny undershirt, his bowtie loose around his neck. He pulls Wallace, who's wearing a powder blue tuxedo jacket and bold chrome shoes, in for a kiss. While they're not exactly coordinated on the dance floor, they look as adorable as ever and very, *very* high up. I gulp. I don't think I'm brave enough for that.

"Maybe we could just stick to the outskirts to warm up," I suggest. Skip laughs and puts his arm around me, then waves across the room. When I follow his gaze, I see Peggy-Sue's party crew. Olivia tags along with us. She's met them a few times before, and while they don't dislike each other, they haven't really clicked.

Peggy-Sue is wearing a pink tulle dress, her hair swept up in an elegant updo. With the way she's squinting, I'm guessing she didn't take Miss Galaxy's advice to just wear her glasses.

"Susie! You look adorable! Oh, and so does your friend! How cute—the two of you match. The sun and stars!"

Peggy-Sue gets close, examining our outfits. "And Skip, you look very sharp, as always."

"Did you just get here?" he asks, not bothering to return the compliment.

"We got here early," Peggy-sue replies. "You have to have the cookies if you make it to the refreshments. They're shaped like tiny burgers! They also did a fizzy punch that hasn't been tampered with *thus far*." She winks. I crane my neck to look over at the refreshments and my stomach lurches.

I knew Eugene would be here. But I wasn't prepared for this.

Eugene is always in the back of house when we go to Lester's. On our trip, I pondered what he might look like in his uniform. In a room of formal wear, glitter, and suit jackets, he stands apart from the crowd, but not in the way you'd think.

Just like when I saw him wearing that lightweight cardigan, there's a softness to him. The pointed soda-jerk hat sits perfectly on his coiffed blue hair.

The cuffed shirt shows off the lines of his thin arms, and the apron pulls in his waist in a way that makes me want to throw my arms around his midsection just as tightly as the apron strings. As good as he looks in a leather jacket, I like seeing him this way.

He towers over both of his parents; I catch him shoot a small smile at his mom while she refreshes the punch. I turn away, hoping I haven't let my eyes linger for too long.

"Oh my gosh, Susie! It's *the song*!" Olivia squeals, jumping up and down.

It *is* the song! The one we—kind of—learned the dance to on Neo Viridis. Everyone else just continues to dance normally or, with slight confusion, float back down toward the rest of the festivities.

"The song?" Skip asks, looking confused.

"From the trip—I guess it wasn't a detail I included in any of the recaps! Did you go to the big festival on the last day?"

He shakes his head, but before he can say anything else, Wallace runs over, pulling Teddy behind him, and Olivia grabs my hand. Before I know it, the four of us are out on the lowest point of the dance floor. The only person we're missing is Eugene.

We stick to the outer circle of the dance floor, laughing as we try to remember the line dancing moves. Step forward, step back, twirl, box-step. Or was it back, forward, box-step? I bump into Wallace, and he spins me around. I fall back into line between him and Teddy. It's hopeless. I try to copy their moves, but I can't remember how we did this on the trip. We laugh and bump into each other before we even get to the second chorus.

I search the room for Skip—hadn't he followed us out here? He's standing on the sidelines with his friends laughing around him.

"Reverse!" Olivia shouts, and we jump backward.

When it's over, the four of us curtsy and bow to each other, and a hand spins me back around into another dance. "What *was* that?" Skip shakes his head. I begin to explain, and he cuts me off with a loud laugh. "You all looked ridiculous."

"You should have joined us!" I tease, spinning back into him. He guides me around the dance floor with his usual ease. Everything from his posture to his subtle movements reminds me of a prince at a ball. Especially now, I should be swooning. "You're a really good dancer, you know."

He spins me out into a dip and smiles down at me. *He knows.*

"Looks like there's another thing I can tutor you in." He raises my hand to his lips before spinning me around again we're carried away in the motion of music, spinning around the outer circle of the dance floor where our feet never leave the ground. Our movements feel slower, more graceful, and thought-out. Hovering above the ground, I don't worry so much about stepping on his feet. But the thing that strikes me more than anything else is that despite how good at this he is, I don't want to be in his arms.

"Maybe we should get back to the others."

"Aw, come on! Just one more dance," he coos.

I hang my head. I know the book says to wait until important functions are over, and I certainly can't break up with him on the dance floor. He studies my face.

"You're not having fun, are you?" he asks suddenly. The smile on his face wavers for just a moment before it returns. It's unnerving. Anyone watching would think he's flirting with me between that smile and the soft whisper. But his eyes tell a different story. He's jealous again. I don't know why. I haven't given him a reason to be.

"Of course, I'm having fun."

"Really? Because I'm feeling like a third wheel. And every time we dance, you seem like you want to be somewhere else." He whirls me around again, spinning me back into his arms, before letting me go. "I'm going to get freshened up. Maybe when I'm back you can start acting like we're—I don't know—on a date?"

He leaves me up against the wall with the others in the garden of unpicked wallflowers. What am I supposed to do now? Just wait until he comes back? Olivia waves from across the room, balancing a cup of punch in her hand while she does the twist with Wallace and Teddy. I shake my head and watch her shrug. I'm glad at least she's enjoying herself.

I should be enjoying myself too. It's not fair. All Skip wants is to have my attention to himself or hang around his friends.

I try to catch a glimpse of Eugene by the soda fountain, but I don't see him. I bet it's almost a relief for him to be behind the counter, working with his parents. I imagine everyone would be trying to work up the nerve to ask him to dance if he were free. That's probably why he decided to work the dance instead of attend. He can enjoy the festivities without being a part of them. That's been his strategy ever since he transferred here, hasn't it? I sigh. That's another thing the two of us have in common: a strict set of rules on how to survive or thrive in high school.

I stare at the floor.

A pair of wing-tipped shoes enter my view. I look up to see Eugene sheepishly grinning at me. My breath gets caught in my chest. His long lashes are dark against his smooth blue skin, and his pouty lips part into a smile. He has no business looking this handsome.

Not in his work uniform, not at a school dance, and certainly not standing in front of me. It's enough to make me feel like I'm going to explode.

"Hi," he says.

"Hey."

"C-can we dance?" Eugene asks. It's a sentence I longed to hear and dreaded all at the same time. I hold out my hand and nod, even though I should be shaking my head. If Skip comes back and sees me dancing with Eugene, he'll be furious. But then again, that wouldn't exactly be a change of pace for the evening.

"I would love that," I say, more candidly than I mean to. I savor the feeling of him intertwining his fingers in mine; it reminds me of bumbling around together while ice-skating.

He leads me out into the dance floor. We stumble together at first, trying to match each other's step.

"I missed you earlier. Uh, I mean, I think everyone did."

"I th-thought I should s-stay away."

"And…?"

Without warning, he leans forward and his forehead presses against mine. The stars from my headpiece knock his hat further down the crown of his head, but neither of us move away.

"I couldn't." The words fill my lungs with nitrous oxide. I'm dizzied by the sound of him and the feeling of his hands on my body.

Neither can I.

The song is fast, and he dances more goofily than I'd expect, flashing an uncertain smile at me every once in a while. I smile back. He spins me, and I bump into his shoulder. The two of us stumble back laughing, edging closer to the center of the dance floor. I can feel the gravity lighten.

My dress flows around me, our movements suddenly slower—and so is the next song.

We're floating higher than I'd let myself all night. My feet barely scrape the laminate floor. My body starts to drift away, and when Eugene's hand reaches out for mine, I take it, unexpectedly crashing into his chest.

Our bodies pressed together, I make no attempt to move, my cheek resting against his neck.

I feel his Adam's apple quake nervously under my skin, heat rising from his body to mine. Trembling, his hands settle at my waist. I look up.

I've never wanted to kiss someone so badly in my entire life, and I'm unsure if the desperation I'm reading in his eyes is the same as my own. Everything has fallen away—the people, the music—and all I can focus on is his eyes. I'm not sure if you can even call this dancing anymore; we're just clinging to each other, neither able nor wanting to look away. The chiffon of my dress drifts around us.

I need to tell him.

"S-Susie," he whispers, and I snap to my senses. We are at the center of the dance floor.

The band strikes up a fast song, and the heaviness of my body return. We slowly make our descent down to the ballroom floor. I'm suddenly aware of the eyes that have been watching us, and painfully aware of what Eugene wants to confess.

"I know what you're going to say," I admit, biting my bottom lip. My feet touch the ground, and regret billows in my chest. "And Eugene ... I made a mistake."

An arm snatches around my waist.

Skip.

"Can you give us a minute?" I say quietly, but my voice is lost to the beat of the music. But Skip just glares at Eugene.

"The line for refreshments is sure getting out of control," he announces loudly, my lipstick still displayed proudly on his face. He leans down to whisper in my ear. "You really do love making a scene."

I want to tell him it was just a dance, but we both know that's a lie. Just like it was never just a jacket and never just soup.

I've liked Eugene this entire time. We danced like that in front of the whole school, and the world just fell away. I didn't think of the consequences or what it looked like in the moment. Every thought was of Eugene.

I didn't even think that sort of thing was possible.

"Let's go." Skip catches my arm, and before I can react, Eugene places his hand over top of Skip's grasp and looks at me pleadingly.

"Don't." His voice echoes weakly across the dance floor. "Y-you don't have to g-g-go with him." It's the most I've ever heard him speak in a crowd this size. His cheeks flush pink, and his hands ball into fists at his sides.

"Eugene..." I take a step toward him. The music feels like it's faded, like time has stopped in this room. But everyone is still sipping punch and dancing while my life blurs into slow motion.

"I'm her boyfriend, okay?" Skip interrupts the moment by stepping between us, poking Eugene in the chest. "She doesn't have much of a choice."

Is that what he really thinks? That I'm just ... stuck with him now? I slip between the two of them. Skip's hand is still firmly on my arm.

"That's where you're mistaken." I pull my arm free and glare at him. "We're over." I start for the door, barely looking back at him.

The band picks back up, and couples part as I storm past them. In ten seconds, I've done everything I told my readers not to in every issue of *The Gazette:*

I danced with another boy.

Made a spectacle of myself.

Broke up in public.

The Space Age Ladies Guide to Romance and Social Affairs would not approve.

I'm not sure that I care.

27.

"Wait!" Skip chases me down the hallway. "Babe I'm sorry— I was just—I hated seeing my girl dancing with some other guy."

"No!" I turn back to face him with the swivel of my heel. "I'm not *yours*, okay?"

His hands raise helplessly in the air. "Okay! Okay!" he shouts. "I get it. You're mad. I've been a jerk all evening." He stomps after me, but I have no intention of letting him catch up.

"We have something special! You're just going to let that go?" Skip continues. I think of each of the letters, the adventure, the promise of finding something, someone back here at school who really cared. But I don't owe him a relationship because he did something nice for me.

Finally, I stop. Standing in the center of the hallway, I take a deep breath.

"Skip, I know you put a lot of effort into those letters, but—"

"I didn't write the letters!" he screams as though the words are tearing his heart out and not mine. He lets out a desperate breath, the sort you'd hear if someone had been drowning. This lie had been killing him.

But it might destroy me.

My knees shake beneath me, and suddenly, the floor feels like it's uneven. I take a deep breath, and another, and another, but the air isn't reaching my lungs.

Skip didn't write the letters. No, that's not possible. He had to have. He told everyone that he was Anonymous.

He kissed me while the whole school cheered.

"I think I'd rather just be Skip and Susie." His words burn in my ears.

Skip stands, slope-shouldered, in front of me. "Your friends just jumped to conclusions—and then what was I supposed to do?" His whole body shakes as he talks, and he lets out a frustrated sigh every now and then. "I mean, yeah, lying wasn't great, but considering who wrote the letters, didn't I do you a favor? Susie, I care about you. I really care, and Eugene—do you know how many friends have written into Miss Galaxy heartbroken that he won't even give them a single 'hello'? I thought that, in a way, I was doing you a favor."

Eugene.

My head is spinning.

What does any of this have to do with Eugene? I need a minute to process my thoughts, but Skip just keeps talking.

"I did what you said. I found an opening and took my opportunity. I jumped! I did what I had to do to finally get your attention!"

An opportunity to jump. Why does that sound so familiar? *Lovestruck Fool...*

The last article I published before this all started feels like a lifetime ago.

"Don't be afraid to let your feelings be known. Be sincere and look for an opportunity to jump in and tell her how you feel."

"You did the opposite of being sincere!" I shake my head. I should never have gone along with this. I should have rejected him the minute he confessed his feelings.

"I'm being sincere now," he says softly. He reaches down to take my hand. "Come back to the dance with me."

I'm not going to make the same mistake twice.

"I can't."

He bites his bottom lip, and finally nods.

"I shouldn't have taken the credit— even if that guy is the worst." He crosses his arms, looking down the hallway back toward the dance. There's a small crowd watching from the doorway, but Eugene is nowhere to be found. I replay every conversation, trying to figure out how our wires got crossed. Where did I go wrong, and how could I not have seen it before?

Eugene wrote the letters.

He was next to me the whole trip, and I never saw it once.

"You really do like him, don't you?" Skip's voice creeps into my ears.

"I do," I say. "Even without the letters, I really do."

"Then I guess we are over." He throws his hands up in the air, turning back toward the gym. I place my hands on his shoulder and give him the satisfaction of a small nod.

"We would be over either way," I assure him.

It's not just the lies and the jealousy. It's the way his heart doesn't fit with the shape of mine. I always liked the idea of Skip, but as for him as a boyfriend, we don't match up. That's never going to change.

"I hope you're not making a mistake." The sincerity in his voice catches me off guard.

"I'm not," I say before rushing down the hall. Going after Eugene is the first thing that hasn't felt like a mistake since I got home.

Eugene isn't with Wallace, Teddy, and Olivia, he's not behind the refreshments table, and he's certainly not on the dance floor. There's one more place at school I think to look, but I'm not confident I'll find him.

My heart sparks when I see the light on in *The Galaxy Gazette.* He's sitting behind the desk with his head in his hands, notes scattered around him.

When we look at each other, time stops just like it did on the dance floor. Eugene, with his ink-stained fingers, wrote me all those letters.

Back when I thought he hated me.

Back when I was sure I hated him.

Standing in the doorway, my knees feel weak. It just took a few short weeks for everything to change, but it has and there's no question about who I have feelings for any longer. I just wish it hadn't taken so long to realize this isn't the kind of thing you can ignore. Pushing down my feelings for Eugene Eris was like trying to pull a star down from the sky— an impossible task I'm a fool for ever trying.

"You!" I gasp.

Silence hangs between us, his dark brow furrowing. His long legs carry him toward me. It seems like he's gotten taller in the few minutes we've been apart. I think about the dozens of missed calls I had from Eugene *that day.*

He got detention because he ran out of class when he heard what happened. Stars, is that because he was looking for me?

"You're Anonymous." Terror grips me before I can manage to say anything else. After everything that's happened, how can I be sure he hasn't changed his mind?

"Yeah," he huffs, sliding his hands in his pockets.

"What do you mean 'yeah'?" I shout flailing my hands in front of my body. "Why didn't you tell me!"

"You ww-wh—you knew, and you picked Skip," Eugene stammers breathlessly. "You told me... you..." He squints down at me while he tries to pick up the pieces of how this happened. 'It w-was always Skip.'"

"You thought I knew?" A sharp pain pierces through my chest. I had said that, and he thought I meant... *Oh no...*

The pieces snap together.

No, no, no, no, no, no... I bury my head in my hands.

"Eugene, no. I'm so sorry." My hands shake, but I try to hold it together.

Suddenly, his hands peel mine away from my face, and his tear-stained eyes meet mine.

"Shhh, it's okay," he whispers in my ear. I bury my head in his chest, and that's all the encouragement he needs for his arms to tighten around me. His warmth is all around me, gentle and steady. The two of us are as close as possible, and still, I want to be closer.

"It's okay, it's okay," he repeats over and over.

"I threw out the last letter," I whisper against his chest. "I was going to forget about Anonymous and tell you how I felt."

I look up at Eugene, and I know I should have kissed him when he jumped in after me at the pool. It doesn't matter what the book says, what the school thinks, what grand gestures were made. He's the one I want by my side.

"Do you still like me?" It's not the question I meant to ask. The moment it leaves my mouth, I glow with embarrassment. I really messed up. And there's a chance, a big chance, that he wants nothing to do with me.

"Yes."

I let out a sigh. We're back to one word replies.

"Susie..." He dips down to look in my eyes. He looks too serious, his brows harrowed, his eyes clear and blue.

I brace myself for the rejection I probably deserve.

"I l-like you a lot."

But I didn't brace myself for that. My head turns sharply upward. He's looking down into my eyes.

"You don't have to say..."

"I like you a lot. Maybe too much." It's hard to think straight, looking into his dewy eyes. None of this is going how I thought or imagined it would, but his arms fall back around mine and his eyes stay locked on me.

It's still early.

"C-can we go?"

I certainly don't want to go back to the dance, but I don't want to go home either.

"Where?"

"The last place I was going to send you," he whispers, and without hesitation, I follow.

28.

We're at Lester's.

They're closed, with all the lights off apart from the sign on top.

There's a big sign at the front that says they're sponsoring the dance with "GO ASTEROIDS!" in colorful letters.

I take Eugene's hand. After spending so many nights in the corner booth with Skip, I'm less than thrilled to be back here. But I trust Eugene. He must have a plan. We walk around to the back of the building. He pauses and looks at my dress.

"*Oh...*"

"Oh?"

He gestures to the ladder.

We're going up, and I'm wearing a ballgown. I test out the first few steps, then hop back down. The dress doesn't seem to be getting in the way, but I'm worried about pulling myself up onto the roof without help.

"Will you go up first?" I ask, a glowing blush already gleaming across the stars on my face.

He climbs up, and I follow. With a swing of his lanky legs, he's hopped over the ledge. It's clearly not his first time climbing up here. He offers me his hand to help me up the rest of the way.

Eugene leads me out toward the neon sign shining beneath the stars, then guides me to sit on the L. My dress spills over the edge. We're both backlit in the warm glow for a moment until I see the edges of his mouth curl into a smile.

"Wait..." he says, heading toward what looks like a circuit breaker. Suddenly, everything around us is pitch black.

The sign has been turned off. And Eugene, with a flashlight he must have had stowed by the switch, makes his way back to me.

I turn to look at the sky and gasp. This is the best view of the stars I've ever seen. He takes the space next to me. The only light I can see illuminates off the pretty constellations on his face. I can't believe I ever thought he was intimidating.

I lean my head on his shoulder, wishing I could have a snapshot of this moment. Him in his soda-jerk uniform and me in a giant silver prom dress, sitting on the L of Lester's looking up at billions of glittering stars.

I want to hold onto this memory forever. I sigh, cuddling closer. Even in this small way, we fit perfectly together.

"I'm glad I'm finally here with you. Sorry it took so long." I sigh, closing the distance between us. It took us this long; I don't want to waste any more time. "There is something I've been wondering though—"

"Oh?"

"Why Dear Galaxy instead of Miss Galaxy?"

"Typo," he replies with a shake of his head, and the two of us burst out with laughter. I guess it's not as deep as I thought, but I'll admit it added to the mystery.

He looks down, uncertain of something. I turn my head to look at him. His deep eyes soften, and he smiles. I wrap my arms around his waist and squeeze a little.

"You can kiss me now if you want," I say. My cheeks barely have time to glow—I've never done anything so forward before—but then our lips meet, soft and sweet. The kiss builds until I'm running my fingers through his hair and pulling him closer. He shudders and the unexpected sound pulls a giggle from my chest.

Stars, I like him so much.

We kiss until we are gasping for air, and even then, I'm not sure that I want to stop. My chest is light and bubbly, and when we break away, I'm glad I took off my lipstick before we started.

There's no denying it. It's the *feeling*. It always has been with Eugene, and I'm a fool for letting the idea of disappointing the readers of *Dear Miss Galaxy* keep me away from something so real. "What are we going to do?"

"C-come to dinner on S-Sunday?"

"No, I mean, yes!" I turn back to him seriously. "But what about everything else?"

My hand slides across his arm until I reach his fingers, lace them in mine, and squeeze. Finally, he looks back at me, having a hard time meeting my eyes. "W-what do you mean?"

"Don't you want everyone to know the truth?"

"The o-only person I needed to know is s-standing right in front of me."

"And everyone at school?"

A gentle smile plays on his lips. "I-I could care less."

"You know what?" My arms wrap tighter around him. "Me too." People will believe what they want to. And it's time for me to stop following a guidebook and write my own story.

"Dear Susie," he whispers, planting a kiss on my cheek, "I-I love you."

"Dear Anonymous..." I murmur against his shoulder—but no, that's not who I want this admission to go to. The person who captured my heart isn't a name signed at the end of a letter. He's the person next to me, brushing a stray hair from my face with the softest smile I've ever seen.

"Dear Eugene," I begin the way I should have weeks ago, "I love you too."

THE END

Acknowledgments

This book is the story I tried again and again to write and rewrite. Over the years, I've had encouragement from friends in person and across the internet. Every kind Tweet, comment, or message as I shared and publicly queried this piece has helped me keep going, and I can't tell you how much I've appreciated all the love and support from both the bookish and vintage communities!

This book wouldn't be what it is without my dear friend Taylor Simonds, who not only suffered through reading my very first draft, but through editing, conversation, and a whole lot of coffee helped me turn this book into the story it is today. Taylor, you are the friend who taught me to dream big as a writer. You're a brilliant author, storyteller, and friend. There's no one I'd rather reach for the stars with, and I'm so glad we get to be on this wild and crazy bookish journey together. Also thank you for giving me the idea of changing the "only one bed" trope to "only one space pod." It will forever be one of my favorite scenes.

As I was writing (and rewriting) *Dear Galaxy,* I always kept a board of pictures of trips with my friends Esther Vanoui and Brittany Ball on my desk. The warm fuzzy feeling

I get when I think about all our adventures together was the rocket fuel that helped me shape Susie's adventures through space. Dressing up, creating, and cheering each other on is one of the greatest joys. Thank you for being my space girls. And speaking of amazing retro ladies, thank you to Designed.By.Shea for the stunning cover design! It's everything I always imagined and more.

A thank you to Matt Lavoie, my darling husband, who always encourages me to tell the stories that are in my heart. Thank you for making it easy to write love stories, always being there to lean on. You've held me tight when rejections knocked me down and danced in the kitchen when there's good news to celebrate. I also appreciated your *"Hey, that's not how space works"* notes. I can't promise I got all the details right, but I can promise I love you to the moon and back.

And of course, I can't express my appreciation enough for the encouragement and excitement the team at 4 Horsemen Publications shared with me for this project! From my impromptu pitch to publication, y'all have been amazing as always to work with!

And lastly, a big thank you and shoutout to my grandmother Rosalie LeRoy for always asking, "When is that space book coming out?" Grandma, I love you! Knowing that this is a story you're looking forward to helped when I needed motivation to keep going. I treasure all the love and support you've shared with me for all my books. This book will be released the year of your 90th birthday, and I hope you enjoy it.

Book Club Questions

1. What planet from our solar system do you wish Susie and her friends had visited?

2. Did any of the clues Anonymous gives surprise you?

3. When did you start to suspect Eugene was actually writing the letters?

4. Which of the characters do you wish had a spin off novel?

5. Would you be brave enough to try a 0-gravity dance floor?

6. How do you think Susie should have handled realizing she had feelings for Eugene?

7. Did you root for Skip for any of his attempts to woo Susie?

8. What themes or symbols did you notice while reading?

9. Which planet from the road trip would you like to visit the most?

10. If you wrote a letter to Miss Galaxy, what would it say?

ABOUT THE AUTHOR

Paige Lavoie is a Halloween-loving cinnamon roll who writes stories about misfits, monsters, and falling in love. Her affection for cozy autumn moments, charming protagonists, and all things cute and creepy reflects in the worlds she creates. When Paige isn't writing, she can be found hunting for treasures at the local antique mall and sipping oat milk lattes under a lacey parasol as she hides from the sun in her home state of FL.

MORE BOOKS FROM 4 HORSEMEN PUBLICATIONS

FANTASY, SCIFI, & PARANORMAL ROMANCE

AMANDA FASCIANO
Waking Up Dead
Dead Vessel
The Dead Show
Dead Revelations

BEAU LAKE
The Beast Beside Me
The Beast Within Me
Taming the Beast: Novella
The Beast After Me
Charming the Beast
The Beast Like Me
An Eye for Emeralds
Swimming in Sapphires
Pining for Pearls

CHELSEA BURTON DUNN
By Moonlight
Moonbound
Bloodthirsty

D. LAMBERT
Rydan
Celebrant
Northlander
Esparan
King
Traitor
His Last Name

DANIELLE ORSINO
Locked Out of Heaven
Thine Eyes of Mercy
From the Ashes
Kingdom Come
Fire, Ice, Acid, & Heart
A Fae is Done

J.M. PAQUETTE
Klauden's Ring
Solyn's Body
The Inbetween
Hannah's Heart
Call Me Forth
Invite Me In
Keep Me Close
Heart of Stone

KAIT DISNEY-LEUGERS
Antique Magic
Blood Magic

KYLE SORRELL
Munderworld
Potarium

LYRA R. SAENZ
Prelude
Falsetto in the Woods: Novella
Ragtime Swing
Sonata
Song of the Sea

The Devil's Trill
Bercuese
To Heal a Songbird
Ghost March
Nocturne

PAIGE LAVOIE
I'm in Love with Mothman
Dear Galaxy

ROBERT J. LEWIS
Shadow Guardian and the
Three Bears
Shadow Guardian and the
Big Bad Wolf

T.S. SIMONS
Project Hemisphere
The Space Between
Infinity
Circle of Protections

Sessrúmnir
The 45th Parallel

VALERIE WILLIS
Cedric: The Demonic Knight
Romasanta: Father of Werewolves
The Oracle: Keeper of the
Gaea's Gate
Artemis: Eye of Gaea
King Incubus: A New Reign
Queen Succubus: Holder
of the Crown
Val's House of Musings: A Mixed
Genre Short Story Collection

V.C. WILLIS
The Prince's Priest
The Priest's Assassin
The Assassin's Saint
The Champion's Lord

YOUNG ADULT

A.R. FARINA
Welcome To Mansfield

BLAISE RAMSAY
Through The Black Mirror
The City of Nightmares
The Astral Tower

C.R. RICE
Denial
Anger

Bargaining
Depression
Acceptance
Broken Beginnings: Story of Thane
Shattered Start: Story of Sera
Sins of The Father: Story of Silas
Honorable Darkness: Story of
Hex and Snip
A Love Lost: Story of Radnar